FICTION CAMPBELL
Campbell, Ramsey, 1946-
author.
The influence

RAMSEY CAMPBELL

THE INFLUENCE

This is a **FLAME TREE PRESS** book

Text copyright © 2019 Ramsey Campbell

FLAME TREE PRESS
6 Melbray Mews, London, SW6 3NS, UK
flametreepress.com

Distribution and warehouse:
Baker & Taylor Publisher Services (BTPS)
30 Amberwood Parkway, Ashland, OH 44805
btpubservices.com

Thanks to the Flame Tree Press team, including:
Taylor Bentley, Frances Bodiam, Federica Ciaravella, Don D'Auria, Chris Herbert, Josie Karani, Molly Rosevear, Will Rough, Mike Spender, Cat Taylor, Maria Tissot, Nick Wells, Gillian Whitaker.

The cover is created by Flame Tree Studio with thanks to Nik Keevil and Shutterstock.com.
The font families used are Avenir and Bembo.

Flame Tree Press is an imprint of Flame Tree Publishing Ltd
flametreepublishing.com

A copy of the CIP data for this book is available from the British Library and the Library of Congress.

HB ISBN: 978-1-78758-374-0
PB ISBN: 978-1-78758-372-6
ebook ISBN: 978-1-78758-375-7
Also available in FLAME TREE AUDIO

Printed and bound in Great Britain by Clays Ltd, Elcograf S.p.A.

RAMSEY CAMPBELL

THE INFLUENCE

FLAME TREE PRESS
London & New York

For Catherine and J.K. Potter
who lit up more of the dark for me
("The last dream tells the truth," says Guilda Kent)

CHAPTER ONE

As the bus out of Liverpool sped up the overpass, the night storm from Wales came across the bay to meet it. Alison Faraday could see nothing of the Seaforth docks or the marina except rain and blurred lights, and she felt as if she were drowning. At the foot of the overpass, the broad Georgian houses of Waterloo were blocks of mud. Under the Five Lamps, five globes skirting a stone angel, a train slipped eel-like through the bridge. Beyond the station the bus splashed past Thompsons Boot Repairers into Mount Pleasant, where the windows of tall terraces dwindled towards the roofs, and Alison was already hauling herself along the swaying aisle towards the exit doors.

The drenched concrete pole of the bus stop crumbled under her fingers as she pushed herself towards the side street and met the August storm. It plastered her raincoat and her nurse's uniform to her as she fought her way along the narrow street beneath sodden embers of sodium lamps. Darkness several storeys high carried windows past the end of the street, as if Queenie's house had floated loose from its foundations. It was a ship beyond the dunes, and the dark bulk from behind which it had sailed was Queenie's house, towering massively over its neighbours. Up among its chimneys and haphazard slate slopes, Queenie's window glared towards the bay. Alison's stomach tightened as she came to the end of the street and groped through the downpour for the gate.

The garden path was slippery with moss. Alison stooped over her handbag to keep out the rain while she fumbled for her key, and then light from the hall spilled across the flower beds choked with restless grass. Hermione had snatched the door open. "Derek was called out to a job, and she's been shouting for Rowan."

Hermione must have run to the door when she'd heard the gate scrape the path. Her small features looked huddled together in the midst of her long plump face; the dents like thumb marks under her eyes seemed deeper than ever. "I sat with Rowan to make sure she stayed asleep."

Alison squeezed her sister's forearms gently, the nearest she could get to a hug while she was so drenched, and heeled the door shut behind them. "It's all right now. I'm here."

"And every inch of you soaked to the skin," Hermione said, the protective older sister. "I'll make you a coffee with brandy in it while you get changed. She's quiet now. I shouldn't bother going up."

"I may just look in to see how she is."

Hermione brushed back her greying hair that no longer curled properly but wouldn't stay straight, and rubbed her forehead as if she could rub away the wrinkles. "I expect you're right," she said heavily. "She'll know you're here."

The hall that was wide enough to drive a car through stretched fifty feet to the stairs. Plaster fallen on the stained-glass lampshade cast shadows like mould on the darkly papered walls. Shivering with the chill of the building, Alison climbed the zigzag staircase, whose treads sagged towards the cracked rear wall of the house. Three dim corridors formed a T at the first landing. She tiptoed down the corridor towards the front of the house and into Rowan's bedroom.

Rowan's white furniture, her bed and chest of drawers and wardrobe, looked almost lost on the expanse of worn carpet that fell short of the pale pink walls. She lay with her cheek on one palm, her long reddish hair trailing over her face. As Alison stroked it away from her eyes she turned onto her back, mumbling "Down the cellar," though there wasn't one. With her eyes shut she looked even more like a delicate eight-year-old version of Derek: long blunt nose, slightly pouted lips, wide forehead, square chin. Alison kissed her long lashes and tucked the sheets tighter, then she plodded soggily to the next room, hers and Derek's.

It was as though their flat in Liverpool had been reduced to a bed-sitter, their bed and three-piece suite and bedroom furniture fitting easily into the room. She peeled off her clothes and was buttoning herself into a dress when the door inched open, and she heard a slow footstep. It was Hermione, slowed down by a brimming mug of coffee.

She watched approvingly while Alison drank it, and lingered when she had. "Shall I come up with you?"

"I can cope with her," Alison said, and then hastily "You've done more than your share." She gave her the mug and made for the stairs as if she wouldn't dream of hesitating. The upward flight leaned even more sharply, and she held on to the shaky banister. At the halfway turn her hand touched the rear wall of the house, and she felt plaster shift under the browned paper.

Three corridors branched from the top of the staircase. Those to either side were unlit, and she heard the storm blundering about in the dark. The further of the two bulbs dangling ahead of her on fattened tangled cords had failed in its rusty socket. As soon as Alison had passed beyond the first bulb, boards giving underfoot beneath several layers of carpet that smelled stale and damp, her shadow filled the corridor in front of her. Silence filled the lightless rooms beyond doors that no longer fitted their distorted frames. The stuffy dark seemed deepest at the end of the corridor, where Queenie's room was. Alison reached for the knob that hung awry in its socket, and eased the door open.

Even seen from the dark corridor, the large room was dim. The browning of the books that were piled against the walls wherever there was space seemed to have gathered in the light beneath the heavy greyish shade. Among the piles of books, black wardrobes and black chests soaked up the glow, which fell short of the corners of the room. Between the door and the far wall, and facing the wide window, Queenie lay in bed.

Perhaps she had been watching the storm or the distant lights of Wales, for the stained velvet curtains and their veils of net were open, but now she appeared to be sleeping, one hand on a book that lay splayed on her chest. Alison's breathing faltered. She had never seen her aunt looking so young: her long sharp wedge of a face with its thrusting chin, her features cramped into half of the face as if the tight thin lips begrudged the others even that much room, looked hardly a quarter of its eighty years. Was she more than just asleep? The room seemed to exhale the smells of disinfectant and old paper as Alison tiptoed forward, suddenly breathless with the childhood fear that Queenie would rear up without warning, all six and a half feet of her. She was just close enough to read the title of the book under Queenie's wizened hand – *The Nurture of the Child* – when Queenie spoke. "You look surprised, my dear."

Her voice was thin as her lips and sharp as her face. She must have been watching beneath her eyelids, Alison realised, angry with her heart for thudding. "If you're taking an interest I'm glad."

"Someone in this house has to. My little girl's safe in bed, I trust, not playing with her dirty friends or with the workman on his rounds, the bright spark."

"He's my husband and her father," Alison said quietly. "And I wish you'd let him do something about the electricity up here."

"He'll do as he's bid in my house." Queenie raised herself on her elbows, her long body sliding stiffly under the greying blankets, and fixed her pale gaze on Alison. "You should be thankful that I harbour him at all after you married beneath you, just like your father. You'll say it was for love," she said, drawing out the last word and shuddering, and then her voice sharpened. "I notice you still haven't brought those masks."

"Queenie, I told you I can't take them out of the hospital. If infection worries you so much—"

"Don't you dare even think it. I'll stay where I've always lived, and God help anyone who tries to shift me." Her right eyelid drooped, spoiling the symmetry of her face, until she raised it with an effort that made her bare her teeth. Then she settled against the pillow, her eyes closing. "Do my hair for me. I don't want to look like a witch."

She was just an old woman, embittered and lonely and now wheedling, Alison told herself. She went to the dressing-table by the window that was shivering with shapeless darkness and picked up the brush and combs. The patch of light around the bed looked smaller than ever. She laid the combs on the musty patchwork quilt and brushed Queenie's long grey hair back from her papery forehead, and Queenie said "Don't stand there like a dummy, tell me about your day."

Alison told her about the little boy who'd been circumcised yesterday, whose parents had still not been to visit him; the four-year-old who'd kept saying "Big one" to a student nurse who had thought he meant his teddy bear and hadn't rushed him to the toilet until it was too late; the six-year-old whose monster puppet had had to ride the trolley down to the theatre to undergo the same operation he had... Queenie bared her teeth again whenever the brush tugged her hair, and looked disgusted by the anecdote about the four-year-old. As a child Alison had always felt drained by her dozens of questions, and now her silence was just as demanding. When Alison had exhausted her day on the ward Queenie peered at her, her right eye opening belatedly. "You've told me more than you know, my dear. You've told me how dissatisfied you are with your life."

"Not with my life, just with the system sometimes. I never thought nursing would be easy, and life doesn't always go the way you want it to."

Queenie let out a breath that showed even more of her teeth. "My father brought me up to expect the best and never be content with less. If more people refused to give up the ideals they were raised with the world might be less hellish." She stiffened as Alison put in the combs, fixing her hair in buns above her ears. "If you ask me, you want to spend less time caring for other people's offspring and concentrate on your own."

Alison lowered her voice to keep her temper. "Rowan has two parents, and we both—"

"I'm saying nothing against the child. She's as near perfect as they come these days. She reminds me of myself at her age," Queenie said, and stared at Alison as if to make sure she realised how much of a compliment that was. "Especially the way she likes nothing better than to sit by herself with a book."

But you never did anything with all your reading, Alison thought, just as Queenie said "You're thinking I could have made more use of my learning. My father always said it was the work of a lifetime to improve oneself without trying to change the world, but now I'll surprise you again. You bring the child to me now and see how much I can improve her reading."

Perhaps she was losing her sense of the time of day. "Maybe tomorrow, Queenie. It's her bedtime now."

"Your sister said that hours ago, and I've let the child sleep until you came. Don't think you can do what you like in my house just because I have to lie up here. Your sister knows better, and so should you."

Alison dropped the hairbrush on the dressing-table and wondered if she was being unreasonable: how long might the old woman have left to spend with the child? Rowan wasn't starting at her new school for more than a week, after all. Before she knew it, Alison was heading for the door. "That's the way, you fetch her," Queenie urged.

Alison hesitated between the twitching window and the glade of light about the bed. Queenie's eagerness had put her on her guard and cleared her head. Sometimes it seemed that Queenie had only to speak for the family to defer to her, but how could Alison have considered wakening the child so late? She turned towards Queenie to refuse as amiably as she could, and the old woman raised herself, her fists gripping the quilt, her pale eyes bulging furiously. The next moment the door slammed.

Queenie leaned forward, her thin arms trembling as they supported her, and poked her face, chin first, at Alison. "Now you give me your word you'll go straight down for her."

"Not this late," Alison said, and strode to the door. A draught she hadn't noticed must have slammed it, she told herself, and in any case it never closed properly – and then she realised that the slam had wedged it in the frame. She gripped the knob with both hands and tugged until she felt the spindle begin to work loose of the knob on the far side. Whatever she did, she wouldn't give in to the fears that were welling up from her childhood and Hermione's; Queenie was just a crotchety old woman, and she wouldn't plead with her to open the door as Hermione once had. She made her hands let go and turned to the bed. "It looks as if we'll have to wait for Hermione or Derek to budge this."

Queenie's lips pulled back in a grimace so fierce they seemed in danger of splitting. "Either you bring the child to me or you can leave my house tonight, the lot of you. Just remember that you wouldn't be suffering my hospitality if not for her and then perhaps you won't be so resolved to keep her to yourself."

"We're grateful to you, Queenie, but you seemed glad to have a nurse in the house."

Queenie stiffened – her knotted neck, the bony pillars of her arms, her eyes that burned like ice. "You think I'm failing, do you? I'll show you. I'll bring the child myself," she said in a voice low and powerful as the wind, and pushed herself up from the bed.

She must intend to open the door. Alison moved to stop her, her nurse's instincts telling her the strain might be too much for Queenie, whose face was already darkening. Or perhaps that was the light, which had dimmed suddenly, a dimness Alison wanted to blink away or brush from her face like cobwebs. She stooped to Queenie, stretching out her hands, and something dark and wide and suffocating surged up from the bed and flung itself at her, throwing her to the floor.

It was only the mass of bedclothes, the quilt and the blankets. They seemed to close around her as she struggled to free herself, choking on the smell of them, of old cloth and old flesh, of stale books and disinfectant. It must be her struggles that were entangling her. She managed to free one hand, and dragged herself over the balding carpet until she had wormed herself out of the tangle of cloth. She shoved herself back on her haunches and levered herself to her feet, and swung towards the bed.

Queenie lay on her back on the faded striped mattress, gasping. Her whole body seemed to be straining to make a sound. Her arms were stiff at her sides, her hands gripping her pink nightdress so hard that her ribs showed through. Her eyes stared past the dimming bulb. They looked blind, drained of colour, intent on something only she could see. A convulsion as ferocious as the one that must have flung the bedclothes heaved her body up on her elbows and heels, and she managed to speak. "Father," she said like a desperate prayer, and then her age flooded her face, her eyes rolled lifelessly awry. As her long chin sagged and her mouth opened emptily, the light failed with a noise as if a moth had struck the glass, and darkness stormed into the room.

CHAPTER TWO

The old couple who lived near the Freshfield squirrel reserve insisted on sharing the food from the freezer Derek had rewired. They couldn't eat it all before it went off, they told him, and insisted on paying him in full. The storm was blustering across to Wales as he drove back along the Southport road. At Hightown, where trees grew almost parallel with the ground, a rescue helicopter whirred above the sea. The flat land was still, except for the changing of traffic lights, dropping a red coal into the blackness of the road as they changed to red above. Frozen chops and steaks shifted in the bag on the seat beside him as the car swung around the curves, and he thought he'd make it on his own if there were a few more folk like those.

He had to make it, and a year ago he'd thought he would, though less from choice than because the contractor who'd employed him had gone bankrupt. All the same, he'd wanted to work for himself since he'd met Alison while he was working at the student nurses' hostel; she was making the most of her qualifications, and he should make the most of his. Many of the contractor's customers had known Derek and appreciated the care he took, and quite a few had promised to support him.

Up to a point, they had – usually up to the point when he sent them his bill. Small jobs paid on time; it was the large firms that made you wait and might be using you to stave off bankruptcy, but if it weren't for them he wouldn't have enough work. He needed the money even more than he had a year ago. He'd needed it then so that they could move out of Liverpool, and now he needed it to take them out of Queenie's house.

They'd stayed in the run-down flat in Liverpool for as long as they'd felt safe. The burning buildings of the eighties had stayed streets away, the street battles three storeys below. But once Rowan started school they'd realised that the National Front lurked at the schoolyard gates with racist leaflets and ten-year-olds smoked heroin in disused shops. Earlier this year a police van speeding along the pavement towards a potential riot had demolished the gateposts of the flats, where Rowan often stood to watch the street. They'd begun to work all the hours they could, desperate to save enough for the deposit on a house, their savings having dwindled constantly since Rowan's unexpected birth – and then Queenie had invited them to come and live with her.

As soon as they'd moved in Queenie had taken to her bed. She'd read all day and had expected Alison to be available whenever she was in the house. Within weeks she was bedridden, which made her more demanding, as if she was determined to prove she still had power. Derek had supposed he would help look after her, until she'd made him realise the extent of her contempt for him. Having to rely on her, to hope they could trust her hints that she might leave the house to Alison, dismayed him almost as much as her power over Alison – almost as much as the thought of her gaining a hold over Rowan too.

He trod hard on the accelerator until he reached the suburbs. Where Crosby became Waterloo the houses crowded together, thinner and shabbier. As he turned along the side road, a buoy tolled beyond the dunes that faced the parade of nursing homes. Out past the marina, the coastguard radar cupped the movements of the night. He parked by Queenie's house, under the last streetlamp.

The street was quiet except for water splashing from a gutter and the slow muffled beat of the sea. He lifted the gate clear of the scraped path and let himself into the house, and made for the living-room, whose window was lit. But the only sign of life in the high gloomy room with its huge cold fireplace was a Lisa Alther novel, face down on the leather settee.

That would be Hermione's book, the kind she gasped and shook her head over. At least she'd come over from Wales to keep Alison company. He made for the kitchen by the stairs. The women weren't in the cavernous stone-flagged room with its black iron range. He left the steaks and chops in Alison's refrigerator and went back along the hall, pushing open doors on either side of him, but all the rooms were dark – the dining-room whose dusty chandelier chimed sluggishly, the sewing-room full of draped machines, the sitting-room with its screens and piano and framed brown photographs. He hoped the women were asleep, getting the rest they deserved. He climbed the wry stairs into the gaping hush the storm seemed to have left in the house.

Rowan was murmuring disconnectedly in her sleep. He lingered outside her room, enjoying the sound of her being herself, and then edged the door open. Hermione was sitting on the bed, one arm stretched along the headboard, her head drooping sleepily towards the child. The door creaked, and Hermione lurched up from the bed, brandishing the stick she had been clutching. "Hermione, it's me," he hissed at her. "Derek."

Her features drew even closer together, and then she managed to smile. "I don't know what I was thinking of. I came in because Rowan was calling, and I must have dozed off."

"Where's Ali?"

"Upstairs. She went up—" She glanced at her tiny gold wristwatch, and her features huddled together again. "More than an hour ago."

"Don't blame yourself, girl. I'll go and see what's keeping her, and how about making yourself a fresh pot of tea?"

"Making one for you, you mean."

"If Ali could see through me like you can I'd still be single," Derek teased her. He might have thought he'd cheered her up except for the glance of panic she gave him as he climbed the stairs. He'd rewired the lower floors without telling Queenie, so that the house would be less of a fire risk, but the top floor was darker than ever. A single bulb made the askew walls into a frame for the dark where her room was. He peered ahead, and then he realised that he couldn't see a light beneath her door.

He went swiftly but carefully along the corridor. The door was wedged, he saw. He knocked softly on a cracked upper panel, not least to hear if Queenie was asleep. It was Alison who responded. "Is someone there? Derek, is that you?"

Her voice was low and strained, just beyond the door. "It's me all right," he called. "Stand out of the way while I budge this."

As soon as he heard her move aside he gripped both uprights of the door frame, his fingertips sinking into the wood, and kicked at the lock. The door staggered inwards, the doorknob split the plaster of the inner wall, and Alison dodged out at once and made for the light in the corridor, muttering "Close the door."

He could see nothing in the room but darkness, which seemed to billow towards him as a wind shook the window. "What about—"

Alison turned as she reached the light. "Gone. I checked her pulse."

He could tell she was smothering her feelings. He closed the door and hurried to her, put his arm round her shoulders, raised her small dainty long-cheeked face by its chin, which had a hint of her aunt's resolve without the disproportion. Her quick smile made him want to hold her tight and stroke her straight black hair that stopped just short of her shoulders, to remind her how much he loved her and admired her. Sensing that she didn't want to linger, he led her down to the next floor, and then the question proved too much for him. "How long was the light out, Ali?"

"A few minutes. Maybe half an hour or so. I couldn't get the door open, and I didn't like to shout in case it brought Rowan up there."

"My God, why wasn't I here?" He didn't want to imagine how it must have felt to her, he wanted her to tell him so that he could help. He was guiding her towards their room, where he hoped she could lie down while he told Hermione not to bother them for a while, when Hermione came hurrying upstairs. "Tea's brewing," she said, and her voice and her face wavered. "What's wrong?"

"Your aunt's passed on," Derek said.

She glanced upwards more nervously than ever. "I want to see."

"The light in there's bust."

"You can change the bulb, can't you?"

She sounded close to hysteria, and he couldn't think how to keep her away from Alison. "I'll be cutting off the power to the top floor. It's a wonder it kept going as long as it did."

"It would while she was alive. You'll let me have your flashlight, won't you? I've got to see."

"We'll both go up while he cuts off the power," Alison said.

She sounded reassuring, though he was sure she needed that herself. "Just let me pull the fuses," he said, "and then I'll take Hermione up if she really can't wait."

But the fuses were stuck fast in the dusty board under the stairs. He was still trying to dislodge them when the women brought the flashlight from his car. Before he could delay the women, they were overhead. He managed to jiggle one fuse loose, and then the other, and heard a muffled scream at the top of the house. He threw the cracked porcelain fuses into the kitchen bin as he ran to the stairs. He liked the silence up there even less than he'd liked the scream.

Nearly all the light on the top floor was in Queenie's room. He was able to distinguish the women, standing just outside the door and outlined by the glow that the flashlight was casting within. The light swung towards him as he trod on a loose board, and then it fluttered back into the room.

An old woman was lying face up on the bare mattress. Death had seized her by her chin and dragged her mouth wide open, had pinched her cheeks inwards as far as they could go. He knew she was Queenie, if only by the way the long pink nightdress couldn't reach to cover her scrawny veinous shins, but she looked older than he would have imagined anyone could look. No wonder the women seemed almost hypnotised by the sight of her, until Alison murmured "Go and look if you want to, Hermione."

Hermione stepped backwards, hunching up her shoulders and shaking her head violently. "Well then," Alison said, "hold the flashlight while I cover her up."

Hermione almost dropped the flashlight. The lit wall nodded towards them, opening its mouth that had swallowed Queenie. Derek made to grab the flashlight until he saw that Alison was trying to make sure her sister's mind was occupied. The light did its best to fasten on the bed while Alison closed the eyes that were gazing blindly at opposite walls. She stooped to gather up the bedclothes, and the light shuddered. "Watch out for her!" Hermione screamed.

Derek thought she was talking to him. He ran into the bedroom and grabbed one edge of the bedclothes to help Alison heave them over the corpse. She insisted on smoothing them and tucking them under the mattress and under Queenie's chin before she would come out of the room, though the flashlight was trembling so violently that it made him feel the floor shake underfoot. "Now what were you saying, Hermione?" she said gently as she stepped over the threshold.

"Didn't you see her move? She's only pretending. It's another of her horrible games."

"It must have been the light, love. She's dead now, at peace."

"Don't you know her better than that?" Hermione crouched over the flashlight as if to protect it. "Look at her," she whispered. "She's listening to us, can't you see? God help us, she's smiling…"

She gripped the flashlight with both hands and poked the beam at the collapsed face. Now that Alison had closed the mouth and tucked the quilt under the chin, the corpse did appear to be smiling, so faintly it looked secretive. "She's up to something," Hermione cried, and then swung wildly towards the stairs, almost smashing the flashlight against the door frame. There was movement at the far end of the corridor.

The walls tottered, the floor reared up. This time Derek caught hold of the flashlight and steadied the beam, and found Rowan on the landing, yawning and digging her knuckles into her eyes. "Mummy, why are you all up here? Why was Hermione shouting?"

Derek closed Alison's hand around the flashlight and murmured "Was Jo and Eddie's light on when you went to the car?"

"I think so, but—" But he couldn't linger while Rowan might see what lay in Queenie's room or be infected by Hermione's panic. He hurried Rowan downstairs to her room and saw from her window that someone was still up at Jo's and Eddie's, three houses distant on the opposite side of the street. "Just put on your coat and shoes, and we'll see if you can sleep with your mates tonight," he said.

"What's wrong, daddy?"

He was touched by her grave look, her willingness to help and be grown up. "The old lady died tonight, and that's upset Hermione."

Rowan clutched her collar to her throat as they stepped out of the porch. The wind from the sea was so cold it seemed to make the stars wince. Jo and Eddie were watching a video, but switched it off when they saw Rowan. "You can sleep in our Mary's bed, give her a surprise when she wakes up in the morning," Jo said, and bustled Rowan upstairs without even asking Derek what the trouble was.

He told Eddie about the death, and declined the offer of a Scotch. "I'd better get back and see how they are," he said, preparing to help calm Hermione so that Alison could let go of her feelings. But when he let himself into the house that felt as if the night were seeping down through the roof, he found the women in the living-room, sipping quietly from large glasses, a bottle of gin and one of tonic on the floor between them. He might have thought they were over the worst if it hadn't been for the way Hermione had stared at the door to see who he was. He might almost have thought she was more terrified of Queenie now than she had been when the old woman was alive.

CHAPTER THREE

Soon after dawn on the day of the funeral, the sun above Wales drove the mist into the mountains. Rowan stood in Hermione's small back garden that sloped towards the valley and the reservoirs, and gazed across the sea and through the gap in the hills of the Wirral peninsula towards Waterloo. Eventually Derek took her into the village to buy a child's telescope. Alison knew he was leaving the family alone to talk.

She wished he didn't feel he needed to. It wasn't just that he was slow to form relationships, though they'd had to encounter each other three times outside the hostel before he'd asked her out. Perhaps he still found family life dauntingly unfamiliar, or perhaps, she hoped, he simply found the cottage overcrowded now that the family was gathering. Hermione was in the kitchen with her mother Edith, making ham sandwiches for after the funeral. Alison stayed in the living-room, which was less than half the size of any of the bedrooms in Queenie's house. Houseplants bloomed on the sill of the mullioned window, on the rough stone mantelpiece, on shelves in alcoves of the shaggily plastered white walls. Her father Keith was sitting on the window seat, gazing mildly at the sky and fingering his chin, the family chin that Queenie's had caricatured. When he patted the cushion beside him she sat there and laid her head against his shoulder. They stayed like that, silently sharing memories that felt drowsy as the longest summer afternoon of childhood, until he reached for his pipe and she sat up. "You'll be pleased about the will," he said. "Sister Queenie had some good in her after all."

"Don't you think she always had? She wasn't vicious really, just lonely."

"She was one because of the other, but don't ask me which came first," he said with a droll blank look. "I only hope her house makes life easier for you and yours."

"I'm sure it should. Only I keep feeling it was so convenient, her dying when she did, almost as if I...helped her go."

He straightened up and tried to make his compact features appear stern. "What started you thinking that nonsense? Come on, tell papa."

"I feel as if I weakened her by making her so dependent on me all at once. She kept herself fit all those years and yet I'm hardly in her house before she's dead."

"If you've been bothering yourself with that I wish you'd told me sooner. She never would have depended on anyone unless she absolutely had to. Take my word for it, she must have been counting her days when she had you move in."

Hermione and their mother came through from the kitchen, Hermione guiltily nibbling a ham sandwich. "Budge over and let Hermione sit down," Edith said to Keith with a hint of rebuke, as if he ought to show her more concern, and Alison couldn't help thinking resentfully as she stood up that she was the one who'd been trapped in the dark.

She had felt trapped for hours. If she had tried to open the door she would only have pulled the knob loose, and so she had stayed as still as she could, waiting to hear someone, anyone, coming upstairs. She'd tried not to look behind her, especially whenever the creaking of the window sounded like movement on the mattress where the dead woman lay, but now and then she'd felt Queenie rising stealthily from the bed, creeping barefoot behind her and lowering her face with its dead eyes staring in opposite directions, so that it would be level with Alison's when she had to turn and look. Whenever Alison swung round, Queenie was face up on the bed, and only the dim glow through the rain on the window had made her appear to stiffen her limbs in readiness to rear up from the mattress. Alison had felt trapped in a nightmare version of the schoolyard game in which you had to turn quickly enough to catch whoever was behind you moving.

Perhaps something like that had happened to Hermione as a child;

her nerves hadn't been the same since the day she had run sobbing out of their aunt's room. All the more reason not to resent the way their mother fussed over Hermione, Alison told herself. "Derek's taken Rowan shopping," she said. "They shouldn't be long."

Edith lowered her head and gazed at her as if over invisible spectacles, her broad ruddy oval face sinking into its chins. "We've been looking forward to seeing our little girl. We were hoping you'd come to stay more often now that we don't do much driving."

They lived in Cardiff, a day's drive away on roads that were never as straight or as clear as they looked on the map. "We will once I'm roadworthy again," Alison said. "My old car gave up the ghost the week we moved to Queenie's."

"We didn't see that much of you when you were driving. Hermione seems to manage, even if she has to close her shop and take the train to come and see us."

Just because they were fifteen years younger than Queenie didn't mean they had fifteen more years of Rowan, Alison reminded herself as Hermione said "Ali's children need her more than children need my shop."

"I certainly hope they appreciate you as much as we do," Edith cried. "Just remember you're welcome any time you feel you'd rather not be on your own."

"You've no need to worry about me," Hermione said, so shrilly that she contradicted herself.

"Well, you know best," her mother said in a tone that managed to combine hope and umbrage, then craned to look out of the window. "Here come Derek and our little girl, and someone else."

"My brother, I expect," Keith said.

"No, it's not Richard. Good God, I believe it's his son."

"It could be Lance, they've let him out of hospital," Keith admitted. "I suppose that could be him under the beard."

It was indeed Lance, whom Alison hadn't seen for years. She and Hermione had always been wary of him. He'd been twenty, and a civil servant, when the sisters were five and eight, but they had never gone with him along the beach at Waterloo to see his secret, even though that would have taken them out of sight of Queenie's house. He'd never harmed anyone so far as she knew, but whatever he'd imagined doing must have consumed him with guilt, for when his father had found his cache of magazines he'd not only denied they were his but begun to deny he was Lance. Now Hermione let him in and said brightly "Hello, Lance. We weren't expecting you, but you're welcome."

It occurred to Alison that he was a childhood fear Hermione could deal with. He had grown entirely bald, his cranium as red as his face, which was hidden from the cheekbones downwards by a thick gingery beard. His suit was civil-service grey but shabby as social security now. "So isn't your father coming?" Edith demanded. "We understood he was."

"He said he would." Lance paused, his pale lips parting within his beard as if he found it hard to breathe. "And then he said he'd left home because of Auntie Queenie, and he wouldn't have her thinking he'd forgiven her just because she was dead."

"We both left home as soon as we were old enough to get away from her living our lives for us," Keith said. "My only regret was that our parents couldn't make their escape too."

"So Richard sent you instead, did he?" Edith accused Lance.

"I wanted to come," Lance said, more sluggishly than before. His slowness was the price of treatment, Alison realised. "I thought someone should, and I wanted to see the family. I hoped you wouldn't mind."

"We're glad you did," Hermione assured him.

"You don't think it's cheeky of me to pay my respects, then? I was always a bit scared of Auntie Queenie. I used to feel she knew whatever I was thinking."

Hermione turned quickly to the window. "Is that the cars?" she pleaded.

The limousines weren't due for half an hour. Derek kept Rowan outside, away from Lance, where she gazed across the bay and pouted because the telescopes had been too expensive. Now and then Derek glanced through the window at Alison, winked at her or made a face like swallowing a slice of lemon by mistake or pretended to jump back from the sight of the family gathering, and she stuck her tongue out at him when nobody was looking: she'd never said that family life had no drawbacks. The family made conversation as best they could, avoiding the subject of Queenie for Hermione's sake and slowing down whenever Lance had anything to say. The limousines came as a relief.

Derek, Rowan and the sisters rode in the first grey car, Lance and the others followed. Oldsters by the factories on the coast road stood respectfully until the limousines had passed. A train on the shoreside railway raced the limousines through Glan-y-don, another caught them up at Ffynnongroew, and then the cars turned away from Talacre and its caravans clustering near the disused lighthouse, uphill through Gronant to the churchyard.

Queenie and her parents had rented a summer cottage in Gronant. When her mother had died there, Queenie's father had had her buried near the place they most loved. He'd moved into the room at the top of the Waterloo house so that he could see where he would eventually rejoin his wife. Bright as the sun was, he would have seen little on a day like this. The bay was a swarm of blinding diamonds, the sandy coast where Queenie's house stood streamed like flames.

The vicar met the party at the door of the chapel, a squat building with plump white walls, and ushered them into the interior, where sainted windows draped colours over the pine pews. It was as calm as Alison hoped Hermione would be. But Hermione peered down the aisle at the coffin. "Who wanted her left uncovered?"

They glanced blankly at one another. "I'll have them screw the lid on," Keith said.

"We ought to say goodbye," Hermione said with some bravado, and stepped forward. Alison paced her, expecting grotesquely to see Queenie's chin first over the side of the casket. The undertakers had tamed Queenie's features and lent her cheeks a slumbering bloom that reminded Alison of Queenie's last days, when she had seemed able to make herself look younger by her unshakable faith in herself. At least she looked more peaceful than Alison had ever seen her – but Hermione stumbled forward, her arms trembling by her sides, and stared into the coffin. "Who gave her that?" she almost screamed.

CHAPTER FOUR

He shouldn't have brought Rowan after all, Derek thought angrily. He'd been afraid that Hermione might lose control, and this was worse than he'd feared. Whatever she was seeing in the coffin, she sounded capable of reaching in and dragging it out. He tried to turn Rowan away from the spectacle, but her head craned around as he urged her towards the porch. There was confusion in the aisle, Edith having grabbed Keith's arm as he made to slip out to the undertaker's men, Lance standing glumly in the middle of the narrow aisle, the vicar peering past him. Derek pushed Rowan as far as the vicar. "Look after her while I see what's going on," he muttered, and squeezed past the others towards the front of the chapel.

Hermione and Alison were gazing into the coffin. Alison was holding her sister's forearm to restrain her. Derek hurried forward, trying to hush his footsteps on the thick uneven flagstones. He could see nothing wrong. The old woman's face was lovingly made up, her hands were folded on her chest, and the undertakers had found a white dress long enough to cover her ankles. "What's up?" he murmured.

Hermione stared at him as if she was afraid to speak. "We're wondering how Queenie comes to be wearing that locket," Alison said.

He'd already noticed it, a heart-shaped gold locket resting on the old woman's chest, its thin gold chain around her neck. "Not just any locket," Hermione protested, lowering her voice when Derek frowned at her. "Alison knows what I mean."

"She means," Alison said apologetically, "it had Rowan's hair in it. I suppose it still has."

Queenie had demanded a lock of Rowan's hair the first time it was cut, and Derek had never understood why Alison had hesitated. "I told you you should have got it back," Hermione wailed, her voice rising. "You never should have given her anything of Rowan's."

If she was going to bring Rowan into it, he'd be taking the child for a walk. But now the aisle was further blocked by one of the undertaker's men. "He says they always leave the lid off unless they're told different," Keith explained. "Anyone who wants to should pay their respects, and then he'll close it for us."

The family came forward before Derek could usher Rowan out. By the time he managed to edge unobtrusively through to her, the undertaker's man was picking up the lid. "We mustn't leave the locket on her," Hermione cried.

"Behave yourself, Hermione," her mother said, low and sharp. "Show some respect for the dead. She must have wanted to wear it, and that's all that need concern us."

Hermione glanced desperately from face to face. Apart from Lance, who'd given the coffin a token blink and was trudging back to a pew, all the adults were willing her to control herself. Alison guided her towards the pews, murmuring "No need to worry, love, I'm not," but Hermione's shoulders writhed as she heard the faint thud of the lid, the almost inaudible squeal of the screws.

During the funeral Derek kept sensing her nervous glances at Rowan. The vicar said that their sister in God was a woman of rare education and a tower of strength to those who knew her, qualities that were seen too seldom nowadays. Derek took Rowan out of the chapel as soon as he felt he could, catching the undertaker's men eating biscuits in one of the limousines, their hands held like trays to catch the crumbs.

Rowan scattered earth on the coffin, since Alison and her parents did. On the drive back to the cottage she wanted to know why you were meant to throw earth like that, but nobody could remember. Hermione stared at her empty hands as if she regretted not having cast earth, whether to placate Queenie or to help fill in the grave.

At the cottage Rowan sensed that the adults wanted to talk, and took a plate of sandwiches and a glass of orange juice into the garden. Even then the conversation only sidled around the subject of the funeral. "At least she's where she wanted to be," Edith said, and Hermione's eyes flickered. Derek couldn't stand the timidity of the conversation any longer. "With her father, you mean," he said.

"He made her think she was the most important person in the world," Lance said, and Derek's innards tightened at his slowness: the cure seemed almost as distressing as the illness. "She wanted to keep him with her always, even when he died."

"That was just a silly business you children scared yourselves with," Edith told Hermione.

"It's all very well for you to dismiss it like that, mother, but you were never that anxious to be left alone with her yourself."

Derek meant to help. "What were you all so shy of? She looked like any old maid to me. What was all that about Rowan and the locket?"

"She used to terrorise Hermione when we were little," Alison said. "That doesn't go away all at once just because the person has."

"I'll tell you something, Derek, that may help you understand," Hermione said as he opened his mouth and closed it again. "When I was a baby they gave her one of my first teeth, and do you know what she said to me when I was old enough to realise? She told me that if I ever did anything she didn't like or said anything against her she'd make me feel as if that tooth was being pulled out. I wonder if you'd want anyone saying such things to Rowan."

"What do you think?"

"It's the first I've heard of it if she said that to you," Edith declared.

"Mother, I did try to tell you, but you said exactly what you're saying now, that it was all nonsense. Only I noticed you never gave her any of Alison's teeth."

The imminence of a family quarrel made Derek uneasy, and he tried to head it off. "No wonder you didn't like her, but you must have realised sometime that she couldn't do what she said she'd do to you."

Hermione seemed not to know where to look, and then she stared defiantly at him. "She did."

"Hang on, you mean she—"

"I mean that if I ever said anything about her I thought she wouldn't like, the tooth that had grown there started aching. This tooth," she said, poking a stubby forefinger into the flesh beneath the left-hand corner of her mouth.

"You poor little sod. Thank Christ we all grow up. How long is it since you felt she could do that to you?"

"The night she died."

Derek didn't know what to say. Distressingly, he felt a twinge of the inner shrinking he'd experienced on meeting Lance. "She's dead now at any rate, Hermione," her father said. "You've no reason to worry about yourself, or Rowan for that matter."

"May she rest in peace," Hermione muttered, "which is more than she let your father have." She gazed wistfully out at Rowan, who was throwing back her head to drain her orange juice. "I was going to suggest that Rowan could stay for the weekend while you sort out Queenie's house, but now that you've heard how neurotic I am I don't suppose you'll want her to."

Derek glanced at Alison, who looked his question back at him. "We'll be staying," Edith said.

"Rowan can stay if she wants," Derek said. When he went out and asked her she skipped with delight, and he felt he'd been unfair to Hermione. He ought to know as well as anyone that it wasn't so easy to shake off what had been done to you as a child. Rowan would be fine, he told himself, with three adults to keep her safe. He closed his eyes and raised his face towards the sunlight, and scoffed at himself: surely there was nothing here for Rowan to be kept safe from.

CHAPTER FIVE

Dear diary, this morning I tidyed my room but Hermione wouldn't let me use the vaccume even though I do at home, but yesterday I helped in the shop becose grandma said I ought to help Hermione chuse what children would like best, then we all went for an evening walk where I like, down Greenfield valley with the old factorys and resevwars...

That Sunday morning, Rowan was sitting in a garden chair outside Hermione's cottage. Writing didn't feel like writing here; it felt like being part of the long September morning, the sound of church bells across the hills, a chiming as minute as the glitter of the distant sea. Now and then pale patches of grass that at first she'd thought were smoke sailed uphill towards her, and then a breeze would spill over her like cream. When she laid the diary on the lawn beside her, an invisible reader turned the pages. She gazed across the bay towards Waterloo and wondered what her grandaunt's house felt like now.

It hadn't felt the same since the night Queenie had died, but Rowan wasn't sure what the difference was. Perhaps it just felt emptier. A feeling of emptiness and being called had taken her upstairs that night, still half asleep, to Queenie's floor. She was sad that she hadn't had a chance to say goodbye. You could be sad when someone died even if you'd been scared of them when they were alive. Though Queenie's room seemed vast Rowan had always felt closed in by the vastness, by the smell of books and disinfectant and by the dusty net curtains that made the outside world look like a faded pattern in the fabric. Queenie would want to know everything she'd done that day, would ask question after question until it was worse than being at school, especially since Rowan had always felt that Queenie already knew the answers. She'd felt as if the questions were gobbling her up.

Once Rowan had been as frightened as Hermione had always tried not to seem. Every night she'd had to say good night to her grandaunt, had had to climb on the bed that felt like a mound of lumpy dust and hug the old lady's bony shoulders. Rowan had closed her eyes as she craned to kiss the old lips, dry as a bird's beak. She'd opened them as she retreated from the bed – and once, just a few nights before the old lady had died, Rowan had frozen, for the old lady had been gazing past her in such dismay that Rowan had been terrified to look.

It had only been the light, which had dimmed momentarily. If Queenie had been frightened of the dark, why hadn't she let daddy fix her electricity? He'd said that by rights it shouldn't be working at all. The memory made Rowan shiver in the sunlight, and she watched birds gather like weights on opposite branches of a sapling until her grandmother called her from the kitchen window. "Come here a minute, lovey. Would you like to take your granddad for a walk while we make the lunch?"

"Or a drive if you want to save your legs," he said from the living-room window.

"That'd be enormous, great," Rowan cried, and ran in to the toilet before anyone could tell her to go, ran out again to her grandfather. "Please may we go to Talacre?"

"Bingo land again, is it? Well, you should choose, since it's your last day."

She giggled at the way he was trying to sound enthusiastic. "I don't mean Talacre exactly. I wanted to walk to the lighthouse."

"Aren't you afraid of Virginia Woolf? Sorry, I expect that's over your head."

"I know who she is, she writes books. My grandaunt had one in her room. When I grow up I want to write books for people to read. I try to now, but the stories won't stay still long enough."

"You're an old-fashioned young lady, aren't you? Not that we'd ever change you for a newer model."

"I do like old things."

"That must be why you're going out with me. Well, let's get to the beach before the tribes of Homo Transistorus begin their bottle-breaking ceremonies," he said, and ushered her out to the small blunt car.

He braked all the way down the valley. On the coast road trees enclosed the car in a deep green tunnel broken by arches of sunlight, and then the coast flattened out beneath a hillside boiling with foliage. Soon the car turned toward the open sea. Beyond a bridge over the railway was Talacre: houses like wheelless caravans crowded in the lee of the glaring grassy dunes; long brick sheds faced the encampment across the soft road. The sheds were penny arcades, souvenir or betting or fish and chip shops, the Boathouse Bingo that boasted Top Prizes and Quality Prizes. Granddad parked near a picture of a pirate with a sack and an eye patch outside the Smugglers Inn, a shed with a line of white arches stuck on to the front, and they made for the beach.

Beyond the caravans a brambly path led through the dunes. Bits of ruined buildings poked through the undergrowth near the beach: here a foundation, there a chimney stack out of which a crow flapped. As the sand grew softer underfoot granddad began to toil, mopping his forehead with his large handkerchief. He clambered over the last dunes and flopped on a bald patch amid the spiky grass. "You carry on. You'll stay where I can see you, won't you, and watch out for horses on the beach."

Rowan ran towards the lighthouse, which stood on a pie of concrete surrounded by fallen walls at the edge of the waves. At first the beach was baked in mud that gleamed metallically, then the sand was exposed, embedded with pebbles that grew larger near the rubble. Two short stretches of wall wrapped in wire netting remained, though they seemed to cut off nothing from anything. Families were settling themselves against the dunes, but the only person near the rubble was a fat lady in a flowered dress, her head like a bag of flesh with hardly a bump for a chin, tied tight with a bow at the collar. Granddad waved and lay back on the dune, and Rowan walked around the lighthouse.

She liked Talacre, where she could play a video game that made her feel she was flying into outer space, but this was better – older, lonelier. She was hoping she would be able to run up to the balcony around the broken lantern and give granddad a surprise. But though the windows in the white shaft were gaping, the doorway was plugged with bricks.

She sat with her back against the lighthouse and gazed out to sea. Flecks of colour, sandy and chalky, trembled on the horizon of the basking water. Hermione had told her that on a good day you could see the house in Waterloo. All days here were good days as far as Rowan was concerned, but she had never been able to make out the house. She was screwing up her eyes when a voice said "What are you looking for?"

It wasn't the fat lady. When Rowan shaded her eyes and glanced towards the redundant wall she saw a girl of about her own age in a long old-fashioned white dress. The girl was holding her chin as if it were a magic lamp and gazing palely at Rowan. "I was trying to see where I live," Rowan said.

"Across the water? I come from there too." The girl moved closer to her but pursed her lips at the prospect of sitting on the concrete. "You wanted to go up the lighthouse, I thought."

It sounded like an invitation. "There's no way in," Rowan said. "I expect it's dangerous."

"I've been up with my father. I could see right home."

"Why, does he work there?"

"A lighthouse-keeper, do you mean?" The girl gave Rowan a look so sharp she felt she had been scratched. "Nothing so paltry. What does your father do?"

"He's an electrician. He calls it being a spark."

A smirk widened the girl's small mouth. "Don't take me for a snob. My father taught me to say good day to everyone, tradesmen included. It keeps them in their place."

She must live in Crosby and go to private school, Rowan assumed, and said angrily "Everyone says he's the best electrician. He takes me with him sometimes, and I've seen how careful he is."

"Does he ever let you help him?"

Rowan was about to boast, but a glint in the pale eyes deterred her. "No."

"I hope he never does. He'd be breaking the law. He could go to prison if you even helped him without his knowing, and besides, you could hurt yourself."

It was none of her business, Rowan thought, feeling vulnerable and responsible for him. "You're here with your father, are you?" she said.

The girl drew herself up stiffly and stared straight into the sun, her shadow falling across Rowan as if her sudden gloom had been made visible. "I don't know where he is."

Rowan would have sympathised, except that she sensed more emotion brooding under the words than she might be able to cope with. The fat lady was being tugged away along the beach by two children, a girl whose mouth was green with lollipop and a boy wearing only a cowboy hat. "With your mum, then?" Rowan suggested. "Is that her?"

"The woman with the filthy children? I trust you're joking."

It sounded like a threat, even though the girl was still gazing into the sun. "Where do you go to school?" Rowan asked without especially wanting to know.

"I don't need to. There's not a teacher in the world who couldn't learn from my father."

Rowan sensed that scoffing might be dangerous. "I've got to go now. My granddad said I had to stay where he could see me."

The girl turned and gazed at her. Her eyes seemed bright and colourless as the sun she had been staring at. "You needn't go yet. Stay with me."

"No, I can't." Rowan put her hands on the hot rough concrete and tried to push herself to her feet, but the unblinking brightness of the girl's eyes made her feel dim and limp. The gleam of a gold chain that hung around the girl's neck and down inside her dress pricked the edge of Rowan's vision, and she managed to look away. She struggled to her feet and almost sprawled on the concrete. Her head felt fragile as a bubble, her legs were wavering, the dunes were shrinking away from the lighthouse. It was only the heat, she told herself, and granddad would know what to do to make her feel better. She heaved one foot forward to keep herself up.

"Very well, if you must," the girl said as Rowan reached out a hand to support herself on the giant neon tube of the lighthouse, which appeared to be yards away. Her palm pressed against the flaking whitewash, and the world seemed to fall together around her; the dunes came back. She made her way carefully down the concrete, and realised that the girl was watching her with an emotion Rowan couldn't identify: surprise, perhaps, but not only surprise. "Will you be my friend when we get home?" the girl said.

An impression of loneliness passed over Rowan like a lingering shadow. "If I see you," she said.

"Don't worry, I'll see you. I'll bring something I think you'll like."

Rowan stepped off the concrete onto the soft sand. "What's your name, anyway?"

"Vicky," the girl said absently, staring past her at the dunes where Rowan's grandfather lay. Rowan looked to see if he was beckoning, but he was still on his back. He blinked himself awake as she went towards him. "That's right, stay where I can see you," he mumbled, and dozed off. Rowan set about searching for pebbles she could use to decorate her patch in Waterloo once he had landscaped the garden. She hadn't noticed when Vicky had moved away, but presumably the girl had taken off her dress: there was nobody in white along the miles of beach.

The next time granddad wakened, he said they should be heading back for lunch. At the cottage Rowan learned that daddy had to fix someone's electricity and wouldn't be coming to collect her until early evening. After lunch she read the books her grandparents had bought her, and had time for a sandwich tea before the car came.

Daddy picked her up and hugged her and then shook hands with the grown-ups. "Has she behaved herself? You can keep her if you like, Hermione," he teased, then seemed to feel he'd been thoughtless. Rowan gathered her suitcase and her bag of pebbles, and they went out to the car.

Once he was driving he didn't say much. She liked just being with him, gazing out at the russet houses and the trees that glowed like the sky before a sunset. All the same, the thought of never again being with him while he worked made her feel sad. She'd brought him tools and bits of wire sometimes, but the idea that he might have been locked up because of her made her almost afraid to look at him.

The car sped onto the motorway as the sun slipped behind the hills. Cars flashed their headlamps at dark cars in the dusk. In the night at the end of the motorway the Mersey Tunnel was lit like a hospital corridor. Halfway through she imagined ships sailing over her head. In Liverpool the van turned along the dock road, where the warehouses were long as side streets and full of tiny unlit windows, and daddy muttered at potholes in the road. Rowan loved being out so late: it made even familiar streets seem new, mysterious. She was looking forward to arriving at the house, because now that she'd been away she knew what it felt like: home. But when she saw the sign outside the house her mind felt suddenly cold and dark. The house was for sale.

CHAPTER SIX

"Derek and Alison Faraday aren't here just now. If you'll leave your name and number and reason for calling, one of us will get back to you..." When they returned from the funeral, several messages were waiting. The estate agent for whom Derek had rewired some properties wanted Derek to call him, and Robin Ormond, Derek's accountant, was on the tape too. "I'm taking it you've had time to bring your books up to date, and I'll call round early Saturday unless I hear from you."

"He didn't know about the funeral and everything," Alison said.

"He's like a bloody robot, him, nothing in his head but numbers," Derek declared, his voice echoing in the wide shabby hall. "I'll do the books if I have time and if I haven't the bugger can wait. We ought to get started upstairs while we can see what we're doing."

"You make a start while I see to dinner." She held his face in her cool hands to detain him. "Don't go worrying yourself about our finances. We're past the worst, I'm sure we are."

He slipped one hand under her hair and clasped her long neck while he kissed her, the tips of their tongues barely touching. "I'll see you upstairs," he said with a wink.

For the first time since they'd moved in, he didn't feel inhibited. The place was just an old house in need of renovation, too big but not unwelcoming. It was such a relief not to feel as if he had no right to be there that he strolled through the downstairs rooms, opening windows to let out the stale lifeless smell. He touched the chandelier to make it chime and walked his fingers over a few keys of the piano, and then he went upstairs.

The top floor smelled mustier than ever. It smelled, he thought, dark. He opened doors, hoping to lighten the gloom, but most of the grimy windows were draped as heavily as the shapes that stood about the rooms. There should be a skylight over the stairs, anything to let in more light. He groped his way to the front of the house and pushed open Queenie's door.

The smell of old books met him, a smell so thick it seemed to dull the evening light. At least the smell of disinfectant hadn't lingered. He gazed at the stripped mattress that retained a depression like a pinched coffin, until he realised he was behaving as if he weren't allowed in the room. He stalked in and shoved up the sash of the large window, and took deep salty breaths while he gazed across the bay at Wales. Thinking of Rowan, he turned to the books.

He didn't read much himself. Trade literature was about his limit, except for a morning paper to read during his coffee breaks. He knew the kinds of books Rowan liked: he often watched her reading, her eyes scanning the pages as if she wanted to devour all the books in the world. He was proud of her for reading so much, and now he wanted to find the books Queenie would have meant her to have. He went from pile to staggering pile, hoping that he wouldn't have to pull out books from low down on the stacks that were all taller than he was. His shadow drifted over them as if the coaly furniture were leaking. He found the children's books heaped by the bed.

You didn't see books like these in the shops, thick spines embossed with gilded letters and sometimes with pictures. He put one hand on top of the pile and the other halfway down, and lifted the books. He was turning towards the door when the pages squeezed out of the books at either end of the armful, flew out of the bindings like pulp out of rotten fruit, and the pile of books sprawled across the bed.

He picked up one book gingerly, a book with a saint on the cover. When he tried to part the wadded pages, they tore like wet bread. All the books were like that, the children's books and those in the other piles he examined, books about faith and will. She'd often talked about that couple, and the first time he'd heard her he'd thought they were friends of hers. There were books in French and German too, and languages he didn't even recognise. "Look at the state of these," he said when Alison came up. "She must have been something special if she could read them."

"They aren't all like that." She opened the top book on a pile near the bed, and then she stared at it. "I don't understand. She was reading this the night she died."

The print was seeping unreadably through the pages, fragments of which stuck like mould to the opposite wad. "Maybe it was a different book," Derek said, raising his voice to jar her out of her dismay. "They don't look worth keeping, anyway. Let's get the tea chests."

They'd kept the chests when they moved from Liverpool. At first Alison examined each book, but after a dozen or so had proved to be rotten she began to throw them in by the handful. "I'll see to chucking them if you like while you sort out her clothes," Derek said.

She wrinkled her nose as she pulled out the first drawer, which was full of underclothes, yellowed and cobwebbed as if they hadn't been touched for years. Two more drawers contained clothes sown with spiders' eggs; the rest were stuffed with books, the pages mashed together. "It's as though the soul's gone out of the room," Alison murmured as she upended a drawer. She opened a black wardrobe so determinedly that it lurched forward. A long white dress billowed at her, and Derek saw it come apart, torn pieces swarming towards her face. They were moths, which fluttered out of the window into the dusk. "I'll leave this until daylight, I think," she said.

When they'd loaded all the books into the chests the darker patches revealed on the walls looked like stains, spreading as dusk deepened. The sense of so much still to be done depressed him. "What this place needs is bloody gutting," he muttered.

"I know what it needs." Alison took his hand and ran her thumb lingeringly over his palm, and led him downstairs to their bedroom. They sat on the bed and undressed each other, traced each other's bodies with their hands and mouths. Alison closed her long soft warm legs about his hips as he slipped snugly into her. The waves of her sucked him deeper, until he swelled and then erupted, so powerfully that they were left gasping. As he came he felt Queenie's floor hovering over them, a huge dark blotch.

After dinner he pored over his accounts. At least Ken, the builder for whom he'd rewired a block of houses that were being turned into flats, had paid him almost three thousand pounds, though the cheque was dated next week. He was still making entries in the ledgers after midnight, writing small to stay between the lines. He felt dwarfed by debts and all the empty rooms.

In the morning Tony from the estate agent's called round unexpectedly to price the house. "And they're talking of rewiring your kiddie's school, so you should let them know who you are," Tony said as Derek followed him through the rooms. The house shouldn't fetch much less than ten thousand, Derek thought, dreading to hear. Tony marched through, jingling his pocketfuls of change, and peered at ceilings, knocked on walls that crunched under his knuckles, scratched his broad stubbly pate. He hummed tunelessly to himself and said not a word until they and Alison were on the overgrown path, by which time Derek's forehead felt stretched almost to splitting. "I'd ask for more than we expect to get and be prepared to accept offers," Tony said. "Assuming you don't anticipate any queries on the will, I can put it in the window at an asking price of twenty-three thou."

That could mean twenty thousand. Twenty thousand would end all their worries, would let them have a holiday for the first time in years and secure them the kind of house they wanted without saddling them with more of a mortgage than they might be able to cope with. Derek shook hands with Tony, hugged Alison and beamed at her as Tony left, promising to send someone who would price the furniture. Derek even beamed at the sight of Robin Ormond's Mini nudging the kerb outside the gate.

The accountant wasn't quite as tall as Alison, but much broader. He wore a pale blue summer suit, and glanced suspiciously at the chair Derek gave him at the dinner table. "You want to get the little woman busy with the duster before anyone comes to look at the house," he suggested, and put on his rimless spectacles that seemed constantly in danger of slipping down his wide flat face. "These are the accounts, I take it. Well, let's see what can be made of them."

He turned the pages of the ledgers slowly, rubbing the corners between finger and thumb. "Dear me. Pah, I don't think so. Oh, really," he mused, then grew impatient. "Have you no receipt for this? I can't make out this word at all. My dear fellow, that isn't how you spell 'calculate'." At the last page he threw up his hands. "Never accept a postdated cheque."

"I've his word he'll honour it. At least it means I've got a date for payment."

The accountant closed his eyes and shook his head. "You should have taken him to court, or threatened to. Better still, don't work for such people at all."

"If I didn't I wouldn't have enough big jobs."

"You're in a bad way then, aren't you?" the accountant said accusingly. "I suppose I'll have to pass these books, but we'll need to be looking at ways to rationalise your business. You could be on course for a major cash-flow crisis. If you don't call in all these debts you may not even have the capital to pay your tax this Christmas."

Derek was tempted to tell him what Tony had said, except that he might cast doubt on it. Better to tell him when they had the money, and then watch his face. Later Tony came to photograph the exterior, and the prospect of the sale sustained Derek through the weekend, while he and Alison cleared out as much of the house as they could. They planned a leisurely drive to fetch Rowan, stopping for lunch in a beer garden on the way, but on Sunday morning Derek was called out to one of the nursing homes beside the dunes. Alison stayed at the house to have dinner waiting for Rowan, and let the light from the hall stretch onto the path like a carpet as Rowan climbed out of the car.

Alison had made scouse, one of Rowan's favourites ever since she'd had it at Jo's across the road, but Rowan only picked at the stew. "I'm sorry, mummy, Hermione made sandwiches for tea."

"That sounds like my sister. Don't worry, babe, the dinner will keep if that's all that's wrong."

Rowan didn't answer that until she was in the oversized bath, Alison scrubbing her back while Derek waited with a towel on the far side of the tiled bathroom. Rowan lifted one foot and watched bubbles vanish from her toes, and then she said "Do we really have to move?"

"Hurry up, Rowan, it's long past your bedtime," Alison said. "The house is much too big for just the three of us, lovey."

"We didn't think you were that struck with it," Derek said as Rowan walked into the towel, and when she gave him a reproachful look, "Go on then, tell us what you like."

"All manner of things," Rowan said like one of her books. "Hearing the sea and the wind when I'm in bed, and the ships saying good night to me like you said they were the first night we stayed here. Being able to go straight out to the beach. And now I thought I'd be able to bring my friends home and play lots of games all over the house. I was really looking forward to living here now, more than anything."

"Let's get you to bed now, you're very tired," Alison said. As the child wriggled into her nightshirt, delaying so as to hide her face, Alison took her hand. "We can't afford to stay, Rowan. We may not be going very far, we haven't even started looking. We won't be living anywhere you don't like."

Rowan's face struggled out of the cotton neck, blinking back tears. "Why can't the people who owe daddy money just pay him?" she cried, and looked ashamed at once. "I'll try not to mind when we move," she said in a small voice.

The accountant hadn't made Derek feel guilty, but Rowan did – guilty and too easily taken advantage of. Could Queenie have led her to expect that the house would be her home? Later, as Alison caught up on her sleep to be ready for the dawn bus into Liverpool, he lay beside her, his head crawling with figures, as if he could find a treasure buried in his calculations: however hard Rowan was trying to resign herself, he knew that she secretly believed him capable of some such magic. It was a pity she couldn't persuade the bank manager, with whom Derek's interviews had been more frequent lately, and chillier.

As he began to sag into sleep he saw all the figures that were chasing one another around his skull turn red.

In the darkest part of the night, Rowan's voice wakened him. She sounded as if she were using a phone in a dream, pausing every so often for a response. He listened affectionately, though he couldn't make out a word, until it occurred to him that she might be talking in her sleep because she was unhappy. He slid sleepily out of bed and padded into the corridor.

Her room was dark. When he pushed the door gently, the light that fanned across the carpet fell short of the bed. He thought the light had quieted her, and then his eyes adjusted. Just as he saw that the bed was empty, he heard her voice again. She was on the top floor.

He scrambled up the warped stairs and stepped into the dark. His first barefoot step on the damp uneven carpet chased away the last of his sleep. He could hear Rowan ahead of him. He groped along the wall, over wallpaper that felt like mould and doors cold and slippery as slate, and came to a greyish rectangle that might have been a standing slab of ice. It gave way to his eyes as he stepped through it, and he saw dim hints of Queenie's room. As the shapes in the room settled onto his vision he saw a figure in white lying on the bed.

Rowan was curled up on the bare mattress, one arm stretched out, the fingers moving slightly as if she felt the absence of a hand she had been holding in her sleep. "Yes, on the beach," she murmured. Derek lifted her without wakening her and made his way carefully along the middle of the unlit corridor. He tucked her into bed and watched until he was sure she was quiet, and then he crept in beside Alison. He mustn't have been quite awake up there, he decided, already dozing. For a moment, as he'd gathered Rowan up, he'd felt as if they weren't alone in the huge unlit room.

CHAPTER SEVEN

As soon as her parents had driven away, Hermione set about weeding the garden. A comedian was telling jokes in Welsh on a television beyond an open window, a mower droned on a lawn, but otherwise the hillside above Holywell was quiet as the evening crept down the mountains. Fat clouds the colours of pigeons and doves flocked above the distant strip of sea, stirring drowsily. Around her the gardens and cottages and fields were paying back the hours of daylight to the pale sky. She might have sat and watched the colours of the landscape rekindling gently, but she needed the work as much as the garden did. She'd made a generous dinner before her parents left for Waterloo, and then she'd eaten too much of it herself. Weeding would keep her from nibbling, from sitting in the cottage like a fat-faced rodent in its larder. She knew she ate whenever she was nervous, but what excuse had she now? Queenie was dead, and so were the terrors of Hermione's childhood, and perhaps that meant it was time to remember, in between worrying while her parents were on the road and being anxious that Alison and Derek might have taken on too much. Even if Queenie had turned her childhood into a nightmare, she mustn't let that rule the rest of her life.

The thought felt like the start of freedom. If she could blame Queenie without flinching, perhaps she could also forgive her; perhaps she could accept, as Alison apparently had, that Queenie had been nothing but a lonely embittered maiden aunt with no understanding of children. "You'll be where I can keep an eye on you," Queenie had said when Hermione had moved into the cottage. Hermione laughed out loud at that, at having been made nervous by it when she'd been thirty years old. She was too old now for Queenie to seem terrifying, she thought, just as the phone rang in the cottage.

She ran in so hastily that a fist seemed to close around her vision, squeezing it dark as she grabbed the receiver. "Who is it?" she cried.

Her urgency had thrown him, for seconds idled by before he said "It's Lance."

"It's you, is it?" she said, and quieting her panic, "What can I do for you?"

His answer was a mumble that she had to ask him to repeat. "Alison's number," he said as if she were deliberately adding to his difficulties.

"Yes, what about it?" She was feeling as protective as she had when she used to warn Alison not to go on the beach with him. "She's pretty busy just now, Lance. What did you want to say to her?"

"About the little girl."

Hermione took a long breath while she chose her words. "I don't think Alison's husband would appreciate your interest, Lance. If you need to talk to someone, you can talk to me."

"It's nothing like that." He must be pressing the receiver against his face out of frustration with her and his slowness, for his voice blundered closer, blurring. "I was thinking about the old woman."

"Queenie? What about her?"

"About her will. I want to tell Alison. It's hard enough for me to talk."

"I'll tell her you're trying to get in touch and then perhaps she'll call you. That'll do, won't it?"

"I hope so," he said, so inadequately that she waited for the rest. "You could remind her I never hurt anyone."

Except yourself, Hermione thought. He'd locked away his fantasies and lacerated himself with guilt, and all she felt once she put down the receiver was pity for him. If he'd believed Queenie was capable of seeing into his mind, he must have been even more frightened of her than Hermione had been. She wondered if he might have aggravated her own fears.

Her parents had. She'd dreaded visiting her aunt all the more for knowing they dreaded it and yet gave in when they were summoned. Eating at Queenie's had been the worst, feeling her waiting for you to drop food on the tablecloth or on the floor so that she could rap the table with her knuckles and cry "Look what the child's done now." She made you feel like an animal at the table, feel as if you'd smeared your mouth or dribbled or that your chewing was the loudest sound in the room. Being allowed to leave the table at last had never been much of a relief; the whole house had seemed neurotically aware of Hermione, waiting for her to touch something she shouldn't, knock over an ornament, peep into one of the numerous rooms the children had been told to stay out of. Long before they left she would be constipated by the sense of always being watched.

She was beginning to feel angry, not afraid. There was no point in pretending Queenie hadn't been vicious. Hermione dug her fork into the flower bed, remembering the night after Queenie's father had been buried. Queenie had never been more vicious than that night, when Hermione had ventured up to sympathise with her.

She had been six years old, and glimpsing the hidden world of adults. The family had converged on the house in Waterloo when it became clear that the old man was dying at last. He and Queenie had lived there alone for years. Hermione recalled him dimly as a bony man with a disproportionately large mild face and a shock of grey hair, who'd sat hunched at the head of the dining table and who had emitted questions now and then, questions which she'd never understood and which seemed to elude him too. He must have been trying to recall his tenure as a professor in Liverpool. She hadn't realised he was dying until Lance had looked into the room she'd shared with Alison, to tell them he was dead.

By then the girls were huddled in Hermione's bed, where Alison had taken refuge from the screams, their aunt's screams, so piercing and desperate they'd seemed to come from all over the house. The floor shook as people ran upstairs, and Keith told the girls to stay in their room. The screams grew intermittent, until the girls were breathless with dread of the next scream. The murmur of the adults overhead seemed far too distant, two corridors and a staircase away. When Lance sidled round the door to tell them their grandfather was dead, Hermione ordered him out of the room, though she would have pleaded with him to stay if he had been anyone but Lance.

During the night Queenie calmed down but refused to leave her father's room. That much Hermione learned in the morning, when Lance's father Richard took Lance and the girls for a walk on the wintry beach. Between then and the funeral the children were kept away from the house as much as possible, but Hermione gathered that even the doctor hadn't succeeded in moving their aunt from beside her father's bed. The family had to give her a drink laced with a sleeping pill before the undertakers could remove the corpse. She didn't scream when she awakened by the empty bed; she didn't speak to anyone, even to ask where they'd taken her father. No wonder the house felt like a trap about to spring. No wonder Edith kept the girls at the back of the church during the funeral.

The pews were full of ranks of grey professors. The church smelled of wreaths and mothballed suits. Edith craned to watch Queenie over the grey heads, and Hermione saw her knuckles whitening as she gripped the pew in front. Suddenly a murmur passed through the congregation, for Queenie had reared up, flinging Richard aside as he reached for her arm, and was running stiff-legged towards the coffin, her arms outstretched as if she meant to hoist the corpse. Edith rushed the girls out of the church, and Hermione couldn't see what happened as the priest and several other men closed in on Queenie, her face glaring wildly above them. Keith and Richard brought Queenie out behind the coffin, but she ignored the ceremony: she stood at the graveside and stared at the sky, smiling bitterly and secretly as if she could see something none of the mourners could. Afterwards the family drove back to Waterloo, where she went straight up to her father's room and lay on the bed. She refused to speak to anyone or even look at them, and the family was unwilling to leave her alone in the house in case she planned to do away with herself.

Hermione had gathered that from Lance. She felt sorry for her aunt then, even when Lance told her what her aunt had cried as she'd collapsed before the coffin: "He moved, he moved." When Hermione had finished her bath and Alison was still playing with their bath toys, she stole up to the top of the house. Perhaps if she comforted her aunt, her jaw would stop aching with the fear of entertaining thoughts that Queenie mightn't like.

At first she knocked timidly, with just one finger. The huge dim passage made that sound dismayingly small, and so did her distance from the rest of the house. Knocking more loudly brought no response, and made her even more nervous. At last she poked the door reluctantly with her finger, poked until the door swung wide.

Her aunt was lying face up on the bed. Her eyes were closed, her hands were folded on her chest. Her chin was thrust up so rigidly that Hermione felt certain she was dead. A ship moaned on the horizon, and the murmur of grown-ups downstairs sounded even further away. Hermione wished so hard it made her head swim that they would miss her and call out to her, because then she could run downstairs. Nobody called her, and she found herself trudging helplessly forward into the room where the furniture looked like the shadows grown more solid, trudging towards the still figure on the bed.

She was close enough to touch her aunt before she noticed the shallow rise and fall of the flat chest beneath the folded hands. She had to swallow before she could speak. "Auntie, are you going to die?" she whispered out of pity, and hoped at once that Queenie hadn't heard.

Queenie's eyes opened so slowly they looked gloating. They were the only part of the long pinched face that moved. Their first glint froze Hermione. She could only stand and shiver as her aunt glared at her with icy loathing. At last Queenie's lips drew back, baring gritted teeth, which parted just enough for her to speak. "So that's what you're hoping for, is it, my little shoat?"

There wasn't so much as a hint of emotion in her gentleness, and Hermione was almost too frightened to speak. "No, auntie, I only—"

"Shall I tell you something you won't relish? I'm never going to die. Never, so don't waste your time looking forward to the day you'll be rid of me. He should have listened to me," she added as if a memory was making her forget who she was speaking to. "You needn't die unless you choose to, and you wouldn't choose to if you didn't let yourself grow old. It's all an illusion, disease and ageing and death. You just need the will to see through it." Then rage flared in her eyes as she noticed Hermione again. "And you dared ask me if I were dying. You deserve to be shown what that means."

Surely she wouldn't if Hermione told her she was sorry, if she pleaded with her not to do whatever was gleaming deep in her eyes. Or if Queenie was beyond being placated, Hermione could scream for her parents; she had only to open her mouth. Then she heard the door close tight behind her.

Perhaps a draught from the window had closed it, but Queenie smiled as though she had closed it herself without moving from the bed. Hermione would have run to the door, except that Queenie's glare was paralysing her with terror even before she understood why. Then she did, and she would have buried her face in her hands if she had been able to move, so that she wouldn't see what Queenie was waiting for her to notice.

A stirring in one corner of the room, alongside the window and out of reach of the meagre daylight that lingered above the sea, dragged her head around to look. She tried to tell herself that the grey mass that filled the corner from floor to ceiling was just a shadow, and then it stirred again as a spider that looked as big as her hand scuttled back under the cornice, leaving its meat struggling in the midst of the web. She felt as if her gaze were caught there too, not least by her fear of seeing the rest of the room. It had aged horribly, cracks clawing at the ceiling and the walls, wallpaper bulging rottenly, furniture sagging forward at her, wardrobes opening like bat-wings that would enfold her in darkness. She began to sob dryly, and then Queenie sat up at the edge of her vision, a tall thin pale shape. Hermione felt a scream mounting behind her locked teeth as she turned to look.

But Queenie hadn't aged, nor had the bed. If anything, she looked younger, enlivened by her power over her niece. She seemed to know all that Hermione was seeing, for she was grinning like a skull. "Look at yourself," she murmured almost tenderly.

Perhaps she was only mocking Hermione; perhaps she wasn't telling her to do so literally. All the same, the child would have fled to the window and jumped rather than look at herself in the mirror. Queenie seemed to tire of her; she closed her eyes and waved Hermione away like an annoying fly. Or was that a last cruel trick to make Hermione think she was safe? As the child reached shakily for the doorknob she saw her own hand, a blotchy hand that looked almost fleshless and far too large. It was an old woman's hand.

She squeezed her eyes shut until they blazed and throbbed, and grabbed the doorknob, tugging until the door lurched at her. It felt as if it had been released, though the frame wasn't warped. She fled along the corridor and fell down the first flight of stairs, bruising her legs. She crawled sobbing down to the next floor as her father ran to her, demanding to know what was wrong. When she realised that he saw nothing odd about her, she was able to look at her hands, her small familiar pink hands. She clambered desperately up her father to hide her face against his chest. "A spider, a spider," she babbled. "I couldn't get out of the room."

She didn't think he ever realised she meant Queenie's room. She wouldn't go to bed until he promised to sit with her all night. When at last she dozed off she awoke to find he wasn't there, and wakened Alison with her screams before he came back. When they went home to Liverpool a nightmare followed her and lurked in her sleep for years. It was a nightmare about waking up – about wakening to find she was as old as she had seemed in Queenie's room.

She plucked a weed out of the earth and scoffed at herself, somewhat tentatively. What was so odd about dreaming you'd be older when you woke up, since in fact you would be? Queenie had made her believe the room had aged, that was all – no great feat when her victim had been just a child. She'd kept her childish for the rest of Queenie's life. She seemed even to have got the better of her afterwards, at the funeral the other day, when Hermione had made such a fuss about the locket.

Queenie must have been wearing it the night she died, and someone had decided she should wear it to the grave. She was letting this view take root in her mind when the phone rang.

It was her mother calling from Waterloo. "We'll be here two days and then at home if you need us."

"I'm sure I won't, mother. Tell Alison Lance was calling, will you? I told him she might be in touch, but I didn't commit her to."

"What was he after?"

"He wanted to talk to her about Rowan, and something about the will."

"He'd better stay away from Rowan. I don't care who says he's cured. And God help him if he tries to make difficulties for Alison now. He'd have been the last person Queenie would have left anything, him and his father, and Richard wouldn't accept anything even if she had."

Hermione said goodbye to her mother and went outside for her tools: it was growing too dark for gardening. She washed her earthy hands and strolled down to her shop. The shopping streets of Holywell were short and haphazard, as if they'd tumbled down the hill into this disarray. There was no clear view along most of them, which was why she stood the sign that pointed to AUNTIE HERMIONE'S on the street corner when the shop was open. As she let herself in, the streetlamp outside flickered on against the swarthy sky.

She pulled the tasselled cord inside the doorway, and the shop lit up, the racks of children's clothes, the crafted toys. When she'd first thought of moving to Wales, to somewhere near her favourite childhood haunts, she'd meant to teach, but while she'd enjoyed her years at training college, teaching practice in a viciously Catholic school near Liverpool had almost given her a breakdown. She would never have expected the children's clothes she made as therapy to prove so popular – popular enough to let her rent the cottage and the shop. Each year she added a few more lines, though never enough to satisfy Rowan, she thought wryly. It had been Rowan's idea to order a carton of Halloween masks.

When Hermione parted the lid of the carton and folded back the leaves, a witch's face sneered up at her. It was grey and deeply wrinkled, and looked as if it would feel like clay. She picked it up by its long sharp chin and hung it in the window, and then she peeled off more layers of the onion of eyeless faces in the carton, green faces with one eye twice the size of the other, skulls with reassuringly artificial teeth. She was sorting out a representative display when a little girl looked in the window.

Hermione gave her a quick smile without really seeing her. The child oughtn't to be out so late, particularly in just a white dress when the mists were already seeping down the mountains. She selected three masks and picked them up by their elastic, and realised that the little girl hadn't moved. She turned to call out that the shop was closed, and her fists clenched so violently that the elastic tore free of one mask.

For a moment she thought that the figure outside wasn't a child but a dwarf with an old woman's long-chinned face. It was just that the reflection of the witch mask was blotting out the child's face, and yet the sight made Hermione shrink back, for the child seemed to be peering through the reflected empty sockets. Then the child skipped aside, into the dark beyond the streetlamp.

Hermione made herself stumble to the door and drag it open. The street was deserted as far as she could see. When she ran to the bend, there was no sign of the little girl. She retreated to the shop and locked herself in. She couldn't have seen what she thought she'd seen, she told herself, fighting to be calm so that she could venture out before it grew much darker. She knew that children liked to make faces, but the child couldn't really have looked like that. In the moment before the child had dodged out of sight, the eyes staring through the reflection that clung to the window had seemed to have turned outwards, staring past either side of the mask.

CHAPTER EIGHT

The train from Prestatyn to Chester was crowded, and at first Lance had to stand. People crowded in, shuffling him further down the car, until he was clinging to a strap above two girls about ten years old. As the swaying of the train swung him towards them, their mother told one to stand up and sat the other on her lap, and stared at Lance until he took the seat. He was clammy and breathless, and now the two girls made him feel as if there were a blaze on either side of him. The doctors were supposed to have shocked those feelings out of him, but even if he no longer wanted to imagine touching little girls, he still felt as if everyone around him thought he did. He closed his eyes and tried not to know where he was, but once the hem of the standing girl's skirt brushed the back of his hand, and once her bare thigh touched him.

In Chester he sat hunched together until the car emptied, then he trudged out of the station, looking at nobody. He crossed the road into the old town, passed through the gate in the city wall and strolled along the Rows, the shopping walks boxed in by overhanging Tudor storeys. Strolling was no use: he couldn't recall what he'd realised at the funeral.

His memory often let him down since he'd come out of the hospital. Sometimes he wondered how much of himself was lost, though it seemed not to matter. But he was sure this did, for he'd told himself so. Something that he'd seen or overheard at Queenie's funeral had lit up like a flashbulb in his mind. He dawdled home beside the river, but the sight of lamps kindling on the bridge while their reflections trawled the water didn't help. When he reached home at last, his father was waiting for him.

As soon as Lance let himself into the small flat that almost overlooked the river, his father levered himself to his feet, his arthritic hands gripping the arms of his chair that was turned to the window from which he'd been watching for Lance. He bumped the chair around towards the room and lowered himself carefully onto the seat, then he scrutinised Lance, his compact face expressionless but for the hint of a frown among the lines on his forehead. "You can get yourself some dinner if you haven't eaten," he said eventually. "I don't feel like eating."

He was making Lance feel as if he'd done something wrong and forgotten what it was. Lance found himself an apple in the fruit bowl next to the histories of Chester between the Roman soldiers on the sideboard, and crunched it while his father wrote a letter to the museum he'd retired from. His father stared at his pen as the nib rested on a gathering blot, and then his head jerked up, flinging back his grey hair. "Well, how were my brother and his wife? What were they saying about me?"

Lance was expecting to be blamed for the torments of anxiety his father suffered whenever Lance was out of his sight. By the time he framed an answer his father was staring at him as if he were making it up. "Keith said he was sorry you weren't there," Lance told him doggedly, "and Edith was hoping the family could get together now."

"Did you remember to say I was ill?"

Lance's hand closed over his mouth, squeezing his beard. "Oh no, I forgot."

"Hurrah, something else for them to lay at my door. My brother even denounced me for leaving home until he realised he could follow. I don't know why you went at all. You couldn't have believed any of them would be glad to see you."

Lance could tell he was attacking himself under the guise of attacking Lance. "I wanted to see Auntie Queenie laid to rest," he said.

"I can imagine how she must have bothered you. If we'd seen more of her you mightn't have turned out the way you did."

"Dad, can't we just talk? I had something to ask you."

His father let the writing pad slip to the floor and stared blankly at him. "Don't you think I wish we could talk as we used to? I thought we'd have more time to share our lives when I retired. I was looking forward to strolling with you by the river on evenings like this. Perhaps you don't appreciate how finding that filth in your room turned everything you'd said to me into lies. Thank God your mother was dead by then and never knew what you'd been hiding."

Lance had sometimes thought his mother suspected more about him than she admitted – that she had been watchful on his behalf. A memory gleamed in his father's eyes until he blinked it away and said "No, this is wrong. We shouldn't spend our last years together like this. You never would have ended up this way if we'd cared for you as we should have. Ask whatever you have to ask."

By now Lance had forgotten, but his father was liable to act as if he were forgetting on purpose, especially recent memories. He managed to think of something else that had been troubling him. "Did granddad really lose his mind before he died?"

"You aren't losing your mind. If there are gaps that's the price you have to pay, and you should realise it could have been worse."

"Yes, but did he?"

"Who says he did? What have they been saying?"

"Alison's husband was saying he must have gone mad."

"What the devil does he know about it? He wasn't there, he isn't even family. My father didn't lose his mind, he lost his wife, and that's like having part of yourself torn off. Maybe when your cousin's husband loses someone he won't be so eager to denigrate people's grief."

"I miss mother too," Lance said awkwardly.

His father clasped his hands together and stared at his whitening knuckles. "I suppose you do. I apologise for saying what I said before. I'm sure that if she were here she'd intercede between us."

Their talk had foundered in embarrassment. Lance retreated to his room, a windowless box in which furniture white as the walls crowded round the bed. Since he'd come out of hospital he often found that memories surfaced when he was close to sleep, but the memory of his grandfather wouldn't give way to any other. Whatever Lance's father said, Lance was convinced the old man hadn't just been mourning.

Throughout his last months he'd accused Queenie of not letting him go to his wife, of keeping him alive because she couldn't bear to be without him. Richard and Keith had told him soothingly that he'd see his wife when it was time, but Lance thought that even they had been taken aback when their father had lingered for weeks on what the doctor told them was his deathbed.

One night Lance had heard him cry out so loudly he'd been sure it was the end, and had raced up to the room to find the old man lying twisted on the bed, shrivelled limbs huddled together, eyes wide and blank. Then the withered body had jerked like a puppet or someone lurching out of a dream. "Let me go, let me go," the old man had begun to moan, a complaint he'd kept up for days until he died.

Queenie hadn't let him rest even then. The family and the undertakers had managed to sneak the corpse away from her for embalming, but when she'd realised that the coffin was about to be closed for burial she'd rushed to the front of the church, arms outstretched, crying "He moved." And he had: the mouth had fallen open as if in a last silent protest at being prevented from resting. Her footsteps must have shaken it open, Lance told himself, but he wished he could forget the episode, not only because it might be blocking what he wanted to remember.

That weekend he went walking by the river, first with his father, who grew impatient with him for not chatting, and then by himself. On Saturday a brass band gave a concert on the riverbank, on Sunday canoeists were braving the weir, but all this only distracted him. Whatever he was trying to remember, hadn't it to do with Alison? If he could help her, perhaps that would make up for the way he used to think about her; perhaps she might even realise that she needn't be wary of him. When he returned home he could tell that his father was suspicious of him for wanting to go out by himself.

On Monday he was able to be more alone, at work. He had been a clerical officer before his breakdown, but he'd come back as a filing clerk. Few of the married women would talk to him, and most of the men were shy of him, as if his slowness and forgetfulness might be infectious. Now he had the task of putting all the dormant files in order, tens of thousands of them in the long basement where shelves stretched almost from wall to wall and rose to the low dim ceiling. Bare bulbs dangled into dusty aisles so narrow that two people couldn't even squeeze past each other, not that there was often anyone besides Lance. He was glad not to be upstairs, where he might be expected to answer the phone; since his spell in the hospital he had lost the confidence. But then how could he phone Alison?

He still couldn't think why he should. Being unable to grasp the memory made his head feel stiff and cramped. Was it about Alison herself or someone close to her? He stood with a handful of files half off the shelf, trying to force his paralysed thoughts to take one more step, and then he started guiltily and moved to vacate the aisle.

But nobody was watching him. He must have imagined it, not only because he would have heard if someone had made her way to the end of the basement away from the door, but because the figure he'd thought he glimpsed had been half his size. The doctors couldn't have quelled his imagination as thoroughly as they were supposed to, he thought uneasily, almost choking on the smell of old paper.

Yet it was that glimpse of a child which made him start awake that night, realising that he'd meant to speak to Alison about her little girl. It was important, he knew, but even the sense of being needed couldn't part the fog of his slowness. Perhaps he would remember by the time he had Alison's number. He couldn't ask his father, and he had to wait until his father was taking a shower before he could call Hermione. Talking was so hard that when he managed to, he said too much. He told Hermione that he wanted to speak to Alison about her little girl.

He tried to pretend he'd meant something else, something about Queenie and her will. Surely that would make Alison call him, and by then he might know what he needed to tell her. His little niece needed his help; he was sure she did. As he waited for Alison to call he grew tense, unable to let memories form by themselves. Even next day at work, whenever he seemed to be close to remembering he felt as if someone was watching him from the shadowy end of the aisle. The homegoing crowds were a relief from the smell of stale paper. But when he arrived home his father was waiting grimly for him. "So you're up to your old tricks," his father said.

"I don't know what you mean."

"Don't try to pretend you've forgotten that too. The quacks said they'd cured you, but I think they've made you worse."

Lance felt his words slowing until he could barely speak. "I never did anything."

"Nor will you while I'm able to prevent it. You didn't anticipate that your cousin might call while you weren't here, did you? If she really didn't know what you wanted with her child she's as great a fool as you are. I should have told her, and told her to alert the police."

Lance felt as if events were conspiring to ensure he didn't speak to Alison, and that made him nervous for the child, a nervousness that felt like being close to remembering. "What's her number?" he said as his father stared incredulously. "I've got to talk to her. I'll let you listen."

"You won't speak to her on my phone," his father said, his voice rising, "or on any other while you're under my roof, and I swear that on your mother's grave."

Lance felt as if his father was driving the memory further out of reach. "Then I'll go and see her."

"You'll stay here or I'll have you taken into custody." When Lance stood up, his father lunged to catch him and fell back into his chair, panting. "Don't you dare leave this flat. Don't you dare touch that door." He was shouting "Come back here to me" as Lance hurried downstairs.

What if he called the police? Lance made himself walk through the crowds instead of running, shrinking against walls rather than risk bumping into someone and drawing attention to himself. When he caught sight of himself in the window display of a children's boutique, his beard poking out like a caricature of his chin, he wished he could cover his face with his hands.

The railway station was crowded. Lance sat with his back against the window of the car, lifting his shoulder to obscure his face, until he realised that the women seated opposite were whispering about him. He expected every moment to see policemen marching down the platform, searching for him on the train that was so weighed down it felt like his slowness made solid. At last it moved, but that didn't shift his thoughts. He had been hoping that now he didn't have to phone he would find it easier to think.

He had to change trains at Hooton. He dodged across the small station and found a newspaper to hide behind. He felt relatively safe all the way to Liverpool, since he had the train almost to himself. But when he changed platforms in the underground station, the platform for the train to Waterloo was deserted.

He walked to the end where the tunnel closed in and stared along the line. Beyond the point where the rails merged with the dark he saw a lamp surrounded by a cramped dim patch of brick. He felt as if he were hiding from the city of Liverpool overhead, the sounds of a speeding police car, a fire engine, a bottle thrown down an escalator. He leaned against the wall above the slope that led down to the mouth of the dark, and strained his ears for the sound of the train. He'd feel safer once he was bound for Queenie's house.

It wasn't Queenie's house now, it was Alison's. He shouldn't need reminding she was dead when attending her funeral had been so difficult for him, knowing he was being watched whenever he was near Rowan. The family was still suspicious of him. He couldn't blame them, but shouldn't they have had their doubts about Queenie too? Nobody seemed to wonder why, if Queenie loathed children, she had made so much of Rowan.

He gasped as if someone had caught him by the shoulder. That was what he'd meant to say after the funeral. He didn't know why it was important, but he was sure it was – perhaps important enough to make up for his life. He mustn't try to think beyond it, or he might lose it. Someone would know what it meant once he spoke up. He was closing his mind around it when he realised he was being watched.

They had to let him call Alison. He was allowed to make one call. He turned reluctantly, feeling the slowness gather in his skull, threatening to stop his words short of his lips. But there were no policemen. The platform was deserted except for a girl of about Rowan's age, who was staring at him.

He could read no expression in her pale eyes, yet when her gaze met his he shrank inside himself. He felt as if she knew all about him – as if she knew that once he would have imagined touching her. Worse still, he felt that part of his imagination stirring. The doctors hadn't shaken it out of him; they hadn't even buried it deep enough. A malicious smile was growing on the little girl's long face, as if she knew exactly what he was thinking. Her fingers wriggled as they hung beside her ankle-length white dress, and he was terrified that she was about to pull it up to taunt him. He would have dodged past her and fled, except that he couldn't bear the thought of touching her. He swung round and pressed his face against the wall, struggling to force his feelings back into the dark and hold on to what he had to tell Alison.

His ears began to roar with the pressure of blood in his head. The tiles of the wall flattened his forehead, yet they might have been miles away. Even when he clenched his eyes shut he could see the little girl, her long secret legs, her knowing smile. The roaring seemed to flood out of him, obliterating his sense of where he was. He thrust himself away from the wall and turned dizzily. He had to get past her, no matter how.

His eyes had been so tightly shut that for several seconds he was blind. His vision cleared just as his right foot wavered into empty space. The roaring wasn't only the sound of his blood. He saw the little girl's smile widen, a smile of gleeful satisfaction, as he stepped helplessly off the platform in front of the oncoming train.

He made a grab at the platform as he fell, and the heel of his hand thumped the edge. He felt his wrist break, driving a spike of pain through his arm all the way to his shoulder. But he'd caught himself from sprawling across the tracks; he'd kept his balance with one foot on either side of the rail nearest the platform. He clutched his broken wrist to his chest with his other hand, imagining how much pain he would be suffering by the time he was taken to the hospital, and stumbled backwards splay-legged as the train screeched towards him.

The brakes would save him, he told himself. The thought seemed as clear as his pain. He could see from the strain that dragged the driver's shocked face taut how hard he must be applying the brakes. Even when the front of the train towered over him like the collapsing wall of a house, Lance thought he could outdistance it. When the buffer shoved at his chest it seemed firm but surprisingly gentle, nuzzling him into the tunnel at a speed his feet could match. Then a sleeper caught his heel, and he fell backwards, his spine on the rail. Before he could heave himself aside, the wheel of the train pinned him and split him open to the top of his head.

It let him out of his body at once, but the agony of it came with him. He felt as if he'd turned into a wound that would never finish widening, growing rawer as it gaped. But he was retreating into the dark, and as the mouth of the tunnel dwindled, the agony began to fade. He would leave his secret thoughts behind with his body that lay at the mouth of the tunnel, he realised: he would be at peace. Then, just before the light rushed away from him and went out, the little girl leaned into the tunnel and stared pitilessly at him, reminding him of his worst fancies and the guilt they bred, leaving him alone with them in the dark.

CHAPTER NINE

A three-year-old was crying because she couldn't scratch her arm through the plaster cast when Derek phoned the ward. "The Southport job's a bugger. I won't be home until nine at least. Jo says she'll take Rowan home from school."

"All right, love," Alison said as the three-year-old began to cry harder. "Would you like to see what's wrong?" she suggested to the student nurses who were sharing a surreptitious cigarette in the corridor.

Both of them stared at her. "It'll be the same as last time," Libby said. "She'll have to get used to being here without her mam."

Alison took her time about replacing the receiver, but couldn't think of anything to say. A kind of indifference was part of the process you had to go through in order to work as a nurse, growing used to suffering even when it wasn't yours – if you felt everything the children felt you would be in no state to help them – but Libby and Jasmine seemed less detached than apathetic. She knew that even if they qualified they might well find themselves back on the dole, but how could they be so uncaring? Admittedly the ward sister wasn't much of a model, trying out her tetchiness and indolence for when she retired in five years, glad to have parents stay with their children so that they could look after other children in the ward. At least the nursing auxiliaries had children themselves and tried to treat the patients like their own, but if Rowan ever had to go into the hospital, Alison hoped the child wouldn't be in this ward.

You had to take care that the system didn't infect you with its coldness, that the size of the hospital and the meagreness of its staff didn't overwhelm you. The ideals you had when you started work gave way to reality, but surely that was preferable to Queenie's way, withdrawing from the world so as to compliment yourself on preserving your ideals. You mightn't be able to change the world, but you couldn't tell how much of the world just doing your best might reach.

One of the auxiliaries was quieting the three-year-old by reading her a story. Alison made her way through the ward, writing on clipboards, holding small hands, listening to confidences, murmuring reassurances. She kept her widest smile for the little boy whose parents had locked him in their flat with a television that had caught fire while they were at the pub. Too many parents treated their children like property, and few neighbours were willing to intervene. The thought of intervention roused the doubt that had been dozing in her mind all day. She was wondering what Lance wanted with her child.

The will didn't mention Rowan. Perhaps Hermione had misheard him, the way he mumbled in his beard. Alison had only been able to reach his father, and she wished she hadn't told Richard so much; he'd sounded as if she had confirmed his fears. Surely if Lance had designs on Rowan he would hardly have tried to contact Alison, but what could be so important that he had overcome his shyness?

When the next shift came on, so many children wanted to say goodbye to her that she had to run to the bus station. Perhaps Lance would have left her a message, she thought, but all the messages on the tape were for Derek. The shrunken voices seemed to echo in the house now that her parents had gone home. She mustn't mind that they'd spent longer with Hermione than with her; Hermione needed them more than she did, just as she needed to feel protective of Alison to distract herself from her own fears: Alison had known that ever since she could remember. They would all be here for Christmas – the house would hardly be sold by then – and perhaps that would help make up to Rowan for not staying. Alison strolled across the road to collect her.

Jo was leafing through mail-order catalogues and watching a soap opera. "I told her she can stay for tea if she likes. Patty's taken them all on the beach."

Patty was Jo's teenage daughter. "I'll just tell Rowan I'm home," Alison said, and made for the promenade. Breezes stroked her face and stirred the spiky grass that crowned the dunes, yachts swayed on the marina by the docks and the radar station. She stepped onto the concrete walk beyond the dunes and saw that Jo's three were the only children in sight on the narrow beach.

She ran down the steps to the sand. The two younger children were nudging Patty and whispering. "Where's Rowan?" Alison demanded.

Patty turned defiantly, earrings jangling, penciled eyebrows high. "Her friend took her away," she said.

CHAPTER TEN

Dear diary, I like my new school becose everyone is frendly and the teacher is nice and were aloud to write our own things sometimes, like now I can write my diary. Soon our class is going to take assembley and I'll be a loanly old lady, thats if were still living in the big house...

Rowan bit the end of her pencil. She had nearly written that she hoped they would live there for ever. It must be hard for mummy and daddy as well, to have to move again so soon, but now that the man who owed them so much money was paying up, mightn't they be able to stay? She missed her friends from Liverpool, but perhaps one of her parents would soon have time to take her in the car to visit them. She drew the house with all its windows lit and ships sailing by under the moon, the way she imagined them when she heard them from her bed, then she coloured in the windows, different colours for different rooms. When she coloured the top floor she thought of sleepwalking up there. Mummy said she must have done that because of all the upset, but in that case, shouldn't they avoid the upset of moving again? No, that was selfish. Mummy and daddy had enough problems. She ought to help by being grown-up.

After school she went into the schoolyard determined not to let her father even suspect what she was hoping. She needn't have made the effort; Jo was waiting instead. "Your daddy's busy, chick. You come home with me and we'll see if there's some sweeties."

"Don't give her more than me like you did last time," said Mary, who was in Rowan's class but who seemed younger than her. Little Paul, who was in the nursery class, said "Sweeties, yum." He ran ahead on the way home, until Jo smacked him when she'd had enough of running after him. He was still howling when they reached Jo's, a sound as sad as the For Sale sign outside the big house that looked almost inconsolable to Rowan, like a child so big and ugly nobody would play with it. Jo let the three of them into her house and hung up their schoolbags before herding them into the kitchen. "Now what have I got for little people who aren't giving me a headache?"

Paul stopped crying at once, and Mary said "Don't give her more than me."

"You can have the most if you like," Rowan said.

"You'll neither of you get any if you start arguing." Jo hurried to the foot of the stairs, her backless sandals flapping. "Patty, just take these on the beach until teatime, will you? They're squabbling over sweets and giving me a headache."

Patty stumped reluctantly downstairs, a trace of cigarette smoke looming in her nostrils. "I'm not feeling well, mam, and I'm doing my homework."

"You can do that later, can't you? You won't be out dancing if it's your time of the month. Just take them for an hour like you used to and see they don't get into mischief."

Patty took the bag of sweets from the top of a wall cupboard. "See you all behave yourselves or you'll get none."

By now Rowan didn't want any. She would have liked to walk to the marina and watch the sleepy yachts, but Patty didn't want to go so far from the house and Paul might have fallen in. Paul and Mary argued about the plastic buckets for a while, and when Mary insisted the red one was hers he kicked her castle down. Rowan offered to take him to the water's edge and show him how to dig a stream, but Patty said he had to stay near her. Feeling small and unwanted, Rowan wandered away from the others to gaze across the bay.

The Welsh coast was quivering with heat. It seemed to gather itself and surge forward into the swarm of light that was the bay. Rowan often closed her eyes so as to open them and make everything look new, but now she had to close them to keep the light from swarming inside her head. She opened them a crack, and found that she must have been gazing straight at someone and unable to see her for the dazzle: a figure in white.

For a moment that was all she could see, in the midst of a blankness too bright for her eyes. She couldn't even hear the waves. I don't like this, she thought, wondering what the heat had done to her now. Then the figure turned to her, and the sound of the waves rushed into her ears, the bay and the sky and the beach flooded back into focus as the girl came towards her across the sand.

It was Vicky, the girl she'd met in Wales. Around her neck and over her dress, which looked exactly like the one she'd worn before, hung an old pair of binoculars. She halted a few steps away from the water, her pale eyes inviting Rowan to go to her, her small mouth smiling. "I promised I'd see you again, didn't I? I've seen you when you didn't see me. I brought these for you, but I didn't think you'd be with dirty children. We don't want them sullying our glasses."

"I had to come with Patty because my mummy and daddy are at work. I only have to stay near."

"You'll see better from the dunes," Vicky said and, lifting the strap over her head, handed her the binoculars. Rowan was trying to focus them when Paul scampered up. "Me look through those," he demanded.

"You're too little, Paul. You might break them," Rowan said.

He began to howl at once, and Patty limped over, groaning. "He was happy playing and now you've upset him. What did you say to him? Where did you get those?"

"My friend gave them to me," Rowan said angrily, for Patty had made her sound like a thief. "I only said he was too young for them."

"Which friend?" Patty said, then shrugged off the question impatiently. "Just you let him have a turn. I'll see he doesn't wreck them. He's giving me a headache, do you mind? If you don't stop tormenting him I'm telling our mam."

Mary ran to them, pulling at her knickers that had stuck in her bottom. "I want a look too."

Paul wiped his nose on the back on his hand and the back of his hand on his trousers, and Rowan was painfully ashamed to be seen with him and his sisters. She glanced about for Vicky and saw her watching from the edge of the dunes. She was pointing at the binoculars, nodding for Rowan to give them to Paul. Her smile was so wicked that Rowan hesitated until Mary said "She's selfish, her, just because she lives in a posh house."

Rowan lifted the strap over her head, feeling guiltily excited, and hung the binoculars around Paul's neck. "Get hold of them, can't you?" Patty shouted when he began to complain about their weight. He looked at his feet through them and almost fell over, scanned the bay and said "Ow" at the light, and then he turned to look at his house. Suddenly he flung the binoculars away from him, so violently that Rowan feared the strap would break, and huddled against Patty. "Give those back," Rowan cried. "You could have smashed them."

He almost threw the binoculars at her. "Some girl with a long face frikened me," he whined. "She made her eyes look horrible."

Rowan was retreating towards the dunes and trying not to laugh when Patty shouted "You're not to go up there. My mam said you had to stay with me."

"No she didn't," Rowan said. "She said not to get into mischief, and I already know not to do that, thank you. I'm only going on the dunes for a better view."

"You stay where you're told," Patty ordered, a cigarette hoarseness tearing at her voice, and came limping after her. Rowan ran up the steps and across the sandy concrete of the promenade, and heard Vicky's whisper: "Here."

As Rowan scrambled over the dune to her, Patty reached the top of the steps, her face ugly with discomfort. "They won't find us," Vicky said. Rowan crouched down, feeling hot and angry, her heart racing. She heard Patty approaching, yelling threats to make her show herself, and then her ragged voice and the complaints of the younger ones swung away across the dunes. "I said I'd hide you," Vicky said. "You can trust me."

Rowan wished she could be just like her, with her spotless white dress, her bare feet sparkling with sand, her long face smooth as marble, her small features that Rowan saw were perfectly symmetrical. She seemed as unlike Patty and the others as it was possible for anyone to be. Patty gave a distant squawk, and then there was silence, not even the sound of the waves. Rowan flashed Vicky a wry smile that meant to say Patty was nothing to do with them, but Vicky gave her an unreceptive look. "You'll be like that soon enough."

"I will not," Rowan said indignantly. "What do you mean?"

Vicky's face tightened with disgust, and she lowered her voice. "Bleeding."

"All girls and ladies do that," Rowan said, feeling unexpectedly superior.

"You won't be so proud of yourself when it happens to you. You'll feel sick and filthy and ashamed of yourself. You saw how that girl looked."

"My mummy says it's natural, part of growing up."

"The older people get, the more lies they tell."

"My mummy doesn't, so don't you say she does."

"Are you sure about that? I saw that your house is for sale. Did she let you think it was your home now?"

"Even if she did, that isn't lying," Rowan said, but it felt as if it was.

"And your father promised to buy you a telescope, but you had to wait for me to bring you these instead."

"How about your father? Does he tell lies too?"

All at once the pale eyes were blank as old coins, and so glaring that Rowan was afraid to speak. She swallowed dryly and touched the binoculars. "Did you really bring these for me?"

Vicky's glare dimmed slowly, and Rowan heard the whisper of sand through the sparse grass. "I told you so, didn't I?" Vicky said. "I don't tell lies. Go up and see what you can see."

As Rowan reached the crest of the dune she saw Patty on the steps, trailing after Paul and Mary, who were running to their buckets. For a moment she seemed to look at Rowan, but the sun must be in her eyes. Her angry head bobbed down step by step, and then there was only Vicky, her dress white against the sunlit dune, watching Rowan palely as she raised the binoculars to her eyes.

She liked old things, but these might be too old. All she could see was a blur beyond a supine 8 of darkness. The oppressiveness made her head swim. She groped for a focusing screw, but there wasn't one. "Just let them work," Vicky said.

Suddenly they did. The view sprang at Rowan, so fast and so clear that she gasped. She was looking at the water in the middle of the bay, and not only the sight but the sound of the waves seemed closer. As she gazed at the slow wide unfurling, the water darkening and then growing more transparent like a promise that she would see into the depths, the dark tunnel that enclosed her vision seemed to vanish. "The more you use them the stronger they'll get," Vicky murmured. "Have a look where we were."

Rowan lifted the binoculars towards Wales. The movement felt like flying over the sea; it took her breath away. The beach at Talacre sprang out of the waves, and she was dumbfounded by how much she could see: dogs chasing each other in a spray of sand, three sunbathers lined up on three towels like the stripes of a flag, children digging holes in the sand. The shouts of children she could hear must be on the Waterloo beach. "You'd see more from the top of your house," Vicky said.

Rowan skimmed the coast road from Talacre to the Greenfield Valley. Reservoirs glinted among the ruined factories as she rose between the slopes to Holywell. Layers of cut-out cottages gave way to the bunched shopping streets, and then she was outside her aunt's cottage.

Hermione was in the garden, stooping to the flower-bed. Rowan watched spellbound as her aunt tugged at a weed. She could see her aunt's hand pressed to the small of her back, could see the old glove on the hand; she could almost hear Hermione's grunt of triumph as the roots came loose, scattering earth. Her aunt straightened up and was gazing directly at her.

Rowan almost ducked behind the dune, Hermione seemed so close. She felt excited and a little guilty, and was no longer aware of holding the binoculars. She was awed by her ability to see so far. She watched Hermione moving her pail of uprooted weeds along the flower bed – she couldn't stop watching. She didn't know how long she had been watching when she realised that someone was calling her name.

The voice seemed so distant that at first she didn't recognise it. Then the sound of her mother's anxiety plucked at her, and she tried to find the beach. She had to close her eyes as her vision swooped back over the bay. She opened them and steadied the binoculars, and was looking at her mother's worried face. The binoculars mustn't work so well at this distance; her mother seemed further away than Hermione had, far away down a long black tunnel. She tried to lower the binoculars, but her hands felt far away too. She couldn't move while she was holding the binoculars; she would fall. Then her mother looked straight at her without seeing her and hurried away along the beach.

"Mummy," Rowan cried, and wrenched the binoculars away from her eyes. The sky tilted, the dune heaved up beneath her. Her cry couldn't have been as loud as she had thought, for her mother hadn't turned. Rowan stumbled down the sandy slope, the binoculars dragging her faster, and clambered towards the promenade, the upward slope crumbling beneath her heels and gritting beneath her fingernails. Vicky was at the top, waiting.

Though her head blotted out the sun, her face was shining. It was expressionless but for the light in her eyes. When Rowan had almost struggled to the top, Vicky moved into her path and stretched out her hands. Did she want the binoculars? Rowan made to lift the strap from around her neck, but Vicky said "They're yours now."

Rowan wasn't sure that she wanted them – and then, remembering how far she'd seen, she did. "May I keep them for always?"

"For as long as you're in that house. If you stay there always you'll be able to keep them always, won't you? Perhaps you can."

She made it sound as if she was about to tell Rowan how. Rowan would have lingered, but she could hear her mother calling. "I've got to go."

Vicky stared at her. More than one slow wave swelled and withdrew on the beach before she moved aside. "I'll come and find you again soon," she said.

Rowan ran across the promenade and down the gritty steps. Her mother was hurrying back from the marina, her face pinched with anxiety. "Mummy, here I am," Rowan cried. "I was only on the dunes. Patty wouldn't come with me. I'm sorry."

Her mother's face changed from worried to angry, and then she was simply relieved. "Didn't you hear me calling you? Don't ever do that again, Rowan. I thought I could trust you not to go wandering off by yourself."

"I was with Vicky," Rowan protested. "I met her when I was at Hermione's. We didn't go far."

"Well, I hope she's more use than Patty. She couldn't be much less." Rowan's mother was gazing doubtfully at the binoculars. "Did she lend you those?"

"She said I could keep them. They're old. I'm sure they're really hers."

"All right, lovey, nobody's accusing her of anything." Rowan's mother hugged her with a fierceness that made Rowan realise fully how anxious she had been. "Come on, we'd better get to Jo's before Patty has her calling the police. You introduce me to your friend on the way."

But when they climbed the steps and ran hand in hand to the houses, there was nothing to be seen on the dunes but roaming sand and tufts of grass. "Bring her home another time. It was kind of her to give you those. You'll have to give her something in return," Rowan's mother said, and for a moment, as the sand dragged at her feet, Rowan wondered what Vicky might want from her, hoped that she wouldn't ask for too much.

CHAPTER ELEVEN

On Saturday there were two letters on the doormat. One was from Rowan, the kind she often wrote.

Dear mummy and daddy, I don't mind where I live so long as Im with you, I want to live with you for ever because I love you most in the wurld and Im glad you let me keep the ~~bind binnocli~~ binocculers,
I hope you meet my new freind soon...

They gave her a kiss each and sent her to play in her jungle of a back garden while they stared at the other envelope. It was from the bank.

"You open it," Derek said. "Maybe you'll bring us luck." He watched while Alison turned over the envelope and lifted the corner of the flap with a fingernail, slipped one slim finger under the flap and peeled it back, drew out the single sheet of headed notepaper and unfolded it, turned it the right way up. Maybe the manager had written to let them know their account was in the black at last, Derek tried to think, until Alison's face went slack and she passed the letter to him. The cheque from the contractor had bounced.

It felt as if he'd snatched the three thousand pounds out of their hands. Derek saw their plans fade one by one like failing lights: redecorating the house to make it easier to sell, the holiday they might have had at Rowan's half-term, a car for Alison, whose old car wasn't worth repairing... The house seemed to bear down on him, a dead weight they would never be rid of, shabby and ugly and unwelcoming. As he tramped along the hall to the phone, creaks and echoes paced him. "Try not to lose your temper," Alison said.

Children were fighting, a woman was screaming at them above the babble of a disc jockey loud as a public address. "Yeh," a voice said.

"You don't waste words, eh," Derek said.

"Wha?"

"Is Ken there?"

"Who wants him?"

"He'll know."

Whichever of Ken's sons it was went away and mumbled, then came back. "He isn't here. Says leave a message."

Derek could hear Ken whistling Beatles melodies amid the uproar. "I won't bother," he said, and leaned on the phone as he called to Alison. "I'm going over to see him."

She came downstairs quickly, folded sheets piled on her arms. "Wouldn't it be safer to have the lawyer write to him?"

"Safer and longer, with bugger all at the end of it, probably. Look, I only want to try and make him understand the fix we're in," he said, and put his hand over her lips. He could still feel her moist breath on his palm as he hurried out to the car.

He drove through Everton, streets of faded shops and cinemas gone bingo, and up the rubbly hill planted with tower blocks. Beyond Everton was Toxteth, black youths with ghetto blasters strutting through the Victorian streets, white youths in cars cruising for women. The window of the Faradays' old flat was smashed and patched with cardboard. Ken lived on the far side of Toxteth, in Aigburth, at the end of a street above the Festival Gardens. Down among the gardens of all nations on the Mersey bank, the Festival Hall gleamed dully, a half-buried zeppelin. A wagon wheel leaned beside the glass porch of Ken's broad pebble-dashed house. Derek rang the bell beneath a carriage lamp and heard voices screaming at the children to shut up.

Purple velvet curtains stirred at the front window, and then the front door was opened by Ken in an oriental dressing-gown. His round face was trying to look blank. "Hello, Derek. Visiting old haunts? We're in a bit of a mess in here just now."

"I can stand it. You don't want me having to shout at you through the glass."

Ken opened the porch door and came out, smoothing his uncombed hair. "I haven't forgotten I said we'd do up your house, if that's what's up."

"Your cheque is, mate."

"You haven't tried to pay it in, have you? Wasn't it dated the end of next week? My mistake. So much on my mind, you know how it is. Hang on here and I'll write you another."

"We can't afford to wait, Ken. We need the cash now."

"You don't think I'd be fool enough to keep that much in the house with so many thieves about, do you? Just tell your bank it's on its way if they get stroppy. What'll they do, kidnap your kiddie if you don't cough up?"

"Your bank's open on Saturdays. You could get me the cash when you're dressed."

"Can't do it, pal. Cash flow problems and some of the prats I have to work with, you know how it is. Don't make a scene, all right? We're nice people round here, we don't have rows in the street. Are you going to let me give you a cheque? Then you'll have to excuse me, I've got hungry rabbits."

He strode round the side of the house, tying his dressing-gown tighter. Derek caught up with him as he emerged from the kitchen with a drooping lettuce. "I'm not leaving until you pay me the three thousand you owe me," Derek said, loud enough to make the rabbits flinch in the hutch at the end of the garden.

"Still after the green stuff? Chew on this if you're that desperate." He shoved the lettuce at Derek, who grabbed it instinctively as Ken unbolted the alley door beside the hutch. "Now then, are you going to be reasonable? My boys will do your house next week if you don't mind them working nights, won't you, boys?"

Derek swung round. Ken's two large sons were behind him. "Yeh," one said, and the less talkative one nodded. "They'd be out of your way before midnight," Ken said.

How could Derek consider letting them into the house when he could see they were ready to menace him? "I want my money," he said.

Ken took the lettuce from him and opened the alley door, shaking his head sadly. "Give him what he's asking for."

Derek backed into the alley and knocked over a dustbin. He almost sprawled on his back. The youths snorted at that, but they weren't smiling as they followed him. As he hauled himself to his feet, his fingers found the neck of a bottle that had rolled out of the dustbin. He smashed the bottle against the alley wall so savagely that Ken's sons retreated a step. He felt a splinter of glass lodge in the side of his hand like a hint of how fighting them would feel, and it excited him, made him determined to hurt them worse. Then he thought of Rowan, imagined her seeing the state he might be in. He flung the bottle away and turned his back on the youths. They jeered at him and flung rubbish after him as he made himself walk slowly to the car.

He'd kept his self-respect, but at what cost? He'd have to use a lawyer now and pay more for the work on the house. He drove back to Waterloo, growing unhappier with himself and the news he had for Alison. But when he found her, sorting through old photographs in a room on the middle floor, she looked so taken aback that he was afraid to ask what had happened. "Lance killed himself," she said.

"Never. When?"

"Days ago, but Richard only just called my parents. Hermione can tell us more about it when she gets here. You don't mind her staying overnight, do you? She sounded pretty shaken."

"Whatever you think, Ali. No joy at Ken's, by the way. I could hardly get near him for his family."

"We'll survive until things improve." She hugged him but only made him feel awkward, as if she were letting him know she realised he hadn't told the whole truth. He was glad when the phone rang. "It's a domestic job in Bootle," he called up to her. "I'll take Rowan along."

Rowan was behind the house, gazing over the top-heavy privet hedge towards the bay. "You'll take root if you stand there much longer," he told her. "Come and see what needs doing to someone's house."

"I'd rather not, daddy. My new friend Vicky may be coming to play with me, and I want to be here in case she does."

He wasn't prepared to feel so rejected. Maybe she thought it wasn't ladylike to carry his tools any more. There might come a time when he didn't know her at all. The idea dismayed him, and he had to make himself concentrate on sketching the rewiring for the newlyweds in Bootle. When he returned to Waterloo, Hermione had arrived.

She was in the front garden, attacking the lawn with shears. "Here I am again, Derek. You'll be thinking you can't get rid of me."

"Don't break my heart. You know you're always welcome."

"Am I? I don't feel it. I don't mean you, I mean the house." She glanced at it as if she expected to see someone watching. "What about you? Do you feel welcome?"

"Rowan does."

"I'm not sure I like that either." She plucked grass off the blades of the shears. "Well, you'll be thinking your neurotic sister-in-law is as bad as ever."

"You need time to get over things, that's all. The bad bits of your past are dead now, aren't they? Queenie and now Lance."

He thought he'd been too harsh, but she nodded slowly as if to convince herself. "Lance, yes. No mistake about that, he was cut in half by a train. The driver said he looked straight at it and then stepped in front of it. How could anyone do that, Derek?"

"Maybe he couldn't stand himself any longer, the shame of it and people knowing."

"That's what his father thinks. But he was coming here, Derek."

"So what?" Derek said, feeling obscurely threatened. "He had to be going somewhere."

"But why would he come all that way and then do that to himself?"

"He'd been talking about Rowan, hadn't he? Maybe when he came that close he couldn't stand what he was thinking about her."

The discussion was making him nervous, the memory of meeting Lance, the sense of Lance's mind as a dark pit that anyone could fall into if they strayed too near. "You do realise that we'll never know what he wanted to tell Alison," Hermione said, and he was about to retort that it didn't matter when Rowan came round the house.

"Where's mummy? Oh, hello," she said to Derek, "I didn't know you were back. Please may I go just on the dunes where you can see me, and look for my friend?"

"Here I am, Rowan." Alison appeared at the open front door with a scraper and a length of peeled wallpaper. "What's wrong?"

She was asking Hermione, who was staring at the child. Hermione cleared her throat nervously. "Did you give her those binoculars?"

"One of her friends did," Derek said.

"You can have a look with them if you like," Rowan said, and reached behind her neck for the strap.

"No, no, I just want to see them," Hermione said hastily. She peered at them, a frown narrowing her eyes. "Perhaps I could just hold them."

Her attempt to sound casual made Rowan dubious. "My friend said I could keep them as long as we live here."

Derek let out some of his growing impatience. "What's the problem, Hermione?"

"They're hers." She was speaking to Alison, almost pleading. "I saw them in her room, I'd swear to it. Can't you see how old they are?"

"Listen, if someone doesn't—"

"She means Queenie, Derek. She did have some binoculars like these. They weren't in her room when we cleared it. Rowan, love, I won't be angry if you say you did, but did you take those from the old lady's room?"

"I didn't, mummy," Rowan said, close to angry tears.

"She used to sit at the top window with them after her father died," Hermione told Derek as if that should convince him. "She'd watch his grave for hours."

"They're Vicky's. Vicky gave them to me," Rowan cried.

Hermione clutched Derek's arm so hard that he gasped. "Who did you say?"

"Vicky. She's my new friend. I met her when I was staying with you."

"Oh," Hermione groaned, swaying heavily against Derek.

He freed his arm and gripped her shoulders and stared into her eyes. "Hermione, you'll be upsetting the child if you don't lay off. What's up with you?"

"It's all right, Derek, I'll look after her." Alison put an arm round her sister. "It's just one of those coincidences, Hermione."

"What kind of coincidence?" Derek demanded.

Alison glanced at Rowan and scowled at him. "It's just a coincidence," she repeated more forcefully. "She's thinking of Queenie, that's all. We only called her Queenie because grandfather used to call her his queen. She was christened Victoria."

CHAPTER TWELVE

The silence seemed to stretch the air until Rowan's ears throbbed. The shriek of a seagull felt as if the air were tearing. Derek muttered under his breath, and then Hermione pulled away from mummy. "Rowan," she said in a voice that meant to sound disinterested, "what's your new friend like?"

"She's nice. I can tell she reads a lot and likes old things. She always tells the truth, and she's awfully clean. Her daddy brought her up, but now she doesn't know where he is."

Everything she said appeared to upset Hermione further. "And you say you met her near my house?" Hermione whispered.

"On the beach when I went with granddad. But she said she lived near here."

"Very near," Hermione said, and swallowed. "Rowan, will you promise me something?"

"What?"

"Just for me, will you promise not to play with this girl you call Vicky?"

"Do us a favour, Hermione," Derek interrupted. "She's got few enough friends round here yet without you losing her one."

"Just until we've had a chance to meet her, then. What about the children who live across the road?"

"Mary and Paul? I don't like them any more. They're never clean. They'd sully me."

"That's her," Hermione wailed. "That's one of her words. My God, you sound just like her."

Rowan suddenly felt as wicked as Vicky had looked when Paul wanted the binoculars – wicked enough to get her own back on

Hermione for making mummy accuse her of lying. She remembered one of Queenie's words. "They're such paltry children," she said.

Perhaps she'd gone too far. Hermione's face began to shake. "They're just words out of the books she reads, Hermione," Derek insisted. "And maybe from the old girl before she died."

"She's at an age when she picks things up," Alison said. "Better get used to it, Hermione. She may be worse when she's a teenager."

"It isn't just that, can't you see? She might be Queenie standing there in front of us. For God's sake hold on to her while you still can."

"I don't need you to tell me what's best for my child and her mind," Derek snapped.

"She's my child too," Alison said.

"I never said she wasn't. I hope that means you'll take no notice of your sister's crazy talk."

He turned away as if he'd said too much. Rowan was ashamed of having caused the trouble, of making them talk about her as if she weren't there. "I'm sorry, auntie, I was only teasing you. Daddy's right, those words are in my books."

"That's good enough for me," her father said. "Clear off then, but stay where we can see you."

Hermione offered nervously to go with her until mummy said there was no need. Rowan ran onto the dunes. If she was becoming more like Queenie, what was wrong with that? If Vicky was like Queenie too, except less daunting, perhaps Rowan had been drawn to that in her. Talking to her ought to dispel any doubts Rowan had, though she wasn't sure what she would ask. But there was no sign of Vicky on the dunes or on the beach.

When Rowan went home, the grown-ups were being polite to one another. At dinner, even the most neutral remark to her felt as if it were directed at another of the grown-ups. She was glad when it was bedtime, even when they came up one by one to give her kisses that felt like unspoken words.

On Sunday Hermione seemed determined to be sensible: she dug the garden fiercely all morning and then proposed to see what could be cleared from the top floor. She strode upstairs as if she had never been afraid to do so.

Her bravado didn't last for long. She obviously disliked the shapes that squatted in the room next to Queenie's, hands on knees under the dustsheets. Soon all the chairs were uncovered except for the one that looked as if someone were sitting quite still beneath the sheet. The seated shape was only cushions – rotten, by the smell. When Hermione tried to move a chair, the fabric gave way and her fingers sank into the spongy greyness that filled the arms. "You'll clear this floor out soon, won't you," she pleaded. "The sooner it's livable, the sooner you can get away from here."

Daddy drove her home that evening. By the time he came back Rowan was in bed, listening apprehensively for the argument her parents seemed to be saving until they were alone. She was asleep before she heard anything. At breakfast they were silent, her father staring at a letter propped against the milk jug. Eventually he told her what it said. "I won't be doing the job at your school, in case anyone asks you. You might think it'd count for something that you go there, but a spark undercut me by fifty pounds."

"Won't we be able to stay here?"

"What the hell do you think?" he snarled, and looked shocked by himself. "I'm sorry, love, I didn't mean to shout at you." She was too upset to go to him, and he returned to staring at the letter. "Fifty pigging quid," he muttered.

"Let your father be, Rowan. Hurry up or you'll be late for school." Her mother shooed her to the bathroom to brush her teeth. When Rowan made to look into the dining-room and say a forgiving goodbye to her father, mummy hurried her onwards. She was too late. Rowan had already heard one of the worst sounds she could imagine ever hearing: her father weeping.

CHAPTER THIRTEEN

At lunchtime on Monday several children came to the shop. Hermione peered out of the back room as the bell rang. Two girls of about Rowan's age were admiring dresses on the racks while some of their classmates crowded at the window, darkening the shop. The bell jangled as girls swarmed in, and Hermione seemed unable to count them or even to see their faces. They made her room feel so like a cramped dark airless box that she stumbled to her feet. "Some of you will have to go out. Anyone who isn't buying something. And don't all block the window. Give the rest of us a chance to breathe."

They stared at her as if she were senile or mad. One, who had just opened her purse, snapped it shut ostentatiously and stalked like a duchess out of the shop, followed by her friends. The shrill bell rang and rang, and then the shop was quiet until Gwen and Elspeth, the craftswomen who made the toys, murmured together in Welsh. "We were saying," Gwen explained, "if you wanted to go home where you won't be interrupted, we could look after the shop."

"I couldn't let you do that. People might think it was an improvement, probably would." Even her attempt at a joke betrayed her nervousness. "If you want to stay, I'd love you to. I'll stay in the back so I don't scare away any more customers," she said, and returned to the latest pile of unsolicited advertising.

Soon all the glossy brochures full of eulogies to plastic toys were in the bin beside her small oak desk. Gwen and Elspeth murmured liquidly in Welsh and glanced at her when they thought she wasn't looking, concern on their sharp but delicate pale faces. Years of living together had made them look almost like identical twins. She couldn't blame them for worrying about her. She would be no use to Rowan in this state.

She had been on her way to this state ever since the child had looked in the shop window, through the reflection of the mask. She'd kept seeing a small figure in the devious streets, and whenever she unlocked the shop she felt there were too many still faces in the window. Then her mother had called to tell her Lance had been killed before he could talk to Alison, and Hermione had remembered what he'd said to her: "the little girl". Perhaps he hadn't meant Rowan at all.

A feeling that she might be needed had sent her to Waterloo. The sight of the house, of its clusters of dull rooftop windows that reminded her of the eyes of an old swollen spider, had made her too nervous to think. The sisters had discussed Lance guardedly, and Hermione had felt less alone for talking. She'd gone out to make a start on the garden so that prospective buyers of the house wouldn't be put off before they opened the gate, and then Rowan had appeared with the dead woman's binoculars.

At first Hermione had thought the black shape was clinging to her chest. She'd seen a bat and told herself it was a kitten. What if they had been Queenie's binoculars? The child was almost bound to have taken something from the house, but why had she insisted that some friend had given them to her? Rowan had gazed innocently at her and told her that the child was someone she'd met when she was staying with Hermione – a child with Queenie's real name.

Nobody had seemed to think it mattered. Once Rowan was out of earshot on the dunes, her parents had turned on Hermione. Rowan was upset enough about having to move without all this fuss about an old pair of binoculars. The damn things weren't even much use, Derek had protested as if that should end the argument: he'd had a squint through them, and the lenses might as well have been plain glass.

Hermione had forced herself to keep quiet until she could choose her words. A night's exhausted sleep had made her feel more capable, so much so that she'd braved Queenie's floor to prove to Alison and Derek that she was over her neuroses and should be taken notice of. But the rooms had appalled her, for they'd felt as if Queenie's death were seeping through them. She'd taken some family albums to browse through at home, and had never felt more eager to be away from Queenie's house.

And now that she was closer to where she ought to be, she was harassing her customers instead of trying to help Rowan. Delaying would only aggravate her fears, and she had to face what she couldn't escape. She stood up, feeling unexpectedly lighter and more lithe, and the women smiled at her as if she'd risen from a sickbed. "If you're staying until we close, could I have a lift to the church?" she said.

They looked relieved and sympathetic. "Any time you'd like to visit the grave," Elspeth said, "just say."

When the children passed the shop on their way back to school, she accosted them. "I'm sorry I shouted at you. I've had a bit of a family upheaval."

"Too many of us came in all at once. We'll come back tomorrow," one said, and Hermione felt like giving them a present each.

She locked the shop at five-thirty while Elspeth brought the Renault from the car park. As they drove to Gronant along the hillside road, a chill like an essence of autumn reached out from the fields, where the edges of leaves were yellowing. At the churchyard Elspeth said "I'll be getting Gwen home, then," as if they weren't living together, though Hermione didn't mind: she rather envied them for what they had. She watched the Renault vanish over the hill, and then she let herself into the churchyard.

It was small and neat, half of it shadowed by the stocky chapel. She made her way over the turf, past flowers nestling against grey headstones, an angel poking the stump of her wrist like a gun barrel out of her stone robe. A weeping willow shaded a patch of ground in the midst of the graveyard, inviolable and inaccessible, and beyond it was the family grave.

The newly chiselled name gleamed at her from the marble pillar above the mound that was blanketed with squares of turf. THEIR BELOVED DAUGHTER VICTORIA, IN HER FATHER'S ARMS AT LAST. Queenie must have worded that herself in advance, or surely her mother would have been mentioned. Hermione shivered at the notion of being lowered into arms beneath the earth – and then she

THE INFLUENCE • 81

remembered that Rowan had said the child called Vicky no longer knew where her father was.

No wonder Queenie had come back if all she had found was emptiness. Hermione believed that when you died you found whatever you expected, but suppose you found only what you were able, consciously or otherwise, to create? Perhaps Queenie, never having created anything apart from her own perfect image of herself, had discovered that she would be alone with it for eternity. Hermione had always thought that the idea of hell presupposed a god, but perhaps hell was yourself after death: perhaps you were judged at the moment of death by that part of yourself you couldn't lie to, the part that knew everything you'd thought and done in your life. Somewhere in everyone was their own severest critic, and perhaps dying released it from a lifetime of constraints to judge what kind of eternity was deserved.

Hermione's jaw twinged, but only because her thoughts were making her clench her teeth. It seemed that Queenie had finished hurting her that way. The rotting of the top floor of her house might reflect a loss of interest too. But she was interested in Rowan – interested enough to make sure she was buried with a lock of the child's hair.

Hermione glanced around her. The willow screened the grave from the road; the nearest cottages were out of sight beyond the hill. Still, it was absurd to plan: not only did she lack the tools, but it wouldn't help the family if she were put away for desecrating the grave. Surely there were legal ways to have the locket retrieved.

Was it just her relief at not having the tools that made her feel contemptuously observed? A chilly scent of rot drifted through the graveyard, and she felt as if the watcher were holding its breath. You've no breath to hold, she thought with bravado so furious that it enlivened her mind. You killed Lance because he would have told Alison why you made your will the way you did, to keep Rowan where you want to be. You haven't tried to kill me because nobody will listen to me, because they all think I'm the way you made me, a neurotic child you scared out of growing up.

The stillness was so breathless that she found it hard to breathe. The willow seemed as fixed as the headstones and the church. She turned her back on the grave, feeling suddenly as if she were challenging the watcher to do more than watch. Perhaps it was that provocation that brought the response.

It sounded like a smothered giggle, not so much childish as senile, an expression of malice that couldn't quite be suppressed. She tried to tell herself she had imagined it, for how could it be where she'd thought it was? Then a voice responded to her thoughts about Queenie and herself, a voice so muffled it sounded withered, and Hermione walked away very fast, not quite running, flinging willow branches aside to make directly for the gate. "That's right," the voice had said gleefully from deep in the mound.

CHAPTER FOURTEEN

Dear diary, Hermione says she found a picsure of my grandaunt Queenie waring her lockit and shed written on the picsure that she wanted the youngest child of the famly to have the lockit when she was dead, so now Hermione wants to have her dug up…

Rowan hoped that wouldn't happen: she would feel guilty and creepy if it did. She didn't want to write about that or about having heard daddy crying to himself. She held her pencil as though she were still writing and gazed across the classroom. Mary was chewing her pencil and shaking her head like a dog at the taste on her blackening tongue. Someone farted, setting off a train of smothered giggles. Rowan hated the school now for reducing her father to tears. She stared at the wall, at the pictures and descriptions of best friends the class had put up before she'd started here, and realised belatedly that Kelly was speaking to her. "Rowan?"

"What do you want?"

"No need to snap. I only wanted to ask if you'd like to come home one night for tea."

Kelly was a large girl who'd befriended Rowan on her first day and given her a bag of sweets. Rowan liked her but suspected that tea with her might rot your teeth. Just now she didn't feel like going home with anyone but Vicky, wherever Vicky lived. Before she could speak, Mary hissed "Don't bother with her, she's stuck up."

Rowan's response was too sharp for her lips to keep in. "Don't interfere, you grubby little shoat."

All the children on Mary's table jeered as if she'd proved Mary right. "You'd think her father was a duke or something," Mary smirked. "He's just an electrician who can't even get jobs."

Miss Frith looked up from her desk where she was reading the *Daily Post.* "Now, Mary, didn't we agree that people aren't always to blame if they're out of work? That's one reason why we learn to read, so we won't be bored if we're out of work and get up to mischief."

Mary and her friends subsided, but not for long. Just loud enough for Rowan to hear, Mary muttered "Her and her mam and dad lived with a crazy old woman who thought she was the queen of England."

The bell for the end of lessons shrilled, and Rowan's voice cut through it. "I'd rather be like my grandaunt Queenie than any of you."

She hadn't meant to include Kelly, but Kelly flounced away, trailing a smell of mints and chocolate bars. Rowan was putting her books away when Miss Frith called her to her desk. "Rowan, we know you're a clever girl who reads well for her age, but school is about other things too. We want to help you grow up. I think we'd be happier if you'd learn to socially interact more, to get on with your peers, which is to say the others in your class."

Rowan's growing dislike of the school focused on the teacher. "My grandaunt said you aren't supposed to split infinitives," she said.

Miss Frith's face stiffened. "Wait outside," she said, and raised her voice and beckoned. "Could I have a word?"

Rowan turned, hoping it was one of her parents, but it was Jo. The teacher closed her out in the corridor, where Paul and Mary picked their noses and made faces at her while she tried to hear what was being said about her. She heard Jo say "They weren't planning on having a child. She was the start of their money troubles."

Mary waited until they were walking home and she was safe on the far side of Jo before asking "Why did Rowan's mam and dad have her if they didn't want her?"

"I never said they didn't, and you shouldn't have been listening." Jo avoided looking at Rowan until they were at the big house, and then she rang the bell to bring Rowan's father to the door. "Miss Frith wants to talk to you and Alison about Rowan's problems at school," she said.

"It's the first I've heard that she's got any." He seemed preoccupied and irritable, but made himself aware of Rowan. "Tell us about them when your mother comes home, all right, babe?" he said, and began to close the door.

"Can't I come in?" she pleaded.

"Can't you play with your friends for a bit?" He saw that she couldn't, and sighed. "Come in if you've got to, but stay out of the way until I tell you different. I'm attending to some business."

As she made for the stairs, along the wide peeled hall that felt like an adventure, he went into the dining-room, where Mr Ormond was scowling at the table spread with receipts and daddy's books. "The best I can say for all this is that it's a sorry mess," the accountant said.

Rowan faltered three stairs up, holding her breath as the accountant went on "I don't suppose it helps much if I say I told you so."

"It helps as much as most of what you say, pal. Seems to me you should have more respect for us poor sods who pay your wages. Maybe I can't spell as good as you, but that doesn't entitle you to wipe your arse on me."

"Come now, that kind of language isn't called for."

"An ambulance'll be called for, you little prat, for you if you don't stop pissing me off."

When Rowan heard the accountant's sharp-heeled footsteps striding to the door, she fled to her room. His car droned away, and daddy called "It's all right now, babe." But it wasn't: in the dining-room he'd sounded brutal and coarse, he'd been someone she didn't know and was afraid to know. At dinner he regretted having lost his temper with Mr Ormond, and mummy was upset about somebody called Julius who had an incurable disease. Usually Rowan felt she could share their preoccupations, but Jo's comment made her feel as if they didn't want her to be there. Eventually her mother said "So, Rowan, is there something wrong at school?"

"Daddy not getting the job," she mumbled.

"Is that all, babe?" her father said roughly. "Don't lose any sleep over it. We'll survive. We'll have to, won't we?"

"Is that all?" her mother said.

She wished she could run up to the top floor and hide, but her own question wouldn't let her. "Didn't you and daddy want to have me?"

"Who told you that? Of course we did. You're worth everything else in the world to us."

"Pigging right you are," her father growled. "Just you tell me who said different and I'll sort them out for you."

"Nobody did," Rowan said, afraid that he might rail at Jo as he had at the accountant. "We were talking about orphans and abandoned children with Miss Frith."

Her mother looked dissatisfied. "That can't be why she wants to see us."

Rowan was silent, though that was the same as agreeing. How could she have let herself think she was unwanted? No wonder her parents hardly spoke to her during the rest of the meal, even if that made her feel as though she weren't there or didn't deserve to be. In bed she lay brooding about school and Miss Frith, who presumably would tell them what Jo had said. Perhaps her rumination made her dream of the school.

It began with the sound of a drill, so tiny that at first she thought it was deep in one of her teeth. No, it was too distant, but then why should it worry her? It was outside the window, towards the school. When she realised that it might be in the school, she slipped out of bed to look.

A tanker soundless as a cloud sailed by. The curtains held her in a soft embrace as she gazed between the houses. The school assembly hall was lit. Now she knew why the sound was painful as a dentist's drill to her: it was the sound of her father's loss. The grinding whined into silence, and after a while a man carried a ladder across the lit hall. She was about to close out the sight of him where her father ought to be when she glimpsed movement at the far end of the assembly hall.

Wasn't he supposed to be working on his own? Surely otherwise he wouldn't have been so cheap. Rowan fetched the binoculars from a dark corner of her room. Looking through them was even more like dreaming: though the man with his big ears and curly hair was closer, she felt all the more detached. She saw him stop halfway up the ladder and peer sharply across the hall, shading his eyes, before he went on climbing. He must have heard whoever Rowan had glimpsed. Whoever it was clearly wasn't with him.

She couldn't see the corridor of classrooms towards which he had stared. She would be able to see from the top floor. Her dream was unusually detailed, for when she crept out of her bedroom she heard the television downstairs, playing an old musical by a local band her parents still liked, the Beatles. She stole upstairs, the binoculars nudging her chest like a baby in a sling.

Dream or not, she might have wished she had worn her slippers. As she went up, the carpet grew damp and chill. On the top floor it felt like the threat of quicksand in the dark. At least her sensations were distant, as though she were hardly there at all. She groped her way along the furry wall to the room full of squelchy furniture, and edged between the vague squatting shapes to the window.

The sash slid up, its weights thumping like irregular heartbeats in the wall. The eyepieces of the binoculars seemed to fit themselves to her eyes and disappear. The electrician had moved along the hall, tacking cable above the picture rail, and was nearly at the right-hand corridor. Rowan turned towards the corridor on the far side of the hall, but nothing looked back at her except paintings, splashier towards the nursery classrooms. Then she thought of the corridor he had almost reached.

It was unlit. The light from the hall reached past the first window and made the wall gleam icily, but the next sample of wall faded from grey to black, and the third window looked stuffed with soot. She wasn't sure if she glimpsed movement where the dimness became dark, movement withdrawing spiderlike into the dark. She only knew that she was growing tense as the man stepped down the ladder.

He set it up just outside the mouth of the corridor, spread its legs and shook them to make sure they were firm. When he leaned towards the corridor, Rowan thought he had heard something, but he was stooping to pick up his boxes of cable-holders and nails. He climbed the steps carefully, arranged the boxes on the platform at the top, stood on the step below it, reached up and placed a holder over the cable, drew back his hammer to tap the nail in. Then, with an unexpectedness that at first made Rowan want to giggle, the hammer flew out of his hand.

Shock had flung his hand up and loosened his grip – shock at whatever he saw rushing at him out of the corridor. Perhaps shock overturned the ladder: could a figure as small as the one Rowan barely glimpsed have snatched it from beneath him? It was certainly shock that made him clutch thoughtlessly for the only support he could reach – the wire of the light overhead.

Rowan saw his mouth twist and gape so wide she thought his jaw would break, and then his body began to jerk. The holder from which the wire hung ripped loose from the ceiling. Yards of cable tore the plaster open, dropping him to the floor. He was clutching the wire with both hands, unable to let go. She pushed the sight away from her with the binoculars when he started to dance helplessly at the end of the wire.

Despite the distance, she saw his face turn black. He was tiny as an insect now, and twitching like one that was almost dead. She turned away, feeling drained, exhausted. She might have curled up on the floor, except that of course she was really asleep in her room. All the same, she had to dream that she tiptoed down the chilly stairs and replaced the binoculars in the corner of her bedroom and wriggled back into bed before the dream could end.

CHAPTER FIFTEEN

What haunted Alison most about Julius was that the single bed was far too big for him. Much of the time he lay there, gazing with bloodshot eyes at whoever came to see him. Blood vessels showed through his bald scalp, blue veins webbed his papery skin. When he had changed into his pyjamas she'd seen that he had almost no penis. His arteries were hardening, and he was suffering from heart disease. He was nine years old.

He looked at least sixty. He had been given a side room off the ward so that the other children wouldn't gawk at him while he waited for the specialist to see him, but even with the door closed the staff was constantly aware of him. He'd affected both of the student nurses: Jasmine had brought him a box of chocolates, and flowers from her seventeenth-floor window box; Libby kept glancing into the side room in case he needed anything and didn't like to trouble the staff. Soon after ten o'clock she came to Alison and moved her stubbly head to indicate that they should talk in the corridor. Once there, she murmured urgently "What's the matter with him?"

"With Julius? Progeria, premature aging. What we call the Hutchinson-Gilford syndrome when it takes someone that young."

"What can we do to help him?"

"Treat the symptoms as best we can, alleviate the pain. The honest answer is, not enough. He's unlikely to see twenty," Alison said as gently as she could.

"If that's the best we can do, why is he in here at all?"

"So the doctors can observe him, Libby. It's a rare condition, and they want to learn all they can."

"But that's awful." Libby fumbled for her cigarettes, pulled one out of the packet, pushed it back in so hard that she snapped off the filter. "That's like using him for vivisection. He's only a child, he can't even make the choice for himself."

Alison thought he had. Though nobody had told him how long he had to live, his instincts might have. Perhaps that explained his calm, however much that seemed like sadness. Children in his state were supposed to be no more advanced mentally than others of their age, but Alison felt he was mature beyond his years. Or was she only seeing him as she believed he ought to be, compensated by nature for the shortness of his life? She didn't feel sure enough to answer Libby, who turned away abruptly as though Alison were conniving at cruelty to Julius and went in to read to him.

Before long the ward sister sent her out to deal with other children, but lingered herself to talk to him with a gruffness that disguised her pity less than she might have wished. Jasmine and Libby were growing more attentive to the other children now. Both of them were busy when it was time to make the hourly entries on Julius's chart, and the sister had been called out of the ward. Alison looked through the glass panel of his door.

He was playing a game on the computer his parents had brought him. The sister must have set up the keyboard and the monitor on the bed table, for he couldn't lift the monitor himself. A gleam reflected from the game danced in his eyes, a faint contented smile had settled on his lips. When Alison saw his smile widen as he broke his own record, she went in.

He watched her while she took the readings and entered them on the chart at the foot of his bed, and she was suddenly afraid that he was about to ask her if he was going to get well. But when she glanced up, his large eyes in his old man's face were calm, so calm that she felt they were sad only for her. "Would you like me to stay and talk to you?" she said.

"It's okay, I was playing," he said, and then with the ghost of a smile "The other children need you more. You can help them to get better."

Watching him play the computer game, she'd thought he was

wasting precious minutes of his life, but now she saw how unreasonable she'd been: he had the right to play like a child if that was meaningful to him. Nobody should interfere if he was at peace with himself, and it occurred to her that his parents were resigned to that. "Well," she said awkwardly "I'm here if you need me."

He smiled so charmingly it pierced her heart. He seemed about to speak, but glanced past her. The door had opened, the disinfectant smell of the hospital surging in. When he frowned, she realised that a child had wandered into the room. She turned to shepherd the child away, and then she faltered. In the doorway, gazing at Julius as though the sight of him had paralysed her with dismay, was Rowan.

CHAPTER SIXTEEN

Earlier that morning Rowan wakened feeling happy and refreshed. She yawned and stretched until the sheets untucked themselves, and then she padded to the window. Though she thought her mother had closed the curtains last night, they were half open. Long skeins of cloud unravelled on the blue sky, a tanker turned ponderously between two tugboats on the bay. Rowan's gaze drifted over the seascape and lit on the school, and then she remembered her horrid dream. She opened the window and let the sea breeze stroke her face until her father hurried in. "Come on, don't be dreaming, we've overslept. I ought to have got you to school by now and be on the way to a job."

He brought her a bowl of cereal to eat while she washed and dressed. As she ran along the naked hall, Jo and her children were straggling out of their house. "Do you mind going with them?" daddy said. "You'd be helping me. I'm mad busy today."

She couldn't refuse when he put it like that. She kissed him through the open window of the car and crossed the road as he drove off. "Please may you take me to school?"

"Of course, chick, you know you're always welcome," Jo said with a heartiness that was meant to deny whatever Rowan thought she'd overheard yesterday, but Rowan sensed how eager Paul and Mary were to tell their friends. She wished she could be like Vicky, not needing to go to school. It didn't matter, she told herself: whatever anyone said about her, she knew her parents wanted her and always had.

She was on the main road when she began to see children she recognised, not going to school but coming back. Jo couldn't ask their parents what was wrong; they were on the far side of the road, beyond the impatient traffic. Rowan felt uneasy, as if the night or the dream were reawakening. The school came in sight, and she saw that the schoolyard and the building were deserted.

The sight seemed to brighten luridly, filling her eyes. Her dream was there before her in broad daylight, and she was afraid to see the blackened puppet on the cord, still dancing. Jo hurried her into the schoolyard. If she saw the figure now, she would be able to make out every detail of its face. But the assembly hall was empty. That was such a relief that at first she didn't take in what a mother emerging from the school told Jo. "No school today. There was an accident last night. The electrician electrocuted himself."

"He couldn't have been much good at his job. Pity they didn't give it to Rowan's dad," Jo said, and frowned at Rowan. "Why the face?"

Rowan was struggling to know how she should feel. "I dreamed that happened," she admitted.

"People do sometimes, they said so on television. It would have happened anyway, chick."

Or had it been a dream? In any case, did that matter so long as it still seemed like one? Rowan waited apprehensively for the horror of what she had seen to catch up with her, until she realised that it wasn't going to. Last night she must have looked away just in time. Her relief gave way to hope. The sooner her father knew what had happened, the better. When she came in sight of the big house she ran across the road to it, for the front door was open.

As she ran into the hall, the dimness closed around her eyes, and she almost fell headlong. Someone came out of the dark to catch her, came so quickly that it was like falling into a mirror, except that the other was wearing a long white dress. "Did you leave your door open?" Vicky said.

Rowan supposed that she must have when her father was hurrying her. She might have resented Vicky's having entered the house uninvited, but she felt more resentful of Jo, who pushed the door wider and blinked at the dimness. "Is anyone in there with you, Rowan? Your mam wouldn't want me leaving you all by yourself."

The idea that Jo was too dazzled by the sunlight to see Vicky amused

Rowan, and she couldn't help sharing a little of Vicky's contempt. "I'm not by myself," she said.

"Don't be clever, Rowan. You just come and play with Paul and Mary where I can see you."

"I don't tell lies. I'm not by myself," Rowan said, and with a sudden wickedness that was Vicky's too "They can come and play here if they like."

Jo stared at her and protruded her lower lip. "You're to tell me if you go out of this gate, do you hear?"

She shooed Paul and Mary across the road and slammed her door. Silence settled on the garden that smelled of the earth Hermione had dug. "I don't care, I wanted to stay here anyway," Rowan said.

When she looked round, Vicky's deep pale eyes that seemed never to blink were gazing at her. "I haven't seen you for a while," Rowan said.

"I've seen you. I've been busy. I should have come if you'd really wanted me to."

She was strange, Rowan thought, but there was a way to find out more about her. "Shall we go to your house?"

"We've no reason to go out of the gate."

"You've been in my house, so now I want to go in yours."

"You needn't worry about that, my dear."

It didn't sound exactly like a threat, nor was it quite a promise. "When?" Rowan demanded.

"You'll see where I live as soon as you're ready."

Rowan might have retorted that she was ready now, except that seemed likely to bring her another slippery answer. She decided to wait until she could tell one of her parents that she was going to Vicky's. "I'll do some jobs for mummy, then. You can help me if you like."

Revulsion flickered over Vicky's face. "You aren't a housemaid, are you? Why don't we give your mother a surprise and go and see her at work?"

Rowan had often wanted to, but her mother always told her to wait until she was older. Her sense that Vicky was capable of adventures she wouldn't have dared herself made her reckless. "Yes, let's. I'll just leave my daddy a note."

She sat under the chandelier to write.

Dear daddy, Ive come home from school becose the ellectrision had an accident which I ecspect means theyll want you now but now Im going with my freind Vicky to visit mummy at the hospittal...

She stopped, because the small sharp noise she'd thought was coming from the chandelier was snickering. "What's so funny?" she demanded.

"I thought you'd be a better speller at your age. It's only the Welsh who double their letters."

Rowan wrote *Lots of love from your Rowan* and then glared at Vicky. "Maybe you think you could do better."

"I'll write it out for you if you like."

"I don't like. I don't want you to do my writing for me." She added some lines of kisses and stood up. "I'll just tell Jo we're going."

"You needn't. She was only interfering. I never—" Vicky's eyes were suddenly opaque. "Let's be off."

"What were you going to say?"

"Nothing to do with you. Don't you want to see where your mother works?"

"We're going to, aren't we? What's your hurry?"

Vicky flung up her hands, and the shadow of one swelled over Rowan. "How long do you expect me to wait?"

All at once the room seemed dark and oppressive and chill. If this was Vicky's impatience, Rowan didn't like it much, especially when her legs began to shiver. Then Vicky turned away, and Rowan stumbled out of the house, her head swimming. The sunlight lit up her mind as she rang Jo's rattly bell. "We're going to mummy," she said.

Jo shrugged. "That's up to her," she said, and closed the door.

The door of the big house closed like an echo. Vicky's white dress seemed to brighten as she crossed the road and made a face at Jo's house. "Wouldn't you like to be able to go wherever you choose?"

"Like you, you mean?"

"You read my mind," Vicky said with a meaningful look.

Just now, riding the bus without a grown-up was enough of an adventure. The streets were full of people she would never meet, every house held secrets she would never see. A man unrolled a carpet along the pavement of a side street, another pasted an eye bigger than himself onto a billboard. A scrapyard was scattered with a giant's fingernail clippings: mudguards. In Liverpool, in the street that led up to the hospital, early drunks seemed to be playing a game, touching all the bases of the lampposts. Vicky led the way into the muggy hospital. "Mummy will be upstairs, I think," Rowan whispered.

Nobody seemed to notice them as they ran up the stony uncarpeted stairs, past a folded wheelchair like a slice of itself. By the time they saw the sign for the ward where her mother worked, Rowan was sweating. Vicky, who looked absolutely cool, pushed open the double doors and followed her in, and Rowan caught sight of her mother beyond a door just inside the ward. She inched the door open, enjoying the surprise she was about to give her mother.

She faltered. There was an old man in the bed, a tiny bald old man with crippled hands. He looked as if his skin had shrunk almost to the point of tearing. What was he doing here? He oughtn't to be in a children's ward. Then his large sad eyes met hers, and she realised he was a child.

She wanted to flee, to run out of the hospital before her mother saw her. She was still trying when her mother swung round and came grimly at her, taking her by the shoulders with a firmness that felt like the threat of bruises and marching her out of the room. "I'll be back shortly," she said to the withered boy as she closed the door, and urged Rowan into the corridor. "What on earth do you think you're doing, child?"

"There isn't any school today," Rowan stammered, glancing about for Vicky. "The electrician had an accident. Daddy may get the job now."

"That's all very well, but do you realise how ill that boy is I was talking to? Don't you know any better than to disturb him?"

Rowan felt her lips begin to tremble as her eyes filled with tears. "I wanted to see where you worked. I only wanted to give you a surprise."

"Well, you succeeded." Her mother patted her face, not too gently. "Now, young lady, don't turn on the taps. I can't waste time on that while there are children here who need looking after. Couldn't you have stayed with Jo?"

Rowan felt as if she hardly existed as a person any more, as if she were just an inconvenience her mother had to deal with, especially when her mother sighed and said "What are we going to do with you? I'd have you read to the little ones, but sister won't let children visit. All the hospitals were like that when Hermione had to go in, and it didn't help me then either. Just wait here."

Soon she reappeared, snapping shut her handbag. "Here's your pocket money early. Go down to the shop and buy yourself something to read. You'll have to stay in the staffroom until I finish work."

Rowan took the coin, which felt cold as indifference, and trudged along the shrill corridor. As she started down the stairs Vicky fell in step alongside her. "You don't look very joyful. Did she send you away?"

Rowan wouldn't admit that, even to Vicky. "I'm sad for that boy. I don't ever want to be like him."

"You won't be yet. It isn't natural to be like him."

That didn't sound as reassuring as it ought to be. All it meant was that Rowan would take longer to wither, for her limbs to turn scrawny and fragile, her hands and feet to curl into useless claws, until she was nothing but a lolling doll to be treated like a baby and pushed about in a wheelchair. "I don't ever want to grow old," she said, shivering amid the mugginess.

A child's cry echoed through a corridor, an overhead speaker paged a doctor, a telephone rang. When these sounds faded, Vicky was still gazing at her. "Maybe you won't have to," Vicky said.

CHAPTER SEVENTEEN

On Thursday evening Derek and Eddie papered the hall of the house. Rowan admired Eddie's deftness in clothing the walls with hardly a wasted inch, but shook her head when they asked if she wanted to help. Even in the sewing-room, where her mother was stripping the walls, she didn't help much. She didn't want to be alone, Derek realised. He was glad when she was in bed and, surprisingly quickly, asleep.

The hall was finished when he went downstairs. He and Alison had chosen a paper embossed with silvery leaves, so that the eye was caught by the fall of light on silver rather than by the irregularities in the wall beneath. He took her hand as Eddie brought in a large white Chinese lantern. "Now you can get rid of that old thing," Eddie said, and clattered up the ladder to remove the stained-glass lampshade. When the lantern was hung, the light turned the hall a dozen different shades of silver. "Now at least you won't be putting off anyone who comes to view the house as soon as they step through the door," Eddie said.

"You must let us pay you for that at least," Alison protested.

"No chance. Call it the present we never gave you when you moved in. If you want to show your appreciation you can let this poor overworked bugger come with me for a drink."

Derek sensed that she wanted to talk about Rowan, but she let go of his hand. "He's never needed my permission."

"I'll stay if you want me to, love."

"Go on, you deserve a drink. Get away from the family and try and relax for a while."

Did she mean that as a rebuke? Eddie must have thought so, for when they were in the smoky pub and being served by a woman whom

Derek had seen meeting her children at the school but who seemed not to want to be recognised, Eddie said "Something up at home?"

"Nothing worth mentioning. How do you mean?"

"Just thought there was an atmosphere in there before."

"It'll be that we don't know how to take what happened at the school. I mean, they've asked me if I want the job and I'd be a fool to myself if I said no, but I'd rather not have got it that way."

"He couldn't have been much of a spark. Better he did it to himself than put our kids at school in danger."

"I reckon," Derek agreed. They found themselves a corner table, and Eddie said "Any interest in your house?"

"If there is, nobody's told me."

"I saw a couple looking, but something must have scared them off. The size of it, most likely. You know what me and Jo were saying you should do? Get outline planning permission for a nursing home. See if your estate agent doesn't think so."

"I might at that," Derek said, imagining the house full of people and light, every bedroom a home.

"If it was half the size I'd make you an offer myself. We could do with more space now the kids are getting bigger. We're starting to get on one another's nerves."

"Oh, aye."

"You should count yourself lucky having just Rowan. Mary's after a room of her own because she doesn't want Paul to see her undressing, would you believe? And she can't share with her sister because Patty's up there watching her portable telly after Mary's in bed. So now we've got Jo calling Patty a selfish cow and keeping on at me about looking for a bigger house, but will she get up off her arse and look for one while I'm out all day working? Will she buggery. Too busy giving the neighbours tea and cakes so they'll order stuff from her catalogues so she can get another free percolator or some other crap. And then she whines on about how she never sees me because I'm out working all hours. They don't appreciate us, do they?"

"Maybe we don't appreciate them."

"What's that? Whose side are you on? You're with your own kind now, mate, no need to be scared to speak up. Get that down you and I'll buy you another, and then maybe you'll talk some sense."

This was an aspect of pubs Derek didn't care for, going out for a drink so as to bare one's home life. Discussing it with Alison was hard enough sometimes. He told Eddie how he'd bounced the accountant and was having to sue Ken. Eddie kept nodding, but looked dissatisfied. "I wanted to tell you, that lampshade was sort of a peace offering from Jo," he said eventually, shouting now that the pub was packed. "She'd have come over herself but she was sorting out the brats. She wanted you and Alison to know she's sorry if she let Rowan hear too much."

"When was this?"

"Didn't Rowan tell you? Perhaps it doesn't matter, then." He went on reluctantly "Jo thought she might have heard her and the teacher saying Rowan wasn't, you know, planned."

"Who says she wasn't?"

"Don't shout at me, pal, I wasn't there. I expect your wife must have."

She wouldn't, Derek thought, and then: she must have. While he was doing his best to keep their secrets, she wasn't even bothering to keep them in the family. At closing time he and Eddie leaned into the dark wind from the sea as they walked home. "We'll have a go at your ground floor on Sunday," Eddie called across the road as Derek stepped into the house.

The smell of soaked wallpaper and bare plaster from the darkness of the sewing-room reminded him of Queenie's rotten books. Alison was lying on the sofa in the living-room, a mug of cocoa by her dangling hand. Her sleepy smile began to fade as she saw his expression, before he said "I found out what the trouble is with Rowan at school."

"It's nothing too bad, is it? She's still recovering from seeing Julius at the hospital."

"It's worse."

"Oh dear, what now?"

"She heard Jo and her teacher saying we hadn't wanted her. I thought we were keeping that to ourselves. If I'd thought you might tell anyone I'd have made you promise."

"You might have asked me, you certainly wouldn't have made me. I told Jo in confidence. She thought she might be pregnant when they weren't planning it, and all I said was how glad we were to have Rowan even though it was by mistake."

"How about how you nearly had to find a second job, Rowan cost so much to keep?"

"Jo may have said we must have had a hard time, and I suppose I'd have had to agree, but that's all."

"You didn't maybe mention we once talked about having her adopted?"

"What do you think? And may I remind you that was your idea, which I wouldn't even consider. I don't think you did really. You'd had too much to drink if I remember rightly, and I think you have now."

"Drink or no drink, I don't go shooting off my gob about how we didn't want Rowan."

"Keep your voice down. Do you want her to hear? I'll have a word with Jo first thing in the morning. I wish I'd never told her, believe me."

"Just never tell anyone else."

"Do you think I would? Poor little thing, she wouldn't even admit it was Jo and Miss Frith she heard. I think she believed what we told her, don't you?"

"I hope she did."

"She must have, surely." All the same, she shivered and drew her shoulders up. "Won't you hold me at least? I know I was wrong. I don't know why Miss Frith wants to see us, but I'll want to see her to make certain this doesn't go any further."

Derek sat by her on the sofa and put one arm around her shoulders, and she rested the side of her face against his chest. "We mustn't hurt each other," she mumbled. "I'd never do anything to hurt either of you. You're all I've got, you know."

Except for the rest of your family, Derek thought, but that thought led to a tangle of doubts. He laid his cheek against Alison's hair, and she moved his free hand to her breast. "We better hadn't say anything else to Rowan," he said. "Only if it looks as if she's wondering how we really feel about her. Come on, let's go up to bed."

And Rowan, who had been wakened by a whisper in her ear or a touch on her face that she thought she must have dreamed, stole away from the foot of the stairs, back to her room. She didn't know how she was managing to tiptoe when her body felt so stiff and meaningless, but perhaps her fear that her parents would realise she'd overheard them was making it work. She'd crept downstairs in search of company just as her father had come home, looking so fierce she'd hidden, and she had heard everything. Vicky was right: they had lied to her – lied about the most important thing in the world. She could trust no one but Vicky. She crawled into bed and lay there, too dismayed even to weep. "I don't want to live," she whispered, and for a moment she felt less alone. She felt as if someone had smiled at her out of the dark.

CHAPTER EIGHTEEN

When the phone wakened Hermione she thought someone was calling her about the message on the photograph. Knuckling her eyes with one hand, she fumbled her bedroom door open. She must have overslept, for the landing and the stairs were brighter than she expected. The sunlight made her blink stickily, the phone bell shattered her thoughts as they tried to form, and so she forgot to be careful. She was only resting her hand on the banister, not holding on to it, when she stepped on the small pale shape.

It was soft and cold under her bare foot. Perhaps it was where the smell of rot and disinfectant was coming from. She wasn't sure whether it writhed, but she did, so violently that she lost her footing. Her nails scraped the banister as she failed to grasp the polished wood. Her other hand flailed at the window beside the stairs, knocking over a potted plant, spraying soil across the highest of the miniature Welsh landscapes that hung above the staircase. But she'd grabbed the ledge. She groped clumsily behind her for the banister and steadied herself on the stairs before she turned to face what she had trodden on.

It was an old rag doll in a frilly white dress. She'd stepped on its face, almost dislodging one eye. Now the bland discoloured face was regaining its shape, the cheek filling out sluglike, the mouth she'd trodden crooked settling back into an innocent straight line. "It has to look as if I had an accident, does it?" Hermione said furiously, and stumbled downstairs to the phone.

Alison was already speaking. "I won't be a moment, I'm just trying to— There you are, Hermione. How are things? How are you feeling?"

What could she say? Shaken and fragile but alive, irate with herself for not having taken care, beginning to feel all the more determined as she realised that the attempt to trip her up meant she was on the right track... "Better than I did, thanks. How's everyone?"

"Rowan, well— Actually, she's why I'm calling. If it's inconvenient you just say so, but she wanted me to ask you if she could stay with you this weekend."

At least then Hermione could keep an eye on her. She didn't think Rowan was in danger physically or would be. She glanced up the stairs and caught her breath. The doll had gone. "All right," she murmured as a challenge. To Alison she said "I'd love to have her. When?"

"Shall Derek bring her straight from school today? Then she'll be out of the way while we attack the house. Thanks, Hermione, you're my favourite sister. A few days in the country may do her good," Alison added as though she were trying to convince herself.

"Don't you worry about her," Hermione told her, wondering what Alison had left unsaid. "I'll look after her as if she were my own."

"That's because she is, love."

Hermione replaced the receiver and then, though her heart still felt painfully magnified by her fall on the stairs, she went upstairs to search the rooms. There was no trace of the doll or of any intrusion. She was on her way to the shop and nibbling a thick sandwich before she realised how wistful Alison's last words had sounded. Perhaps Alison felt hurt because Rowan wanted to come again so soon. The empty eyes of the backs of the masks in the window grew dimmer as the day wore on, but it wasn't the masks that Hermione sensed watching her. The attempts to injure her or frighten her seemed both childish and senile, and at least they meant Rowan was being left alone, she told herself.

As she climbed towards home the mountains were greying, the stone swallowing the grass. A house rattled like a trap as it let a car into one of its front rooms. Hermione was hurrying until she saw that Derek's car wasn't at her cottage, and then she ran: her phone was ringing. The key scratched its way into the lock, and she knocked the receiver out of its cradle. "Hermione? Is that Hermione? Hermione, is that you?"

"Unless it's a burglar, mother. Are you well?"

"Oh, trundling along. Getting used to slowing down and watching the days change. They've asked me to be secretary at the Women's Institute, mind you, and already three of the members want your father to look at their gardens. And at least I've time to sit and think."

"That's the attitude, mother."

"I've been thinking a lot about you."

"Oh yes?"

"No need to sound as if I shouldn't be. If it's any consolation to you, I wish now that Alison hadn't given Rowan's baby hair to your aunt. I won't accept that it did any harm, but it's certainly caused too much fuss. But Hermione, it's all in the past now. Won't you try to accept that for your peace of mind and everyone else's?"

"Believe me, I've tried."

"Try a bit harder, I beg you. Just count yourself lucky that we care enough about you that we managed to get that photograph of Queenie back from the solicitor. You could have been prosecuted for forgery if your father hadn't told him how upset you were."

"So nothing's going to be done," Hermione said dully.

"Put the idea out of your head, child, or if you can't do that, have a word with your doctor. Queenie almost split the family, we mustn't let her do that now. Just let her lie, that's all I'm asking."

They were saying their goodbyes when Derek's car drew up. Hermione had begun to think of putting Rowan off, but she couldn't help feeling relieved. Rowan ran to her, the binoculars dancing blackly on her chest, as Hermione opened the front door. The child's hug was unexpectedly fierce. "I get the idea she's glad to see you," Derek said as he lifted the small suitcase out of the car.

While she made him a coffee, she learned that he would be rewiring the school after all, and why. "Be good for Hermione," he called up to Rowan, who was unpacking. He was at the car when she darted out and gave him a quick kiss, but ducked under his arms as he made to hug her. As he drove away, Hermione saw Rowan at the bedroom window, her face blotted out by the binoculars, their huge eyes full of gathering clouds as they lowered to follow the car.

She served Rowan a candlelight dinner. As the dusk turned the hills into heaps of ash, the child's long face seemed to grow flawless in the soft light. She was obviously troubled about something, but Hermione couldn't tell which of the subjects she herself raised it might be: school, her father's second chance there, the house in Waterloo? They were in the kitchen, washing up the dishes, when Rowan blurted "We went to see where mummy works."

"You and your father?"

Rowan shook her head, and Hermione grew tense. "Was it your idea or your friend's to go?"

"Why do you keep getting at Vicky? She's my friend, my only friend. Why can't you leave her alone?"

"Rowan, you mustn't talk to me like that." At least now Hermione knew it had been Vicky's idea, but Rowan's vehemence dismayed her. "Aren't I your friend too? And what do you think your parents are?"

Rowan turned to the draining-board, and a long pale face pressed itself against the window. It was her reflection, taciturn as a mask. "Rowan," Hermione said "whatever happened at the hospital, talking about it might help."

The child shivered. "I saw some little boy who looked older than my grandaunt," she mumbled.

"That's very rare, dear. You aren't likely ever to see anything like that again," Hermione assured her, and played games of Gwen and Elspeth's draughts with her until Rowan was tired enough for bed.

Soon Hermione was in bed herself, awake. If the encounter at the hospital was part of a plan, what about the accident at the school? When she managed to doze she was wakened twice by Rowan's voice, talking in her sleep. The second time she thought a whisper responded, and she had to stumble to the child's room in the dusty dawn to see that she was alone.

She overslept until Rowan brought her a cup of tea. At the shop her lack of sleep felt like a vacuum in her skull, a constant threat of pain behind her lumpy eyes. She was grateful to Rowan for showing customers where items were. Sometimes the child seemed to be in two places at once, especially when they were alone in the shop.

At closing time the board that said AUNTIE HERMIONE'S came scuttling down the street, but that was only the rising wind. Rowan was bouncing a ball Hermione had given her to keep. "Now what shall we do?" Hermione said.

"Please may we go for a walk down the valley?"

"Right now?" Hermione hadn't yet made dinner, but Rowan's eagerness to return to her favourite haunts seemed reassuring. "Maybe it'll clear our heads."

Beyond the flinty parking lot by the road through Holywell, a gravel path led down the valley. Below Saint Winifred's Well, a Norman shrine whose gift shop sold blinking Christs and various sizes of saint, trees reared over the path, roaring softly. Grass and ferns and thorny creepers spilled over the gravel, and soon the narrow path was tunnelling through green, which smelled like foggy leaves and felt chilly as autumn. "Don't go out of sight, dear," Hermione called as Rowan chased her ball.

Rowan picked her ball out of the blackberries and gave her aunt an old-fashioned look. A wind swooped through the lashing trees at her. As she brushed her hair out of her eyes with the hand that held the ball and tugged her skirt down with the other, she looked older than her years yet intensely vulnerable, dwarfed by the trees. Hermione took her hand quickly. "Just walk for a bit so your poor old aunt can keep up with you."

She had to let go as the path grew twisted and narrower. Overgrown banks obscured the view ahead. The path descended steeply through a dimness like soaked moss and emerged beneath the darkening sky, at the end of the causeway that bordered the first reservoir. A chimney as high as a house stood beside the path, displaying a dark archway Rowan liked to gaze up. Hermione was relieved that she seemed to feel too grown-up now.

On the side of the causeway further from the reservoir was a sheer drop to a ruined factory. Thick jagged walls topped with weeds stood here and there on the grey foundations. On some of the walls tangles of dry vines flexed their spidery legs in the wind. Hermione wanted to ask Rowan to give her the ball for fear that it might bounce to that edge of the causeway, but she couldn't risk making her resentful when she needed Rowan to trust her. She managed not to grab at Rowan when, halfway across the causeway, the child let go of her hand.

Rowan went to the railing above the reservoir so swiftly that Hermione's heart stuttered. Some yards from the wall was the opening through which the reservoir drained, a plughole at least ten feet in diameter. Water poured down a quarter of the rim and trickled down the rest into the foaming darkness, over grass and stalactites of moss that grew on the inner wall. Rowan leaned over the railing. "Is dying like that, do you think?"

"Good gracious, dear, I wouldn't know. I'm not quite that decrepit, am I?" Hermione was being too studiedly jovial, she knew, but the child had taken her off guard. She thought that death might be very much like falling into a greedy darkness. Even if you passed through to whatever you expected to find, could that include other people? Suppose Queenie couldn't find her father because he was engrossed in his own afterlife? Perhaps life after death was an endless lonely dream, and whether it lasted for the moment of death or eternity didn't matter: its kind of time would have nothing to do with life awake, even if one were to invade the other. Her thoughts seemed to be plunging into the slippery dark. "Let's move on, shall we?" she said as soon as she felt steady enough to walk.

They strolled back past the chimney and followed the path downwards between empty windows shivering with weeds. A wall patchy as the sky towered over the path through an overgrown bank. The branches of the tree that stood against the wall had scraped pale an arc of bricks. Rowan strayed ahead in the premature dusk, bouncing her ball. "Don't go so fast," Hermione panted, cursing the weight of her body, the prickly heat that swarmed over her as she tried to run into the wind. Rowan vanished around the side of a building like a huge stained broken tooth, and Hermione ran faster, her legs aching. She grasped the mossy corner of the building and pushed herself around it so that she could see the next stretch of path.

And then she shuddered to a halt and clutched the squelching wall.

Rowan's ball had rolled into a clump of grass that sagged over the path, and she was stooping to retrieve it. She seemed unaware of anything else, of Hermione or the trees that threw themselves back and forth above her with a sound like a stormy sea. She didn't seem to notice the figure that stood close behind her, a little girl in a long white dress.

Rowan straightened up and walked on, bouncing the ball on the squeaky gravel, and the other followed, gleaming like a tombstone under the sunless sky. As Hermione heaved herself away from the wall, she saw that though the wind was tearing leaves off the trees and dragging so hard at her clothes that she staggered backwards, it didn't trouble Rowan. The child and her companion might have been walking inside glass, their hair and their dresses were so still.

They were almost at the next bend, past which the path was out of sight beyond the high bank. Hermione flung herself after them, her heart pounding so furiously that her blood drove all thoughts out of her head. Then, just as Rowan reached the bend, her companion looked back at Hermione, and smiled.

The smile seemed to blot out the world. That Hermione recognised the face was terrible enough, the long pale face that resembled Rowan's all too clearly. The pale eyes stared at her as if she were a dog that would have to look away before they blinked, if they ever did. The smile was telling her that there was nothing she could do, despite all her knowledge. The power of that contempt settled about Hermione until she could no longer hear or feel the wind. Then Rowan vanished beyond the trembling grass of the bank, and the other turned like a figure on a music box and followed her. At once the wind almost hurled Hermione to the ground.

She fought her way into it, appalled that anything so insubstantial could be so difficult to overcome. When she struggled round the bend, digging her fingers into the muddy bank, Rowan was alone on the path. "Rowan," she called shakily, but the child didn't look back. Hermione was afraid Rowan was ignoring her or cut off from her somehow until she realised that the wind which was flapping Rowan's clothes was also blowing her own voice away. She drew a breath that filled her throat with damp. "Rowan," she shouted "let's go home now."

Rowan dawdled back to her, bouncing the ball. Hermione grabbed her hand as soon as it was within reach. Once they turned, the wind was behind them, but she wished they could go faster up the steep path. Whenever bushes flourished the undersides of their leaves she thought a pale figure was rearing up at her. As the clouds began to break, the snatches of light at the path ahead, and then at the deserted streets of Holywell, were pale shapes too.

She slammed the front door and sat Rowan in the kitchen with a glass of orange juice while she searched the cottage, and then she halted in the living-room, staring at the photograph album she'd brought from Waterloo. She turned to a photograph of her aunt at Rowan's age, gazing into the lens with a wilfulness that had survived the browning of all those years. She slipped it free of the corners that held it, and made herself carry it into the kitchen. "Rowan," she said as though her mind were on some other subject entirely, "do you know who this is?"

Rowan looked up, licking orange from her upper lip. She glanced at the photograph, and her face grew innocent at once. "I couldn't say, auntie."

Hermione turned away hastily. She hurried back to the album, almost crumpling the photograph as she replaced it in its plot. The face of the child behind Rowan on the path had been even more symmetrical, a perfected image of that childhood self. Having recognised it wasn't what dismayed her most: it was the knowingness with which Rowan had avoided the truth. She'd seemed just like Queenie except for the face.

Except for the face – "God help us," Hermione whispered, and sat down quickly lest she lose her balance. At last she knew why Rowan had to seem like Queenie. "So that you won't be noticed," she muttered, and waited for the mocking whisper to tell her she was right but helpless. There was no whisper, only a watchful silence, and she knew she had to act now, while she could. She had to do what she could hardly bear to think of.

CHAPTER NINETEEN

As soon as he came back from Holywell, Derek set about stripping the staircase wall. He strode up to the top floor and began to peel the paper off while there was enough light for him to see by. He was pulling down the first strip when the weight of sagging plaster tore it loose. Lumps of plaster clattered against the metal legs of the ladder, shaking it under him; dust the colour of pale flesh blinded him. He held on to the ladder until he could see and then, though he was coughing, he began to laugh. Under the doddering plaster the bricks were sound and dry. "Do your worst, you old sod," he mocked the wall, and moved the ladder down two stairs to attack the next stretch of paper.

He was halfway down when Alison came to look. She made a face at the mess on the stairs and gave him a kiss which plastered her mouth like a clown's. After dinner she helped him strip the rest of the staircase wall. They laboured downstairs with cartons of rubble, and then they took a bath together and made love lingeringly. Afterwards Alison lay and gazed at the ceiling. "It just feels empty now," she murmured. "It feels as if it's waiting for someone to move in."

She was asleep before they could talk about Rowan. In the morning he had to make an early start on rewiring the top floor, since he would be working at the school next week. He'd lifted floorboards to expose the dusty innards of the house when Tony rang from the estate agent's. His contact in the planning department thought there should be no objection to another nursing home, and a contractor who owed Tony a favour had agreed to work on the house for cost. Derek felt better than he had for months, maybe years.

He was drilling the walls on the top floor when the phone rang again. He hoped it was Rowan, because then he would know she was over whatever had made her so taciturn on the drive to Wales. But Alison told him it had been her mother.

By mid-afternoon he'd finished threading the top floor, and soon he was training wire down the exposed bricks above the stairs. Shortly before dinner he was able to shout down to Alison to switch on the circuit breaker. When the entire top floor lit up around him, he wished Rowan had been there to perform the ceremony. He felt as if he'd conquered the house.

Alison had brought a property newspaper from the estate agent's. During dinner she wanted him to look at photographs of houses. He agreed with most of those she'd marked. At last he said "What did your mother want?"

Alison pointed to her mouth and chewed to show she couldn't speak. She seemed to take her time about swallowing. "There won't be any exhumation, you'll be glad to hear."

"I should damn well hope not. That's what your mother said, is it?"

"Yes."

"That all?"

Alison frowned at his impatience. "No, not quite."

"Don't bother telling me if it's a family secret."

Alison reached for his hand across the table. "Why do you say things like that, Derek?"

"I just don't feel comfortable with them sometimes. Don't let it bother you."

"It does. I can't help that. I don't know what more we can do."

"Maybe you try too hard. I could have done without a family conference on what we were going to call Rowan."

"I quite liked involving them. She's my parents' only grandchild, you know. I wasn't aware that you resented them so much."

"I never said I did. I just wish I didn't feel expected to check whatever we do with them first. We even had a conference over what we were going to do about this house, for God's sake, as if we couldn't decide for ourselves." He felt bewildered by himself, arguing like this when life was going well for them at last, and yet he seemed unable to stop. "I notice you keep saying your family."

"Our family, then." The corners of her eyes glittered under the chandelier until she dabbed at them. "You've no reason to feel excluded, you know. They're the family I've always had, and I wouldn't change them for anyone, but I chose you."

"You still haven't told me what your mother said."

"You know perfectly well, Derek. She said Hermione wrote that message on the photograph."

He thought of Rowan, running away from him to Hermione. "I know she's your sister, but I wish we hadn't let Rowan go to her this weekend."

"Dear me, Derek, what do you think Hermione's likely to do to her? She only wrote that message because she cares about Rowan so much."

"Seems like a crazy way to care."

Alison's voice sharpened. "What was that, Derek?"

"Listen, I'm not getting at you or your parents, but even you've got to admit that the rest of them are pretty odd."

"You don't need to mince words with me." She seemed angry that he had. "Say what you're thinking," she said.

"Fair enough, I will," he said distractedly, staring at Wales under the gathering darkness and wondering when Rowan would call. "I think there may be a crazy streak in your family that missed you and your father. That can happen, can't it? You should know, you're a nurse."

"Don't you try to bully me. That won't convince me, you know."

"I shouldn't need to. Don't tell me you can't see it for yourself." When she stared tight-lipped at him he burst out "Your grandfather thought your aunt was keeping him alive when he ought to be dead, and if you ask me she thought she was never going to die at all. And your cousin chucked himself under a train. Reckon that's normal, do you?"

"Who else have you in mind, Derek?"

"I already said, not you. But if you mean your sister, I'm not arguing. All that stuff about her tooth and then about that pigging locket, and even about Rowan's friend, about a child, for God's sake. I know she had a rotten childhood, but so did I, what with my mam dumping me on her folks whenever she wanted a man round while my dad was away at sea and then her folks treating me as if it was all my fault. I nearly jumped off a bridge onto the railway once. Never told you that before, did I? But you can't use your childhood as an excuse for the rest of your life."

"Derek, if you really believe— No, I won't say it."

He was meant to know, and it infuriated him. "I'm telling you, I wouldn't have let Rowan go this weekend if I hadn't felt bad about the row I had with your sister, as if that wasn't her fault too for going on about Vicky and the binoculars and all that other crap."

Alison sat forward so violently that the chandelier rang. "You wouldn't have let Rowan go to my sister? She has two parents, if you'd care to remember."

"I know that. We aren't talking about that." He saw that she was about to say it wasn't up to him to choose the subject, and so he blundered on "I just want to keep you and Rowan safe from all this craziness."

Her stare grew softer but no friendlier. "Derek, I know you mean well, but you mustn't try to undermine relationships I've had all my life. Queenie almost split the family. I hope for the sake of our marriage you don't want to. And as long as we're discussing irrational behaviour, we might remember the way you went after Ken like some young ruffian in the street and seemed proud of it too."

"Look, I'm not blaming anyone for anything. Or if anyone's to blame for the way Rowan is, I am as much as anyone. I wish I could spend more time with her. I will when I can if she wants me to."

"What do you mean, the way she is? Are you suggesting she's mentally ill?"

"I just mean she's a loner, the way I used to be." He refused even to consider what Alison had said – he wished she hadn't brought it up. "Let's call this the end of the round and go back to our corners. I want to phone and see how Rowan is before she goes to bed."

"Can I trust you to talk to Hermione without upsetting her?"

"I managed yesterday. You phone if you think you've got to protect her from me, but I want to talk to Rowan." When Alison turned to stare across the bay he went into the hall, past the shifting of silvery leaves. The argument had been Hermione's fault, he thought. He had to take time to put away his anger before he dialled her number. After a while he dialled again slowly, to make sure of the digits, and stood there listening and gazing up the stairs at the dark. He waited as long as he could before he went back to Alison. Though it was almost Rowan's bedtime, there was no reply from the cottage.

CHAPTER TWENTY

Dear diary, they can make adverts look oldfashuned on televishun so I ecspect they can do it to picsures, becose Hermione showed me one that looked like Vicky ecsept it was too old...

Rowan let her pencil stray above the page. She hadn't written what she felt. Out beyond the window, dusk was settling like mud into the bay. Over in Waterloo the first lights were sparkling, lights of houses that looked distant as stars. That sight used to make her deliciously homesick, but now it reminded her that her parents hadn't wanted her, that she was a burden to them. She felt as if she didn't belong anywhere.

The only person she could tell was Vicky, except that now Hermione had managed to make Rowan uneasy about her. Hermione had taken a dislike to Vicky without even having met her, all because of the binoculars. That was just Hermione being odd as she sometimes was, and she might have rubbed something on the photograph to make it look older – but where had she got a photograph of Vicky, and how did she know what Vicky looked like? Rowan would rather ask Vicky than her aunt, since Vicky always told the truth. She was watching the lights multiply beyond the bay when the doorbell rang.

She ran to the window too late to see who came into the cottage. She heard murmuring downstairs but could make out no words until Hermione called to her. "Rowan, dear, would you get your coat and come down?"

Rowan undressed the hanger in the wardrobe and hesitated at the top of the stairs, for Hermione was saying "I do hope it isn't inconvenient, but you did say that if I had to go to Gronant I could get in touch with you."

"I said so. Is that the child I hear coming?" A woman Rowan knew but couldn't place stepped into the hall and eyed her. The woman's face was sharp but delicate as china, her eyes made up as though the china had been painted. "Here she is."

Hermione appeared, buttoning her coat hurriedly. "Rowan, you remember Elspeth. She and Gwen make the toys for the shop. You're going to stay with her while I go somewhere."

Something about her urgency made Rowan demur. "May I just phone home so they'll know where we are?"

"No time now. We shouldn't be long, we should be coming back here to sleep."

How could Rowan believe her when Hermione was pretending not to be nervous, so brightly that even Elspeth seemed suspicious? All Rowan could do was be hurried out of the cottage by Hermione and down the path to the squat red French car.

As they drove along roads sunken in shadows of hedges, Hermione began to chatter. She used to eat when she was nervous, but this was worse. She kept trying to point out sights to Rowan, who was watching the lamps of the far coast as they glittered across the dark cold fields. Hermione fell silent as they passed the graveyard outside Gronant, stones glimmering like clouds over a moon, then recommenced chattering at once, almost stammering. "Here we are, Rowan, nearly there now. You'll be good, won't you? Perhaps Elspeth will let you watch television. I'll be as quick as I can."

The car coasted down into Gronant and halted in front of a small newish house like a sketch of a cottage, squeezed onto the corner of a lane. "I'll just get the child into the house and then I'll run you to the hotel," Elspeth said.

"Don't trouble, Elspeth, I need the walk. I'll come in and see Rowan settled, and then I'll be off."

Elspeth frowned at her when she struggled out of the car, and seemed even more annoyed when Hermione bustled down the path of cobbles the size of eggs to the brass knocker. Gwen opened the door. Her face was at least as sharp as Elspeth's, but seemed to soften as she let out the light to them. "Stay for a cup of something if you like, Hermione," she said.

One room with polished pine walls took up most of the ground floor. The curvy wood of the sofa and chairs looked stuffed with flowered bags of the lavender that scented the air. Hermione darted to a bookcase that slanted across one corner of the room. "Here, show Gwen and Elspeth how well you can read." When Rowan leafed through the collection of folk tales in search of one she might like, Hermione cried "Any one will do. She'll read you the whole story, won't you, Rowan? Just listen to her."

Gwen sat down smiling, and Elspeth followed suit reluctantly on the opposite side of the room. The story was about two girls, one of whom was made of sticks, though in the illustration they looked like bones. As soon as the story was under way, Hermione made for the door. "I'll see myself out. Rowan, you keep right on to the end."

The front door slammed, and Rowan read on, too self-conscious to look up. She hardly knew what she was reading, though her voice was sure enough. When a dog barked behind the cottage Elspeth started to head for the kitchen window, but Gwen clucked her tongue softly at her. Rowan finished the story without knowing which of the girls in it was alive at the end. When she turned back to reread it, Elspeth protested "Whoa now, you've sung for your supper. Breakfast's not until tomorrow."

"That was excellent, young lady. How old are you? Only eight? You read like someone older."

"That's all very well, but can you read Welsh?"

"Some words, when they're like English spelled wrong."

"Like Welsh spelled right, you mean," Elspeth snapped. "You won't get far round here with that attitude."

"Now, Ellie, she's only visiting."

"And why is that, may we ask? Where's your aunt gone, Rowan?"

"I don't know. Nobody told me."

"She's gone to see a friend who was taken ill at the hotel, hasn't she?" Gwen said.

Elspeth gave her a furious look and stalked into the kitchen. The back door opened, the dog barked. After a while Elspeth came back, disgruntled with having found nothing. Rowan pored over the book so as not to draw her hostility. Gwen brought her a glass of milk, but she felt out of place, especially when the women began to talk Welsh. She didn't know if they were talking about her, and that made her feel hardly there at all.

It must have been hours later, for she was halfway through the book even though she could recall nothing of it, when Elspeth spoke to her again. "Put that away now or we'll have your aunt saying we let you ruin your eyes. Gwen wants to teach you something."

"What?"

"Just listen for a change," Elspeth said impatiently, and Gwen struck up a lilting song in Welsh. After a few bars Elspeth joined in. Rowan liked it, but felt they should have their arms around each other's shoulders instead of singing from opposite sides of the room: was it her fault that they weren't doing so? The song ended on a high sweet note. "What did you think of that, then?" Elspeth demanded.

"Lovely," Rowan said, and since that apparently wasn't enough "I liked it very much."

"Let's hear how much, then. You try."

"Listen again," Gwen said, taking pity on her, and repeated the first line. When Rowan attempted it, it made her tongue flutter like a bird in her mouth. They went through the first verse line by line, and then Rowan did her best to sing it through. She was quite proud of herself until she saw Elspeth scowling at her as though she'd inadvertently sung something rude in Welsh. How could she get the song right when she didn't know what she was singing? She felt less present than ever, as though even her voice wasn't her own any more, and desperate to talk to someone she knew. "Can I call home?" she blurted.

"No need for that, is there? Your aunt will be back soon, according to her."

"Why do you want to, dear?" Gwen said.

"I haven't spoken to my mummy and daddy at all today. I want them to know where I am."

"You'll just be telling them you're at my house until your aunt gets back, will you?"

"Our house," Gwen said gently.

"Oh yes, our house, tell everyone," Elspeth complained, and lapsed into Welsh. Rowan shrank into herself as they began to argue: half of it sounded like spitting. She couldn't understand how she had caused all this by asking to phone her parents, but she was afraid to say anything further. She was wishing desperately that Hermione would return when someone knocked at the front door.

"I expect that's your aunt," Gwen said, and made for the hall. Elspeth eyed Rowan ominously until Gwen came back, looking puzzled. "Rowan, there's someone here who says she's a friend of yours."

It felt like salvation. "Vicky," Rowan cried.

"Oh, were you expecting her?" Gwen said reprovingly. "She wants you to go to her house."

Gwen sounded dubious. She and Elspeth murmured in Welsh as Rowan grabbed her coat and darted into the hall. Vicky was waiting for her beyond the open door. Against the night, her white dress and long pale face looked even brighter than the hall. As she saw Rowan coming, her eyes seemed to deepen and fill with the light from the house. She turned away at once, and Rowan had followed as far as the gate when Elspeth demanded "Where do you think you're going?"

"Just with me," Vicky said from beyond the streetlamp. "She'll be gone no longer than her aunt, I promise."

Elspeth narrowed her eyes at the dark and frowned, then shrugged as if she weren't grateful to be relieved of Rowan. "Be sure that you know what you're doing," she said, and closed the door.

The night was chill and restless. Beyond the island of light on which the streetlamp stood, the houses made no sound, but the trees took long irregular breaths and stooped out of the sky. Rowan stayed close to the lamp as Vicky glanced back. "How did you know where I was?"

"I saw you leaving in the car, and I knew where that woman lived."

"You mean you've come all that way? How?"

"There are buses, you know – just not very often. I'm here, isn't that enough? Or would you rather go back in there?"

Rowan didn't want to antagonise her under all the circumstances. "You said we could go to your house."

"Let me show you something first." Vicky took another pace away from the lamp, and held up one hand. "You forgot these."

They were the binoculars, their lenses glinting like black ice. Rowan stiffened. "Did you go in my aunt's house?"

"Don't you recall leaving them in the garden? Maybe you'd rather they were ruined after I gave them to you."

"Of course I wouldn't, don't be daft. I didn't mean to leave them," Rowan said, unable to remember where she had. Vicky was already striding away, and so Rowan followed her, across the main road and up a flinty path between the gardens of two houses screened by trees. As the glow of the houses sank beneath the shaking leaves, it seemed to let the night wind reach Rowan, who clutched her coat tighter. Almost at once she could hardly feel the wind or the prickly path. Vicky led her up into the steep dark and waited for her on a flat ledge surrounded by grass that glistened as it threw itself flat beneath the wind. There she handed Rowan the binoculars and pointed across the bay. "See how strong they are at night," she said.

Beyond the Wirral peninsula, a sleeping dragon chained with light, the lamps and windows of the far coast merged into threads, bright insects that trembled as if they were preparing to swarm into the air. The sight made Rowan unexpectedly wistful, and she felt more outcast than ever. "Use the glasses," Vicky urged.

As soon as Rowan lifted them to her eyes, the night closed around her. That must be the eyepieces, but she felt as if she were riding the night towards the lights. The peninsula swam beneath her, and then she was across the bay. There were the docks, the radar tower surveying the dark, the dunes bunched like huge dim fruit, the rank of pastel nursing homes, all grey now. She seemed to glide along them, and there, where the mouth of the side street gaped darkly, was the house.

The top floor was lit. It looked like a crown or a beacon, but it didn't feel as if either was meant for her. Her gaze strayed downwards to the lit front room. The curtains were drawn, but not entirely. If she peered through the gap she might see her parents. For a moment she yearned to see them, as if she'd been away for months, and then she remembered what she'd overheard. They might be talking about her now, and she didn't want to see. She let her hands fall.

At first she thought the strap of the binoculars had snagged, because the view of the house didn't shrink. It must be an after-image, and it felt plastered to her eyes. She squeezed them shut and opened them. The nighttime landscape reassembled itself blurrily around her, the glow of the houses streaming mistily up through the swaying trees, but everything looked flattened as the fans of light. "Why did you stop?" Vicky hissed in her ear. "You were there."

The threat of her impatience was almost enough to force Rowan to lift the binoculars, but not quite. "I don't want to any more. You said I could see where you live."

The wind flapped over the hills and slithered through the grass. Trees nodding over the lights below sent darkness sweeping uphill. Rowan felt suddenly even lonelier and more vulnerable. "No, I don't want to," she stammered as if that might fend off whatever was making her uneasy. "I'd rather see where my Aunt Hermione is."

Vicky was silent until Rowan glanced at her. The gleam in her eyes seemed deeper. She began to smile, lips pressed tight, as she turned to lead the way downhill. "All right, you shall," she said.

CHAPTER TWENTY-ONE

As soon as Hermione was outside the house she dug her knuckles into her forehead. She should have loitered out of sight nearby until they were all inside, she shouldn't have gone in. She was sure they'd all seen how nervous she was growing; she had almost panicked in case Elspeth insisted on driving her to the hotel. But she was out now, and the women were listening to Rowan – surely they still were, though Hermione couldn't hear her. She hurried down the cobbled path, wiping her slippery hands on her coat, and made as much noise as she could in closing the gate; then she tiptoed back and dodged around the side of the house.

The path there looked as if it might be composed of loose slate. It was crazy paving, she told herself, and took a step, so tentative that she swayed against the house. She supported herself against the whitewashed wall as she crept to the back garden. The floodlight on the next house doused the garden with the shadow of the hedge, but she could make out the shed on the far side of the lawn. It was the only place in Gronant she knew there was a spade: Elspeth often talked about digging the garden. She stepped onto the small neat lawn, and a dog barked.

Hermione recoiled against the wall of the house. The dog was under the floodlight, beside a pair of French windows. If anyone parted those curtains they would see her flattened against the house like a moth. Gwen or Elspeth might lean out of the kitchen window beside her, and what would she say then? She shook all over and crammed her fists against her mouth before she could burst into hysterical laughter. The dog had settled itself. As soon as she had gulped down her mirth she padded across the grass.

The flashlight in her pocket bumped her thigh all the way to the shed. She unbolted the door with fingers that felt swollen and rigid. The hinges were so thoroughly oiled that the door came towards her faster than she was expecting. The dog made a sound in its throat. She leaned forward and peered into the dark. In the far left-hand corner, caged by a rake and a fork, was a spade.

When she stepped on the floor of the shed, the tools stirred. If they fell they would start the dog barking in earnest. She lunged across the plank floor and grabbed all three handles. She was close to hysteria again, because at first she couldn't distinguish which handle belonged to the spade. She groped downwards until she felt the edge of the head, which was trapped behind the others. She set about disentangling the fork and the rake, forcing herself to take her time, and then she froze. She was being watched.

She made herself glance towards the house. The kitchen window was unlit, and she was sure the curtains hadn't moved. She was being watched from somewhere closer in the dark, because she had realised the danger to Rowan. She slipped the spade from behind the other tools, almost thumping the handle against the roof, then she tiptoed over the creaking planks, closed the door, inched the bolt shakily into its socket, dodged across the lawn and hid beside the house, out of reach of the floodlight, while she debated how to hide the spade.

There wasn't room under her coat. She pressed the cold head against her chest and crossed her hands over it, and found she was able to walk, though not as fast as she would have liked. She stole along the path and out of the gate. She gave the house a last nervous glance and willed Rowan to be reading, then she embraced the spade and hurried onto the main road.

Trees brushed the steep pavements with shadow and brought darkness lurching out of gardens as she climbed the winding road, and yet a stillness seemed to pace her beneath the gusty trees, an icy stillness that felt like the absence of the mocking whisper she'd once heard. A car sped up the hill, and she shrank away from the kerb. Lance must have fallen under the train because he had been taken unawares, she told herself.

She toiled to the crest of the hill and hastened downwards. The lights of Gronant were cut off by the hill, isolating her with a lone streetlamp. Nevertheless the sight of the churchyard was almost a relief. Surely nothing more substantial than fear could threaten her in there.

Beyond the gate the grey path led to the stocky unlit chapel which, she tried to think, would be watchful on her behalf. She unlatched the gate and closed it behind her. Clutching the spade to her chest, she ventured onto the grass. Headstones gleamed and dimmed, flowers in vases shivered on graves. The robe of an angel stirred with shadow, as if a small figure might be peering out of the stone folds. The willow seemed less peaceful now than secretive, its tent of branches parting to give glimpses of darkness within. She was beside it before she was able to see the family grave. That meant that she wouldn't be visible from the road, she reminded herself, and stumbled forward, turning the spade head down.

The grave was in the shadow of the willow. Light from the streetlamp flashed between the branches, picking out words low down on the marble pillar: VICTORIA...HER...ARMS... The turf on the mound was still distinguishable as squares. Hermione inserted the edge of the spade under the nearest and leaned her heel on the metal, and then all her limbs locked. Her resolution had brought her this far, but she could no longer avoid realising how much she dreaded what she planned to do.

It was for Rowan. She had to do it while Rowan was still herself. But perhaps doubt was even harder to deal with than fear: was she really planning to dig up the family grave because she thought that Rowan was being made to seem like Queenie so that nobody would notice if Queenie took her place? Put that way, here at the graveside with the night surging at her like a cold impalpable sea, the notion seemed almost too grotesque to contemplate, the delusion of a lonely woman too eager to find someone else to care for now that her little sister had made a life for herself – except that she had seen Rowan's companion face to face. She was right about Vicky, she was the only person who had seen through her, and surely that must mean she was the only person capable of guessing her scheme. She willed her body to relax. The spade dug under the square of turf and peeled it back.

She lifted the rest of the turf and laid the squares where they would be out of reach of her digging, then she sidled round the marble pillar to the side of the grave from which she could glimpse the road. She took a deep breath, heartfelt as a prayer, and drove the spade into the mound.

It went in so far she almost lost her balance. She remembered the pulpy chair into which her hands had sunk, as if the failure of Queenie's will to live had spread rot through the upper rooms. She gritted her teeth and heaped the spadeful beside the grave, dug again and trod hard on the spade, reassuring herself that it couldn't sink all the way down to the coffin. In any case, there was a lid; she mustn't imagine how the spade might cut straight through Queenie, severing her body like a worm. She stamped on the metal with a fierceness that bruised her heel but couldn't quite stun her thoughts.

The next layer of earth was packed harder. Despite the chill wind, she was soon so hot that she had to drape her coat over the marble pillar. It waved the empty sockets of its arms while she stooped over the grave, more and more precariously. She was putting off the moment when she would have to step into the hole she'd dug. At last she had no choice. She clung to the spade with one hand and the pillar with the other, and let herself down into the dark that smelled of moist earth.

It yielded beneath her weight, but not far. There was still earth between her and what lay face up beneath her. She reached for her coat and managed to pull the flashlight out of her pocket. She propped the flashlight against the pillar, facing the unevenly quadrangular pit. Yellow light fastened on black glistening lumps of earth at her feet. She glanced warily towards the road, where there hadn't been a car since she had left the pavement, and moved to the foot of the grave.

The willow was behind her now. Whenever shadows scuttled over the heaps of earth that hemmed her in, she thought someone had peered out between the dangling branches, but she could never catch sight of a watcher. Being watched should mean there was no danger beneath her, for how could it be in two places at once? Before long she was hardly aware of the movements: she must be almost on the coffin – close enough to dread what she was stepping on as she edged along the trench to point the flashlight downwards more sharply. At the end by the willow the fan of light grew wide as the grave, but so dim that it was able only to make the earth glisten sluglike. She retreated there, her jaw aching until she managed to unclench her teeth.

As she poked the spade into the earth, gingerly in case it was about to strike wood, she felt both sick and, grotesquely, famished. Nothing like hard work to give you an appetite, she thought helplessly, and leaned all her weight on the spade. It sank in a few inches and stood there. It had reached a surface more solid than earth.

The halting of the spade seemed to spread through her body, freezing even her thoughts. The willow lurched towards her, hissing and rattling its branches; shadows swarmed over the heaps of earth that walled her in the trench. For Rowan, she thought, and swayed forward as if she were starting awake. For a moment she thought the lid had shifted beneath her, but the spade had slipped on the wood. Between fury and panic, she began to fling earth out of the trench.

It didn't take long to uncover the lid. She glanced about at the shifty night, the headless scarecrow of her coat, the streetlamp peering through the willow, and then she set about scraping the last of the earth from the glimmering lid. Every so often the spade would clank. She stared at the scraped wood displayed in earth like sodden plush, and made for the brighter end, poising her spade to use as a screwdriver. Then a chill seeped through her from the soil to the roots of her hair, for she'd realised why the spade had kept clanking. All the screws were half out of the lid.

She grabbed the flashlight as if it were a lifeline on which she could haul herself out of the grave, and made herself train the beam on the screws. They poked out of the coffin, dripping earth, daring her to turn them further and lift the lid. She thought distantly of Rowan, and then of herself, of the way Queenie had terrorised her when she was Rowan's age. Wasn't she still doing so, confronting Hermione with the screws so as to make her incapable of lifting the lid? "I can see through your tricks," Hermione whispered, and reached shakily for the nearest screw.

It was gritty with moist soil. As soon as she had extracted it and dropped it near the foot of the pillar she rubbed her fingers together, shuddering. She did that automatically each time she removed another screw. She was beginning to wish she'd dug a wider trench: though there was just enough room on the left-hand side of the coffin for her to perch on the earth in the grave, she was nervous of slipping onto the lid now that it was held by so few screws. She paced along the yielding strip of earth and stooped to lift out a screw, another, a third. Now there was only the one closest to the pillar, and if she sprawled onto the coffin the lid might swing away from her on the pivot of the screw, dumping her into Queenie's lair. That was what Queenie would want her to think, she told herself, and snatched out the last screw and shied it towards the pillar. Before another wave of apprehension could inhibit her, she squatted on the strip of earth, gripping the flashlight between her shaky knees, and poked her fingers under the lid.

One heave and it came up, so easily that she almost overbalanced. It thumped against the far side of the grave, spilling earth into the coffin. Hermione stood up as quickly as she dared, grasping the flashlight with both hands. She longed to clamber out of the trench to recover from the shock of having almost lost her balance, but then she might not be able to force herself back in. She swayed against the wall of the trench to steady herself and gazed down, eyes twitching, at the long pale shape that lay beneath her in the coffin, beyond the reach of the flashlight beam. For Rowan, she thought fiercely, and let the beam sink into the coffin, past the fat white ridges of the lining, until it settled on the object in the box.

Her grip tightened until the flashlight began to shiver. Her throat closed around her held breath. She'd expected Queenie to have worsened, but not like this. The long face had withered to the bone around the shrivelled eyes, which were almost black, and the mouth, exposing all the teeth and the blackened gums. The hair was spread out around the skull. The face was almost all grin, a dead grin with tiny eyes, staring up out of a nest of grey hair.

She had to look away from the face to find the locket. She forced her gaze and the light away, though her arms trembled. The beam swung further than she meant it to, jerking at the folded hands on Queenie's chest. There was barely enough left of them to be called hands, and they were spattered with earth that the lid had dislodged. Hermione dragged the light back to the neck.

It was gnarled and peeling as a dead branch, and dismayingly thin. She strained her eyes until they stung, and then she held on to the edge of the grave and lowered herself to one knee on the narrow ridge beside the coffin. Still grasping the crumbling edge, she leaned precariously towards the coffin and lowered the flashlight until the lens was almost touching the circle of bright light on cracked dead ropy flesh. Nothing gleamed. There was no chain around Queenie's neck.

Hermione got down on both knees, her right knee resting on the rim of the coffin. With the casing of the flashlight she probed at the chest above the hands in case the chain had broken, leaving the locket concealed. When she was sure that the locket wasn't there she continued to prod the corpse, more viciously now, to show that she knew she was being watched and didn't care. She'd faced the worst, and it couldn't harm her, it was only loathsome. She could even make out the watcher at the edge of her vision, a small pale shape beyond a grave to her left. She let her face take on all the contempt she was feeling, an unexpected rush of it that she could scarcely cope with, and then she raised her head and looked straight at the watcher.

Her hand clenched on the wall of the grave, tearing loose a fistful of earth. The small figure who was watching her, and clinging to a granite cross as though it could barely support her, was Rowan.

She looked ready to turn and flee if Hermione even spoke. Hermione was overwhelmed with shame and panic. She might have ducked out of sight if she'd thought Rowan hadn't recognised her. Queenie had tricked them both, she realised with a fury that made her head swim: Queenie, who was Vicky, and who must be the shape that was moving at the edge of Hermione's vision. But Vicky had miscalculated, she thought as she swung towards the movement, trying to focus on it.

She'd strayed where Hermione could confront her in front of Rowan, and that might even show Rowan the truth.

But the moving shape wasn't Vicky, nor was it beside Rowan. It was much closer to Hermione, which was why she hadn't been able to focus at once. It was a hand, a shrivelled hand piebald with earth. Though it was jerky as a puppet's hand, it was able to close around the back of Hermione's neck.

She flinched convulsively away from its touch, and tried to scream as if that would help her twist out of reach. But a pain deep in her innards had sucked breath into her, pain that bowed her over herself and sent her sideways into the coffin. She was still gripping the flashlight, which thumped the lining of the coffin and showed her Queenie's grinning head. The head was rising from its nest of hair.

The hair stuck to the lining. It tore free of the grey scalp as the corpse sat up stiffly, a bald grinning doll with no eyes worth the name. Perhaps it was mindless as a puppet, but its fleshless grin fell open in what might have been a soundless scream of triumph as it clasped its arms around Hermione's neck and pressed its face against hers.

CHAPTER TWENTY-TWO

Rowan didn't ask the question until she was back at the main road. She followed Vicky down the flinty path between the trees that hid the lights. Vicky waited for her next to the splash of a streetlamp, but Rowan lingered just inside the gap between the hedges of the lit houses. "How do you know where my aunt is?" she said.

Vicky put her hands on her hips and gazed expressionlessly at her. "I thought you trusted me."

"I do, but I still want to know things. You always seem to be where I am whenever I'd like you to be."

"Then you should be grateful, shouldn't you?"

"I've said I'll be your friend, but I don't like you knowing more than I do."

Vicky glared at her so harshly that Rowan almost retreated between the shivering hedges. For a moment she thought Vicky was about to say "How dare you speak to me like that?" or even "Don't you know who I am?" She held her breath until her ears throbbed, and then Vicky's face softened, her voice turned almost wheedling. "You could know everything I know if you'd trust me."

"I've told you, I do."

"You didn't just now when we were on the hill. You were nearly home, you could feel you were. It would have been so easy to go on, I should have made sure it was, but instead you had to come back."

Rowan was lost. If all this was about the binoculars, she was beginning to feel they were more trouble than they were worth. "I thought you wanted to be there forever," Vicky said.

That made Rowan even sadder than she had been on the hill. "I did before," she whispered, not wanting to be heard.

"Before what, Rowan?"

Rowan felt as if she weren't being allowed to hide something she was ashamed of. "Before I heard mummy and daddy talking. They never wanted me."

"They had you because they were careless, you mean."

"I suppose so," Rowan said, but Vicky's eyes were telling her to go on. "I feel as if I'm making everything that's going wrong for them worse, and I think they think so too."

Vicky beckoned her off the path, over the uncertain rim of the glow beneath the streetlamp. "Suppose you could always be with them and yet never be a problem?"

Rowan felt betrayed. Vicky shouldn't make her imagine such things, especially when Rowan had shared her worst secret with her. "I expect that's what they'd like."

"Wouldn't you? Suppose you could always stay the age you are now and never have to leave your house? Suppose you could always watch over your mother and father, be there waiting when they came home and never cost them a penny?"

"Suppose we were in fairyland and dreams came true."

Rowan meant to be sarcastic, but Vicky's eyes brightened. "That's it exactly. It would be like dreaming your best dream, the one you always wanted to dream, except it would be real and never end."

Her eyes were so bright that Rowan felt as if, should she look away, she would see only darkness. It was like being unable to take the binoculars away from her eyes, this being surrounded by darkness with a single light ahead, except that the binoculars were on her chest, in her hands as she groped for something to hold on to. "That's the ticket," Vicky murmured. "Let's go back where we were."

She was speaking so low that the words might have seeped into Rowan's mind before she was aware of hearing them, if she hadn't sensed how Vicky was concealing her impatience. Why should it be so urgently important to Vicky that they go up the hill? Rowan squeezed her eyes shut and kept them shut as long as she dared before she opened them. She was under the streetlamp on the empty road, along which a wind roared like an invisible bus. She was there, however flattened it seemed. "I want to go to Hermione," she said.

"Then you'll get what you're asking for, my dear."

Vicky turned her back on her at once, to head uphill. "She said she was going to the hotel," Rowan protested.

"That's as may be. You still don't trust me, but you will."

Rowan felt as if she had rejected something Vicky valued deeply, though she had no idea what it might be. If so, she had realised too late. Vicky was striding uphill like a parent daring a child not to follow – like the adult she increasingly resembled. Rowan followed, because if her aunt hadn't told the truth she was even more anxious to see where Hermione was.

She had to trot and sometimes to run, though even then she couldn't quite catch up with Vicky. Shadows roamed the deserted road, and she promised herself that if Vicky led her much further into the dark she would refuse to go on until she knew where they were bound for. She panted up the sloping pavement, and felt safer as she saw the church below. She felt safe until Vicky halted, one hand on the churchyard gate.

She would have hoped her aunt was in the church, except that the church was dark. Even the church was less reassuring when she remembered the last time she'd seen her aunt in there, lurching at the coffin. Vicky put her finger to her expressionless lips, and then her mouth grew even thinner as she unlatched the gate.

Rowan couldn't hear the latch. Only her sight seemed to work. The willow stirred among the graves like a spider sensing its prey, and then it grew so motionless that it might have been petrified by the stillness of the stones. Rowan felt frozen too, for she'd glimpsed movement through the branches. A wide flat head on a thin neck had wavered out of the ground and lain down with a soft thump on the earth. It was a snake, she thought, a huge snake that had slithered out of a grave and might come writhing through the grass in search of her. Yet that seemed comfortingly unreal when she realised what she had actually seen: a spade. Someone had been digging a grave in the dark.

Surely it wasn't Hermione. She would rather Vicky were tricking her because Rowan had turned down whatever she was offering. But when at last she managed to turn away from straining her eyes, Vicky looked both pitying and accusing. "You asked me to bring you," she said tonelessly, and opened the gate wider.

Rowan could only step onto the gravel path. If her footsteps were half as heavy as they felt, they ought to be making enough noise to warn Hermione, give her the chance to bolt before Rowan had to see what she was doing – except that Rowan could barely hear her footsteps herself. When the willow was between her and the gaping earth, she stepped off the path onto the grass, and couldn't hear herself at all. She felt diminished, outcast, hardly even there.

She stole past the willow to a granite cross and hid behind it, clinging to it until her hands felt glued to it by frost. The binoculars stirred with each of her shaky breaths, and she gripped the cross harder in case she was tempted to use them. She could already see too much. She could see her aunt, stooping and straightening laboriously, stooping again in the glowing earth.

She was picking objects from the grave and planting them beside the marble pillar that she'd dressed in her coat, as if for company. Rowan had a nightmarish impression that she was gardening, plucking pests out of the grave. Hermione dropped a last glint by the pillar and took hold of the flashlight that lay there. Its glow sank beneath the earth, and Hermione followed it. There was a silence that stopped Rowan's breath, and then she heard a large soft thud in the grave, and a faint rain of earth.

It seemed to shrink her until she was nothing but sight and hearing, helplessly aware. The glow of the flashlight hovered like mist in the open grave. As the willow flexed its branches, leggy shadows scuttled towards the grave, so purposefully that Rowan wanted to cry out a warning. Then her aunt straightened up in the trench.

She had been digging for the locket, Rowan realised. She had a sudden dreadful suspicion that if Hermione saw her she would run to her with the chain she'd taken off the corpse and fix it around her neck. She had to flee, or at least hide behind the cross. But she was struggling to make her stony body move when Hermione raised her head and met Rowan's eyes.

It wasn't only being seen that paralysed Rowan then, it was that her aunt looked at least as caught out as she felt herself. The embarrassment that flooded through Rowan and made her face blaze was her aunt's as much as her own. It seemed that neither of them might ever move again, that they would stand there with the other statues while the wind shook the grass. Then Hermione turned her head, and seemed to clutch at the back of her neck with one hand. The next moment she ducked into the grave.

The glow within the heaped earth wavered and steadied. The trench gaped silently under the pillar, where Hermione's coat flailed its handless arms. Rowan tried to call out to Hermione to stop hiding: it was stupid, and it was frightening her. "Come out, I saw you," she might croak, but her throat wouldn't let out even a whisper. Anger and panic made her hands into fists on the cross. She shoved herself away from it and faltered towards the grave.

Vicky was nowhere to be seen. Rowan both resented being left alone like this and was glad if Vicky hadn't seen what her aunt was doing. She avoided the willow as she crossed the trembling grass and stepped gingerly onto the long thin heap of earth beside the grave. Her shoes sank into the heap as she leaned forward and looked into the trench.

As soon as she saw what was there she felt as if she were falling into the dark. Hermione was lying in the coffin, whose white interior was spattered and stained with earth, a mass of fat white ridges that made Rowan think of the flesh of a grub. The flashlight lay close to Hermione's face and shone pitilessly on her open eyes and mouth. Rowan willed her to blink, wished and then prayed that she would blink, until she couldn't avoid seeing how slack and unresponsive Hermione's face was. Hermione would never lie there if she knew that she was doing so. Her eyes were dead to the light, as she was.

The sight seemed to let the graveyard seize Rowan. Death was everywhere. She was surrounded by death and darkness. She'd said when she had overheard her parents that she didn't want to live, but she hadn't understood then what dying meant. Death was the sight of Hermione's body, empty and ugly and left behind, nothing but an object any more. Rowan glanced up wildly as if she might see where Hermione was now. But it was Vicky who was watching her across the grave.

Rowan straightened up, her feet sinking further into the heap of earth, and tried to speak. When her voice didn't work, she pointed despairingly into the grave. Vicky continued to gaze at her with an indifference so intense it looked accusing. "I tried to make it easy for you," Vicky said.

Rowan felt bewildered and abandoned and, worst of all, guilty. Could she have somehow helped cause what had happened to Hermione? The thought was so dreadful that it paralysed her mind. Then something like hope allowed her to look away from Vicky, and down. She'd glimpsed movement below her.

Hermione was moving: her face turned towards Rowan. It was slacker than ever. The flashlight displayed how soil had fallen in the open mouth. Hermione's head was moving only because something beneath her was.

Rowan tried to drag her feet out of the heap of slippery earth as a head appeared beneath, straining up from the shadow of Hermione's. It was a bald head whose scalp looked patched with mould. Beneath its shrunken eyes and the string of gristle between them, its mouth yawned like a trap. Hands that were almost all bone and blackened skin clutched at the near edge of the coffin to heave its crushed body from under Hermione's corpse. Rowan knew it was death, fleshless and grinning, that was hauling itself inch by creaking inch towards her, to seize her and pull her down into the grave.

She flung herself backwards, too violently. Her feet lost their grip on the loose earth. She staggered towards the cross, so hastily that she fell. The granite crossbeam struck her head like a hammer. The last thing she saw as the world drained away into the dark was Vicky, watching her in triumph.

CHAPTER TWENTY-THREE

At half past nine Derek tried to find a television show to watch, less for himself than for Alison. It would be his fault if she was worrying – his fault for attacking her family and making her nervous. He never would have if he'd known they were about to have so much trouble in contacting Hermione. She and Rowan must be visiting, or perhaps they were down at the shop, where there wasn't a phone: in any case, what harm could come to them in Holywell? They'd be home next time he phoned, he assured himself, once the television show was over.

But the television hadn't much to offer: three hours of golf on one channel, the end of a kidnapping film on another, a politician and a gerontologist disagreeing about ways to help the aged, a lull in a cricket match. Unexpectedly he found *Shane*, a film he hadn't seen since he was Rowan's age, but as he prepared to watch until the next commercial break he realised it was dubbed in Welsh. He was about to change the channel when Alison said irritably "Settle on something, for heaven's sake. I might have liked to watch the programme about old age."

He hadn't been sure she was watching, crouched as she was over the last book Rowan had been reading. Her face seemed longer than ever, weighed down by thoughts, closed against him. He sat on the arm of her chair, though it protested. "Listen, I'm sorry I said those things about your sister and all."

She moved almost imperceptibly away from him. "All who, Derek?"

"You know who I mean. I meant who I said. Don't let's argue any more. All I'm saying is I'm sorry I upset you."

It wasn't all he felt: he was afraid that their marriage could lose its balance, its way of letting one of them be calm when the other needed it, not that he had any reason to suppose they were going to need it now. "I'm sorry if I spoiled anything for you," he said awkwardly.

"All right, I hear you. Now I'd like to watch that programme."

He changed channels and sat in his chair. The politician and the doctor were still arguing. He couldn't take in what they were saying; their disagreement felt like an extension of his argument with Alison, and made his forehead ache. Alison's hands were clenched on Rowan's book, her thumbs stroking the cover as if that might grant her a wish. He closed his eyes and willed Hermione to call, and then he heard the plastic cover crack in Alison's grasp. As unobtrusively as he could, he sidled out of the room.

He wouldn't lose his temper with Hermione. He might pass a remark about her not letting them know that she was taking Rowan somewhere, but he would make it sound like a joke. He counted twenty pairs of rings and dialled again. This time he lost count of the sounds. They sounded monotonous and distant and meaningless, empty as the cottage must be. Why did he have to feel so worried now, when life had been going right at last? Appalled by his own selfishness, he replaced the receiver clumsily and stormed into the living-room. "I don't care if she is your sister, she ought to have let us know where they were going."

Alison jumped up and switched off the television, then swung to face him. "Don't you think I feel that way too?"

Had he been pretending otherwise so that he could believe he was protecting her? "Maybe I was by myself for so long I don't notice when I'm not," he said.

She held his arm tight with both hands. "You're right, we shouldn't quarrel. We'll be giving our Rowan a bad example."

"When she gets home."

"Tomorrow."

"I'll pick her up about five, shall I? We'll tell Hermione not to make dinner and then we can have ours with Rowan. I like the three of us eating together, specially now she's growing up."

"So do I," Alison said, and shivered. "The house seems so empty tonight without her."

"We've no call to worry really, though, have we? Hermione wouldn't let anything happen to her."

"She'd die first." She led him to the sofa, where she sat and gazed at the obsolete wallpaper. She breathed slowly a few times and then said "When you keep ringing, could her phone be out of order?"

"I can always hear it, love."

"They must be late coming back from somewhere. I'll be having a word with her about not letting us know they were going. What time is it now?"

"Almost ten."

"Let's give it another ten minutes. Fifteen, say. She's bound to call as soon as they get in."

She snuggled against him and he put his arms around her, laid his cheek against hers. Once, in her room at the nurses' hostel, they'd fallen asleep like this and wakened when it was dark. He'd had to clamber out of her window and flee in a crouch round the building, expecting any moment to be mistaken for the burglar who'd broken into the adjacent hostel earlier that week. Now he and Alison could lie in each other's arms and dream for as long as they liked, no matter what the hour, and he was reflecting sleepily that they always had this when Alison stiffened. "It's no use, I can feel something's wrong."

The room seemed to darken, the shadows in the highest corners staining the walls. "Like what?" he demanded.

"I don't know, but that doesn't matter. Don't you dare say this is craziness or I'll never forgive you."

"I wouldn't, Ali. But what can be wrong? If anything had happened to your sister, Rowan would have called us, or gone to the police and they would have. You know she'd be sensible."

Alison gazed at him so dully that at first he didn't realise she was agreeing with him. "Do you want to call the police?" he said.

"Give it another few minutes." But she was on the phone to Hermione almost at once. She hung on longer than Derek had, and his head felt brittle with thoughts that chased one another unstoppably: Hermione should have called, if they were going to be home late she ought to have phoned on the way, she would have if she could... "I don't think there's even a police station in Holywell," Alison said unevenly. "They'd have to come from I don't know where."

"When they mightn't need to. Why don't we go ourselves?"

"We can't both go. One of us has to stay by the phone."

He could imagine her doing so literally, for hours. "I'll go then, shall I? I'll call you as soon as I get there."

"All right, you go," she said as if she were humouring him, though they both knew that was a pretence to keep their spirits up. "I hope you have a wasted journey," she added, and kissed him hard, clung to him, pushed him away. "I hope I'm being as irrational as you must think I am."

During the last few minutes he'd ceased to think so, but he thought better of telling her. He gripped her hand until he was out the front door, and then she watched him from the lit hall. Beyond the dunes the lights of Wales quivered. At least he wouldn't be waiting helplessly, at least he would be doing what he could, yet the thought of the roundabout route he would have to take, when Wales was close enough to see, dismayed him. He started the engine and turned the car, and Alison held up one hand as if she couldn't wave. Then the house swallowed her and the light as she closed the front door.

CHAPTER TWENTY-FOUR

There was a reason why Rowan didn't want to waken, if she could only think. Trying to think might waken her before she knew what it was. Better just to lie here in the dark and drift back to sleep until it was daylight and safe to start remembering – better to stay as deep in the dark as she could and ignore her discomfort, whatever it was. Some part of her felt like a threat of unpleasantness, but perhaps she could rearrange herself gradually enough not to waken. She moved her limbs gingerly, just enough to feel them and the bed.

It wasn't her bed. It was lumpy and prickly, and far too cold: she seemed to have thrown off all the bedclothes. She was going to waken in a bed that wasn't hers, she thought apprehensively – she wouldn't be able to run to her parents for comfort – but then it must be her bed at Hermione's, and she could go to her aunt while she remembered the nightmare that was troubling her. The thought of Hermione made the nightmare loom at her, and she jerked away from it, wakening at once.

And then she tried to cower back into the dark, but it wouldn't let her hide from all that she was seeing. She wasn't in bed, she was lying on frosty grass. A few yards away, a willow drooped. A streetlamp glinted through its branches from a pavement beyond railings. Thin stripes of light stretched across the grass; here and there they climbed crosses and rectangular stones, which seemed to be emitting the grey light. She was in the graveyard. The nightmare was real.

She wanted desperately to hide, though she hadn't yet remembered what she would be hiding from, but she felt frozen to the earth. She managed to raise her head, and caught sight of the granite cross beside her – the cross on which she'd knocked herself unconscious. The memory allowed her to reach up and touch her head, which wasn't as bruised as she feared. Then she remembered what she had been fleeing, and she jerked back in panic, crouched in the shadow of the cross.

The open grave ahead of her was no longer glowing. Long thin shapes stirred on the ridge of earth at the foot of the trench. She flinched before she realised that she wasn't seeing fingers groping over the edge of the grave, only snatches of streetlight through the restless branches of the willow. But something had been moving in there earlier. Suppose it had crawled out while she was unconscious and now was closer to her than she knew?

She fumbled for the cross behind her as if holding on to it might keep her safe. Her hands sank into earth instead, earth beneath which there must be something like the shrivelled body she'd seen writhing. She flung herself forward, away from the greedy earth, towards the open grave. She had to see what was there; she felt as if she couldn't stop herself. She wavered to a halt before she could trip over the ridge of dug earth, and stared in.

The flashlight was nearly spent. Rowan had to lean over the trench, her fingers shrinking from the upheaved earth, before she was sure what she was seeing. She prayed she was wrong even when she made out Hermione's vacated face, staring at the flashlight as if she were waiting for it to fail entirely. Please don't be dead, Rowan pleaded, please God don't let her be dead, and then she realised what her grief had delayed her from realising. Hermione's was the only body in the coffin. Terrified that she was about to scream and betray that she was there, she fled towards the gate.

As she dodged the willow and the gravestones she peered fearfully behind them, and then she remembered she should be afraid of Vicky too. At the very least Vicky had known what would happen, had brought Rowan here to see it and had looked triumphant when she had. Whoever Vicky was, Hermione had been right about her, and now Hermione was dead.

The streetlamp was no refuge. The light felt lifeless, one with the graveyard it was keeping unnaturally bright, the neon gravestones, the petrified grass. She ran out of the gate and up the hill towards the houses.

She felt as if she weighed less than she should, perhaps because she no longer had the binoculars. Vicky must have taken them. Vicky had said she had tried to make it easy for her, which presumably meant she was no longer going to. At the top of the slope, trees bent towards her as if they would flail her into the mouth of darkness whose crooked tongue was the road. But there were houses down beyond the next streetlamp. As she fled towards that light, she felt so numb she could hardly believe she was running at all.

When she reached the houses she felt more alone than ever. Porch lights made the gardens into moats of shadow, isolated the houses on islands of light and warned her not to trespass. A dog whined and snarled as Rowan raced downhill, though she hadn't realised she was making any noise to speak of. She knew she mustn't go to strangers, even to ask to call her parents as she yearned to do, but she did know Gwen and Elspeth, a little. They must be wondering where she was. The thought filled her with unexpected guilt that spurred her faster down the hill.

But the French car wasn't outside Gwen's and Elspeth's. They must be searching for her. She was dismayed to find that she felt easier now that she didn't have to tell them about Hermione, for she couldn't help suspecting that if she had heeded her warnings about Vicky, Hermione might still be alive. Surely Rowan's parents wouldn't need to be told about Hermione right away, surely they were worrying about Rowan by now and would just be glad to hear from her. They were somewhere in the frayed thread of light that was glittering at her across the bay, and she could call them from the Gronant phone box.

Hedges stirred on either side of her as she fled downhill, dodging marshy shadows. The next curve gave her the sight of the red box, between the post office, whose window was full of pet foods and washing powders, and the Gronant Inn. She was already hearing her mother's voice. It wouldn't matter if it was angry or relieved or both: she and daddy must be missing Rowan by now, despite what they'd said when they hadn't realised she was listening. But she lurched to a halt yards short of the box. Someone was in there.

The dozens of small windows were whitened by frost or by the streetlamp, but she could see that whoever was inside was very tall. She mustn't run away just because when the door opened she would be alone on the deserted road with them, or even because she felt she was being watched through the glass. She retreated across the road. The long thin dark blotch that must be the head followed her movement. Now she saw that the figure was almost as tall as the box. She imagined how the box would look if it were laid on the pavement, the tall thin shape lying in it, ready to sit up and show her its face, and then she sobbed in terror and flew down the slope.

The road grew steeper, the bends sharper. It twisted between high rough garden walls that held back the lights of their houses from her. She glanced back, terrified of seeing the shadow of a figure stretching round a bend, but she had seen no movement when she reached the coast road at the foot of the hill.

The road stretched both ways into the dark, between the hills behind her that rose to mountains and the fields ahead that stretched to the water. The lights across the bay had begun to drown in mist. A night wind passed through her like a shiver that felt as if it would never end. She stared miserably at the signpost on the far side of the road. Fflint was towards the distant lights, but she had to go away from them, to Prestatyn. That was where the nearest railway station was.

She looked back at the lights of Gronant, afraid both to leave them behind and to see a shadow creeping down the hill or rushing down at her. She made herself proceed onto the coast road. If only she still had the binoculars she would be able to see her destination as she left it behind. She imagined gliding home across the bay, and for a moment she felt as if she could, even without the binoculars. She shrank from the thought and set off into the dark.

Before long, hedges rose on both sides of her, blotting out the blurry glimmer of the hills and fields. Soon they towered above her, blotches of foliage overhanging the road as though the black sky had sagged like an old ceiling. Whenever the leaves stirred they sounded to her like a withered object shifting in a box. She would have run along the middle of the dim tarmac, but mummy had said you should never walk in the road.

At last the hedges gave way to trees in the grounds of a hotel. The hotel was dark. If the doors had been open and lit, she would have asked to phone. She had realised belatedly that Gwen might have stayed at the house while Elspeth searched. Wouldn't it still be quicker to go back than onwards to Prestatyn? She was wavering, afraid to make the wrong choice, when she heard a car.

She mustn't try to hitch a lift. If the car stopped, she mustn't get in or even go near. She was almost relieved when she saw that it was coming from Prestatyn. She dodged into the mouth of the hotel drive as the car slowed. The driver hadn't noticed her: he was slowing for the junction opposite the hotel. As the car swung away from the coast, the headlight beams stretched back towards Gronant. In the moment before they were snatched away, Rowan saw movement on the road.

It was only a glimpse, but it seemed to leap at her. A figure was crawling towards her at the limit of the headlights. It appeared to be using one hand to drag itself along the tarmac while it held something grey to its scalp with the other, like a wig. All the same, it was coming dismayingly fast. With a scream that her fear seemed to deafen her to, Rowan flung herself away from the hotel, where she couldn't believe there was any refuge, and fled into the dark.

She thought she fled for hours towards the false dawn over Prestatyn, and she lost count of the number of times she looked back. Hedges clawed at the air as if they had missed seizing her, but she could make out nothing on the road. She seemed hardly to move past the hills and the fields; she felt as if the vast deserted night were holding her back. If anything, the night seemed even deeper when the glow of the town began to tint the fields. At last the road turned towards a bridge over the railway. She leapt desperately up the bridge and glanced back. The tarry gleam of the road was still bare as far as she could see, yet the lights of the town weren't nearly reassuring enough.

To her left a street of boarding houses paralleled the railway. She remembered walking through the town once with Hermione: perhaps the memory was why the small hotels looked so blank and unwelcoming in the relentless light. She remembered signs in English, but now they were all in Welsh, and the only one she understood – Y Ffrith, the beach – was no use to her. Supposing she found a hotel that was open, the people there might fail to understand her or even refuse to. She felt abandoned in a foreign country, picked out by the light as not belonging – but there ahead was a link with the world she knew: a telephone box.

She was searching her pockets for change when she saw that the box only accepted plastic cards. She dug frantically in her pockets. She'd had all the money her father had given her to spend in Wales, but she must have dropped it in the graveyard. She had no money for the train home.

There was nowhere to go but the station. Surely the staff would let her phone home or do so on her behalf. It was all right to speak to strangers if they were in uniform: you knew what kind of person they were meant to be. She hurried down the glaring lifeless street to the next footbridge, beside the shoe shop. She'd thought it was called the Cosyfeet Station Shop, but now its sign was in Welsh. Upended slippers gaped against the inside of the window like blind pairs of Mickey Mouse eyes. She turned away uneasily and caught sight of the words British Railways at the entrance to the bridge.

She felt almost home until she read the sign. *Mae British Railways Board yn hysbysu drwy hyn nad eu cyfrifoldeb hwy yw'r llwybr hwn*... She no longer wanted to meet anyone in uniform; she was afraid they might ask her questions that would mean no more to her than the sign did. She had to force herself to climb the rough shaky planks of the bridge.

Beyond the bridge, a few streets of small houses and shops led towards the meeting of black sky and black mountains. Even the taxi stand that served the station was deserted. The main street was brighter than the small platform of the station, but she felt exhausted. She trudged down to the platform and peered at the awning that overhung the booking office. Mustn't Caer be Chester? She sat on a bench on the Caer side of the platform, with her back to a timetable in Welsh.

She couldn't sleep, even if she had dared to. She must be so tired that she'd passed beyond tiredness. She would have stared along the line on which the train should appear, except that now she had time to be afraid that the thing she had glimpsed on the road would come crawling down the line in the opposite direction, clutching whatever it had found to cover its peeling head. Whenever the swings in the playground by the tracks rattled their chains she peered nervously at them, but Vicky was never there. She tried to imagine how mummy and daddy would hug her when she reached home, but the night seemed so unrelenting she thought it might never end.

It must have been hours later when the dark began to change, seeping forward, growing paler, cutting short the tracks. By the time she realised this was mist, it had merged with the dawn in a greyness that crept down the mountains and closed around the town. Soon it had blotted out the town itself, isolating her on the platform with a few further yards of railway between dripping embankments. If there was any activity in the streets, she couldn't hear. If anything was hiding from her just beyond the grey wall that felt like growing blindness, she mightn't know until it was too late.

At last she heard a sound, a faint breath that turned into an approaching squeal. She couldn't tell where it was coming from until the huge blank face of the train loomed out of the mist. She dodged around the booking office for fear that the driver would see her, and huddled against a poster mottled with dew.

The train screeched to a halt, and there was silence. The train ought to take her to Chester, but how could she make sure that it did? She would have gone to the engineer and told him her plight, except that she couldn't shake off her fear of foreigners, even in uniform. She tiptoed to the corner of the building and peered along the platform, and saw that a carriage door was open about midway on the train. The windows were grey with condensation, and she could only pray that the car was empty. She darted to the open door and dodged in, and hid between the musty seats.

CHAPTER TWENTY-FIVE

Derek had never driven so fast into Wales. On the motorway he was up to ninety miles an hour. He slowed to eighty on the Queensferry bypass, and braked to the limit through Shotton and Flint and the occasional village. Now and then he passed a phone box and was tempted to call ahead, but driving made him feel less helpless. All the way into Wales he didn't see a police station or a single police car.

He had to slow once he turned off the coast road. Ruins and dark reservoirs sank beneath heaving trees, and he thought how much Rowan loved walking down this valley. He'd take her for a walk here soon, he promised himself, and the promise helped him suppress a surge of panic. He shifted gears to send the car faster up the tortuous road into Holywell.

Faces peered at him out of Hermione's shop, but they were only masks. The shop looked dusty in the harsh light from the street, as if it had been locked for months. Dresses Rowan would love to wear hung emptily in the shadows. He'd buy her one, he vowed as he drove up the hill.

He sucked in a breath as he parked opposite the cottage, for he'd glimpsed a light in Hermione's bedroom. He slammed the car door and told himself to keep his temper, then he swung towards the cottage. Her window was dark. If he got her out of bed, too bad: she hadn't had time to fall asleep. He was striding to the cottage when he realised the light had been the reflection of the streetlamp.

He rang the bell and waited, then he leaned on the button and hammered with the knocker. When he stopped at last, the only sound was of the thin chill wind. His palms were suddenly icy with sweat; his mouth was growing dry. He might have asked the neighbours if they knew where Hermione was, except that although it wasn't yet midnight, all the cottages were dark. He trudged round to the kitchen window.

Pots and pans and a drop of water swelling from a tap above the metal sink glimmered as his breath spread grey over the pane. The drip fell, silenced by the glass. Feeling bereaved of ideas as to what to do now, he reached for the handle of the back door. The door was unlocked.

If Hermione had forgotten to lock it, where had she been taking Rowan in such a hurry? Suppose she had cracked after all? His hand clenched on the chilly metal and snatched the door open. The drip fell again, a sharp dead sound. When he switched on the fluorescent light, the kitchen glared like a walk-in freezer. He hurried into the main room, and a smell of old paper came at him out of the dark.

He groped for the light switch and stared into the room. Plants bowed their faded heads on the mantel and the windowsill, shadows like cobwebs darkened the whorls of the plaster. The smell was coming from an old photograph album on the Welsh dresser. Remembering that Hermione had forged the message made his stomach writhe as he ran upstairs.

The rooms were deserted. Rowan's nightdress lay flat on her bed. He'd make sure she caught up on her sleep after this, he promised himself fiercely, and faltered on his way down to the phone. Speaking to Alison would release all the fears he was still trying to suppress. Then his eye was caught by the message board nailed above the phone. Among the listings in Hermione's warily careful script was one for Gwen and Elspeth. Might Hermione have told them her plans for the evening? He grabbed the phone and dialled the Gronant number.

It had barely rung when it was answered, in Welsh. That and the urgency in the woman's voice unnerved him. "Can you speak English?" he demanded, and wondered if he'd offended her. "I mean, would you mind? I've got the right number, have I? You make stuff for Hermione, don't you? I'm her brother-in-law."

"You mean you're Rowan's father."

"Yes," he said, and experienced another rush of panic.

"Is she with you?"

"No she isn't. Why?"

"You're her father, aren't you?" she said, and almost as accusingly "Then why are you calling?"

He'd meant to avoid harming Hermione's reputation, but he had to know the truth. "She's supposed to be staying with Hermione, but we haven't heard from them all day. I thought you might have an idea where they are."

"They were here. I'm Gwen, by the way." She fell silent, and then she said "Hermione left Rowan with us while she was meant to be visiting someone down at the inn. But nobody there knows about it, so it doesn't look as if she was."

He was afraid to ask what she was leaving unsaid, but he had to. "Where's Rowan?"

"Do you know a friend of hers called Vicky?"

"Yes," he said, and his forehead suddenly felt tight as drying paper.

"Then you must know where she lives," Gwen said with relief. "That's where Rowan is."

"How do you mean? Who took her there? Vicky lives somewhere round Waterloo. How can Rowan have gone all that way and not come home?"

"No, she lives round here. I'm sure that's what she said. It was Rowan who wanted to go to her house," she said defensively.

"You let Rowan go out at night with someone her own age and didn't even ask where they were going?"

"I'm sorry, I know I should have. We've no children of our own. Elspeth has been driving round for hours. She said she was going to ask at some of the houses."

He could hear how upset she was, but that seemed to steal feelings he felt more entitled to. "You should have called the police. I will."

"Where are you in case Rowan comes back here?"

"Hermione's."

"Will you be staying there?"

"Yes," he said as if she had trapped him, and made her dictate her address. He pressed the receiver rest down with his thumb while he found the police number on the message board, and dialled with a carefulness that felt like putting off the moment when he would have to speak.

Whoever answered questioned him so slowly and closely that he sounded half asleep. Was he the father of the missing child? What was the child's name? What was the child's address? Was that where he was calling from? Where was he calling from? What was he doing there? Was that the address the child was missing from? Who had told him that the child was missing? What reason did he have to think she was? Had he checked her friend's address? Every question drew Derek's forehead tighter around his raw fears. "We'll send someone as soon as we can," the policeman said at last, and Derek could only phone Alison.

The phone rang once in Waterloo. "Who's there?"

Her haste caught him by the throat. "It's me. I'm at Hermione's. They aren't here. They went to visit the women who work at the shop, then your sister went off somewhere. They let Rowan go with this Vicky without getting her address. I've called the police."

"You think that's necessary?"

"It might be, mightn't it? I mean, wouldn't you have? Just in— just to be safe."

"Of course I would have, for that reason. Vicky has relatives over there, hasn't she? She must have, to have been there when Rowan first met her. Someone must know who. Will you stay at Hermione's in case someone calls? I'll be here, obviously."

"Call me if you get lonely."

"Don't say that or I will be. Let's not call each other unless there's news, all right? Keep the lines clear."

"Good night for now then, Ali. Don't—" He swallowed his advice to her; it would only make her feel worse. "I love you," he said.

"I love you. And Rowan loves us both, and we'll all remember this night when she grows up."

"You'd better believe it," he said fiercely, and patted the rest until it cut her off. He wondered suddenly if Rowan might have left a note, but all he could find in her room was her diary. On today's page she had written that Hermione had shown her a photograph that looked like

Vicky. The idea fed his panic, the sight of her painstaking script made him feel close to weeping. He was still searching the cottage, though by now only to prevent himself from brooding, when the police arrived.

Had the child and her friend ever gone off like this before? Had he any reason to be suspicious of the friend or any relative of hers? Had he any idea where the child's aunt might have gone? Could he provide them with a photograph of the child? There was a framed one in Hermione's room. "Don't worry, sir, we'll be in touch as soon as there's anything to report," the policeman who was driving said.

Derek was staring at the hole in the dark where the taillights had been when a woman in her sixties looked out of the next cottage, tying the cord of her dressing-gown. "You're Hermione's brother-in-law, aren't you? Anything wrong?"

"She took my little girl to Gronant and nobody knows where they are," Derek said, feeling as if every repetition made the situation worse.

"Will you come in for a cup, or shall I sit with you? I'm up anyway. My husband has to go to work."

"You couldn't sit in her cottage for a bit, could you? I just thought where Hermione may be, but it's not worth telling the police if I can go myself."

"I'll have to see the old man off first."

Derek called Alison. "No news yet, love. The police are on it now. The lady next door is going to be here while I see if I know where your sister is."

"Are you going to tell me where?"

"I think she may have gone after that locket," he said, trying to be vague.

Her silence made him yearn to be holding her, except then she would have sensed his panic. "You may be right," she admitted. "Don't be any longer than you have to be, will you? Next time I may take more notice of what you say about her."

"So long as you don't stop taking notice of yourself, love," Derek said, and sent her a kiss. The plastic felt clammy against his lips. He was lingering by the phone when a milkman came to let Derek know his wife would be around as soon as she was dressed. Soon she arrived with her knitting, and Derek gave her Alison's number in case there was news. "No need to rush, I'll be here," she said.

The wind had dropped. Mist shrank the fields beside the road and waited at the limit of the headlights. The idea that Rowan could be out on a night like this almost forced him back to Hermione's, where at least his would be the voice she heard if she phoned for help – but if Hermione had really had a photograph of Vicky, might she have found out where the girl lived? While he struggled with his doubts his body went on driving, treading on the brake when he saw a small figure step back against the hedge ahead, but it was a gatepost leading to darkness. The road climbed towards Gronant, and as it rose out of the fog he saw lights fluttering under the trees against the sky at the top of the slope. People must be searching, he thought, and tried to be hopeful – and then he saw that the lights were on top of a police car and an ambulance.

As he drove up the slope he felt as if he were leaving his heart behind. He had to park before he reached the vehicles, because his hands no longer felt able to control the wheel: he'd seen two men carrying a stretcher through a gate. As he stumbled uphill, headstones wavered like failing neon as the pulse of light touched them. He was almost at the gate when a policeman with a flickering blue face blocked his way and said something in Welsh, and then "Can I help you, sir?"

The men had laid the stretcher down and stepped into a grave. They were going to lift out a body onto the stretcher, as if life were somehow running backwards. "What's happening in there?" Derek stammered.

"I'm not at liberty to say, sir. Please move on."

"I've got to see. I may know her." Derek could hardly speak for praying that it wouldn't be Rowan on the stretcher. "That's my wife's family's grave."

A second policeman came forward, and conferred with his colleague in Welsh. Eventually the one who'd stopped Derek said "You'd better see if you can identify her."

Derek had already seen enough, and hated the surge of relief he experienced. The body that the men were heaving out of the grave was certainly not Rowan's. He hurried across the graveyard, his bluish shadow leaping feebly ahead, and halted by the willow. Hermione looked as if she were screaming in a nightmare from which she was unable to waken. One of the attendants was trying to close her mouth, and Derek was afraid he would have to break her jaw, especially when the blue light made it seem to jerk. He might have fallen into the willow if a policeman hadn't gripped his arm. "It's my wife's sister," he muttered.

The attendant pulled a sheet over her face, and she was carried to the ambulance. As a policeman brought planks from near the gate to cover the trench, Derek lurched forward and glanced in, then recoiled from the sight of the bald blackened shape that lay crouched in the whitish lair of the box. The policemen closed the coffin and arranged the makeshift lid over the grave and then, grotesquely, placed No Parking cones at the corners farthest from the marble pillar. The sight made Derek nauseous, and he had closed his eyes when a policeman said "If you'd like to follow us when you're ready, sir, you can make your statement at the police station."

Derek forced his eyes open. "I've got to find my daughter."

"You can tell us about that at the station, sir, and perhaps we'll be able to help. Please don't be long."

How was it possible that they didn't know about Rowan? Had someone called them to the graveyard before Derek had phoned the police? They waited by the gate, murmuring in Welsh. They must be giving him a chance to come to terms with what he'd seen, but he could tell they had their doubts about him. If he made them check that he'd called earlier, surely they would let him go for now. The pulse in his throat felt like a threat of sickness as he turned towards the gate and stepped into the shadow of the willow. The tree seemed to gulp the lights of the streetlamp and the vehicles. The shadow closed around him like black water, deep and chill, and a small pale hand took hold of his arm.

CHAPTER TWENTY-SIX

As soon as the station receded into the fog Rowan scrambled onto the nearest seat. Whoever had closed the door from outside wouldn't see her now. She'd eluded Vicky and anything else that might have followed her from Gronant. She would be safe until Chester, where she would have to change trains.

Faded brownish seats swayed in the dingy light that clung like frost to the grimy windows. The train smelled old and stale and damp. As far as she could see, she was alone except for the driver. Cars reeled back and forth beyond the connecting doors as if they were striving to line themselves up, and made her feel unstable. She could trust the train, but she wished she could see where she was going – wished that the fog would give her even a hint of home.

She tried to rub the window clearer, but even when she tried to breathe on the glass she could make no mark. The grime was on the outside, and beyond that was the fog. Clumps of wet grass swelled out of the fog, sketching fields and a golf course, and then the bay came sweeping towards the railway and ran beside it for miles. Last time she had been able to see Waterloo, but now there was only the fringe of the sea, grey sluggish waves that looked weighed down by fog. She felt as if the familiar names, Waterloo and Crosby and Bootle and Seaforth and Litherland, had been wiped out by the weather. Soon fields pushed the sea away to be swallowed by the fog.

Her staring out had made the train appear flat, thin as cardboard, so shabby that it seemed on the point of wearing away to nothing. It made Rowan feel hardly there, hardly anywhere, in danger of being unable to fend off the memory of last night, the nightmare she needed to forget until she was safely home. Even when bushes flared out of the fog, green leaves turning yellow and orange and red, they seemed no more real than a film projected on the screen of the window. The prow of a ship loomed over the train, the keel beached in dank grass. It was a restaurant Hermione had promised to take her to when she was older. The next moment it had folded into the fog as if it had never been there at all.

Buildings broke through the fog on the side of the track away from the retreating sea, windowless brown buildings like cartons with too big an idea of themselves. Beyond them she glimpsed headlights drowning on the road along which her father had driven her to and from Hermione's, and then the road was obscured by houses with long narrow gardens dark as moss, boxed in by brick walls. Lit windows displayed scenes misty as television commercials: a man dabbing at his just-shaved face, a woman rocking a baby in her arms beside a cot, an old man dodging from room to room of a house and switching on all the lights. It was too early for children to be up, she thought, and wouldn't anyone who got onto her train at Flint want to know why she was? The train rushed into the station, and she was wondering whether to hide in the toilet when she realised that the train wasn't slowing. It raced through the chalk sketch of a station and out into the fog.

So long as it stopped at Chester, she needn't mind where else it did. A scrapyard ragged with fog sped by, a motorcycle glared at her out of the murk, dripping trees raw with autumn reared up, buildings that looked lost at sea sank into the fog. Houses crowded towards the railway as it approached Shotton, and the train blared its horn at the station. Only Chester mattered, Rowan told herself, but suppose the train wasn't meant to carry passengers at all so early? Suppose it wouldn't start to pick them up until it was past Chester? She pressed her face against the glass as the train sped into Shotton, and willed it to stop here as well, just to reassure her. The houses slid away, making room for a platform the colour of fog. The train wasn't slowing; nobody was waiting. Rowan sat back, rubbing her face to try and rid it of the cold flat sensation of the window, and a figure rushed at her across the platform, trailing fog.

She had only a glimpse as the train swept by, of a figure in uniform with grey hair trailing over its shoulders. She was glad that the train hadn't slowed after all. Then, as her car raced under a bridge at the end of the platform, she heard a door slam further down the train.

Surely nobody could have boarded at this speed, but someone was back there. Rowan crouched on the seat and peered around it, through the connecting doors. Fog flooded by on both sides of her, sweeping away telegraph poles and greying tufts of grass. She could see no movement beyond the door except for the pitching of the carriages. She pushed herself away from the upholstery, which felt soft and damp, and was swaying to her feet in the aisle when she saw a figure coming towards her down the train.

It was wearing a dark uniform with a peaked cap. At first that was all she could see as her mind chased its tail in panic, telling her to run and hide, see first, run and hide… The two carriages between her and the figure seemed to shrink around her vision, twisting it as they jerked back and forth. He must be the guard, she thought, and he'd been on the train all the time. If he didn't let her phone her parents he would surely call them himself, and they would promise to pay her fare. Why then was her panic growing as she watched the figure swing itself towards her down the carriage that looked starved of sunlight, dying of the lack? It was moving almost like a monkey, grabbing the backs of seats on either side and swinging itself between them up the aisle, its long grey hair streaming under the peaked cap. It reached the first set of connecting doors, and she saw it clawing at the glass before it managed to slide them back. It skipped forward into the carriage next to hers, and she saw the face beneath the cap. Despite the ragged hair that trailed over its shoulders, it had a baby's chubby face.

Perhaps it was so old that it looked like a baby again; perhaps that was why the round face, pale as a snail's belly, was slack and drooling. She knew only that it summed up everything she was terrified of. She watched helplessly as it swung closer, raising its legs so that she saw its thin bare ankles, white and blotchy as though with mould, above the shoes that seemed in danger of falling off every time it swung. She saw how delicately it had to take hold of the seats, because its blackened nails were half as long as its fingers. It was just a few seats away now, too close for her to escape even if she could move. Then it looked straight at her, and its small pinkish eyes lit up as a wicked smile puckered its toothless mouth.

Rowan choked on a scream and flung herself away from the end of the carriage, and almost sprawled full length. She fled along the lurching aisle, not so much supporting herself on the seats as fending them off. She almost fell again as she lunged at the door to the next carriage before it was within reach. The motion of the train helped slide the door open for her, and she glanced back in terror to see how much distance she'd gained. The uproar of the train must have blotted out the noise of the far doors, for the baby's face was grinning at her from beneath the peaked cap perched on its matted hair and licking its lips with its swollen loamy tongue, close enough to touch.

This time she couldn't even scream. She flinched across the roaring gap between the cars, swayed on the narrow walkway as the next carriage lolled out of alignment, squeezed past the door as it jerked open, clutched the inner handle with both hands as the train threw the door shut again. She leaned all her weight on the handle to keep the door shut, but it felt as if she might be dislodged at any moment. Praying that the door would stick, she raised her head unwillingly and looked through the glass.

The baby face was flattened against the window of the door across the gap. The blackened tongue stuck out of the slackly grinning mouth and squirmed against the glass. The peaked cap had slipped forward, almost hiding the gleeful eyes. It only wanted to terrify her, she told herself desperately, just as Vicky had wanted to. She thought of letting go somehow, of being able to sail away from the train like going through the binoculars, and clung to the handle as if it would hold her back from the temptation. Then she saw long cracked mottled fingernails creeping around the edge of the other door, in the moment before the car went dark.

A trench had closed around the train, high chiselled walls patched with sodden moss and weeds. The train was racing into Chester. If she could keep the door shut until it reached the station, surely she might be safe – but she had just remembered what lay between the trench and the station when the train rushed into it, into the tunnel.

Rowan squeezed her eyes shut and clutched the handle so hard that she couldn't distinguish her hands from the metal. In the midst of the hollow roar of the train she heard a sliding sound, and then something pale pressed into her face. It was daylight, which meant that the train was out of the tunnel, but the tunnel was only the first of two. The second must be longer, because she was still in the dark when the door began to slide stealthily out of her grasp.

She tried to make herself strong as a stone, prayed that she could be until the train reached the platform, but the door was creeping open with a horrid gentleness, and she no longer seemed able to hold on. She strained to heave the door shut on the long-nailed fingers that she knew were spidering around the edge. They must be capable of reaching for her, seizing her while the pink-eyed baby face flattened itself against the glass until it was ready to drag her into its embrace. Suddenly she wanted to let go, either of the door or of her struggle not to do what Vicky had wanted: she would have given anything to be somewhere else, but now she realised she didn't know how. Then the grey daylight flew into her closed eyes as the train lurched, and the door slid out of her grasp.

She felt herself falling blindly, and grabbed at whatever could support her: something soft, covered with cloth. She thought she might never dare open her eyes, but when she did she found she had clutched the back of a seat. She was facing the doors, which had slid shut again. There was no sign of her pursuer except for a grey drooling patch where its mouth had been squashed against the glass. She fled towards the nearest door that would let her onto the platform – if the train stopped.

Mail vans gleamed as though they had been painted red that morning, and then the station lumbered into view. The train was slowing. Rowan prayed that it would stop, prayed so hard she couldn't think of words. Fog drifted across the platforms, where she could see blurred figures, most of them in uniform. The sight threatened to paralyse her. As soon as the train was alongside the platform, she jumped.

She had to run along the platform for fear that she would lose her footing, and it seemed safest not to stop running. She dashed past the uniformed figures without daring to glance at them, but they seemed not to notice her. Nobody was collecting tickets at the barrier. She dodged past the shuttered bookstall and out into the street with a panicky backwards glance to make sure she wasn't being followed. Beyond the station, steps led up to a road above the tracks, and a sign glittering with dew indicated a way to Liverpool across the bridge. She raced to the top of the steps and stared down at the deserted road outside the station, and then she fled over the bridge.

CHAPTER TWENTY-SEVEN

Five minutes after Alison had put down the receiver, she wanted to call Derek back. Even supposing he found Hermione, what could he do besides fly at her for wandering off in pursuit of her obsession instead of taking care of Rowan? Wasn't he doing exactly the same? He must be so close to his feelings that he couldn't see the chance that having someone stay at Hermione's had given him. She dropped the percolator on the draining-board, screwed the cold tap shut, and ran to the phone in the hall.

The woman who responded announced the number so slowly she must be reading it from the dial. "Is my husband still there?" Alison pleaded. "I'm Hermione's sister."

"Don't worry, dear, your hubby's well on his way. Won't you try and get some sleep? No need for us all to stay awake. I'll give you a call the moment there's any news."

"Thank you," Alison said dully, and made herself move away from the phone before she could be tempted to phone her parents. Her head felt large and empty as the house for lack of sleep, with a brain that was uselessly bright as the top floor, but sleeping would be like forgetting Rowan. She filled the percolator and watched it boil, she poured herself a coffee and took a sip that scalded her lips, and then there seemed to be nothing to do except, agonisingly, think.

She felt as if all the fears that had ever wakened her in the depths of the night had become all that was left in the world. She ought to have insisted on meeting Vicky when she'd had the chance. She would have found out more about her if she hadn't been reacting against Hermione's obsession with her. Even so, couldn't Rowan be at Vicky's now? Perhaps at this very moment she was dreaming, and daylight would bring her home.

Alison gulped coffee and parted the living-room curtains to gaze over at Jo's. Of course the house was dark at this time of the morning. If anyone saw Alison now they might take her for some old woman, wandering through her rooms because she'd lost the ability to sleep. She stared at the locked-up houses, at Eddie's car, and then she realised she could borrow it as soon as Eddie came over to carry on decorating, if she hadn't heard from Rowan by then. She could go over as soon as it was daylight and ask one of them, not Patty, to stay in her house.

Waiting was harder now that there was something definite to wait for. She poured herself another mug of coffee and wandered from the stony kitchen to the gloomy living-room. The television had closed down hours ago, and the newspaper seemed full of reports about children who had come to harm. Every time she thought of Rowan she experienced a spasm of sharp fear. Though she was afraid to do so and afraid to think why she was, she trudged up to Rowan's room.

She would have lain on the bed in the hope that might make her feel closer to Rowan, except that to feel calm would be to risk falling asleep. She gazed at the Muppet poster Rowan had had since she was three years old, the shelves piled so haphazardly with books that it seemed moving any one of them would dislodge them all, the chest of drawers with the toe of a sock drooping from the drawer that would never quite close, eight years' worth of dolls huddled in the corner nearest the bed. Suddenly the room seemed so empty that she wanted to weep, and she could hardly bear to look at the bed. Then she saw something under the sheet where it was pulled taut over the pillow.

Rowan must have left it there when she was making the bed. It was a folded sheet of the flowery notepaper Hermione had given her last Christmas. *To my mummy and daddy*, it said, and Alison had to close her eyes and take several deep breaths before her hands were steady enough to unfold the paper.

Dear mummy and daddy, I love you and I realy dont mind if you dont buy me things becose you cant aford them, I wish youd told me about father Christmass not being real sooner becose then I wouldnt have ecspected so many presunts, Ill try not to cost you so much and you dont need to give me any pockit mony as long as we can all live together and I dont mind where,

Lots of love from your,

Rowan

Alison stared at the note and the lines of kisses at the bottom, and suddenly her hands were as steady as stone, and as cold. She'd thought for a moment on Thursday night that someone was listening to her argument with Derek, and now she was certain that Rowan had been. No wonder she'd asked to go to Hermione's. Perhaps now she wasn't with Vicky at all, perhaps she had run away into the night because she thought nobody wanted her. Alison let out a sob that scraped her throat and resounded in the empty bedroom, and stared upwards with eyes that felt like embers. She might have been going to pray, but overhead was only Queenie's floor, bare and stark. She was taking shuddering breaths that felt like sobs when the phone rang.

She managed to let go of the note with one hand as she jerked, her heart thudding. She saw herself place the note carefully on Rowan's pillow. That took two rings of the phone, and then she was running down the shabby corridor and grabbing at the banister so as not to fall on the canted stairs. She snatched up the receiver and heard the pips begin.

It was a pay phone. It must be Rowan. Thank God you're safe, she thought, stay where you are and I'll come and get you, whoever I have to waken so I can borrow a car. The pips choked on a coin, and Derek said "Hello?"

"Derek." Her voice felt lifeless in her mouth. "What is it? Where are you?"

"At the police station. They told me this phone would be quicker, I'd have to wait to use theirs. Listen, love, I'm sorry. Try and keep calm. They found Hermione. She's dead."

Alison leaned her forehead against the metallic leaves of the wallpaper and let out a despairing sigh. "How?"

"It was what I thought. She was at the graveyard. She'd dug up

– you know. They think it must have been too much for her, for her heart. But—"

The pips cut him off. She imagined him fumbling for another coin, cursing and perhaps wasting time in his haste. She made her hand into a shaky fist and drove it between her forehead and the wall, as if the sensation might help her keep control. She was gripping the receiver so hard that the mouthpiece dug into her lip. She had heard in Derek's voice that he had something else to tell her, and she was afraid to learn what it was.

CHAPTER TWENTY-EIGHT

The road beyond the railway bridge led under falling leaves past a mile of hotels. Whenever Rowan looked down, the sodden tapestry of the pavement entangled her vision in colours and patterns. People must be going to church, for she kept seeing figures emerging from the hotels ahead. They were always walking away from her, and so she never saw their faces. Whenever she glanced nervously behind her there was nobody, no movement to be seen except the slow fall of dying leaves through the retreating fog.

Though she was running, she didn't feel tired. Perhaps she wasn't moving as fast as she thought she was; perhaps that was why she couldn't catch up with the procession of figures. In any case, she didn't think she wanted to: even if she met a policeman in uniform now, she would be afraid to see his face. The hotels gave way to suburban houses, beyond which a roundabout interrupted the road. She hesitated at the intersection, then darted across, staying well back from the procession that filled the misty road ahead.

Their clothes and their hair and the little she could see of their bodies glowed white as mist under the strengthening sun. A second roundabout marked the beginning of the motorway to Liverpool. By the time she reached the roundabout they had left the road and were dwindling across a sunlit field. For a moment she wanted to follow them, for the sight of them made her breathless, filled her with a yearning she didn't understand. They seemed to brighten as they grew more distant, until they were a cluster of light that vanished into the fog. She had to get home to her parents, to safety and comfort and, at long last, sleep. She turned aside, down the concrete ramp, and stepped onto its grassy spine.

She felt as if she were walking on the sky, on thousands of rainbow stars that grew brighter as the sunlight did. They were tiny drops of water, clear and still as crystal. If she stooped to any one of them she might be able to see into its world, but that seemed too like being tempted to let go, as Vicky had wanted her to. She was almost glad when the wedge of grass that led down to the motorway narrowed to a weedy strip between crash barriers.

It led as far as her vision could reach. The fog was shrinking from the sun, exposing the sparkling fields on either side and a sign ahead that told her it was twenty-five miles to Liverpool. Daddy took twenty minutes or less when he was driving, but how long would it take her to walk? That didn't matter, she told herself. At the end of it she would be home, safe, able to sleep.

She glanced up the ramp to make sure nobody was following, and then she stepped between the barriers. They were as high as her waist, and so were some of the weeds and grass. The greenery must be soaking her, but she couldn't feel it; she must have walked so far that her legs were numb. The only sign of life as she picked her way along the narrow island was the music-box chiming of distant church bells. She thought of being trapped between the streams of weekday traffic, racing one another at close to a hundred miles an hour with hardly a car's length between some of them and only the low barrier to protect her, and hoped she would be off the motorway before they appeared. She stopped short of admitting to herself that she was hoping she would be off the motorway before night fell.

She sidled around concrete posts that supported overhead gantries, she edged past the metal stems of speed signs. She thought she had walked only a couple of miles when she realised that the sun was at its height. The waste of concrete stretched ahead of her and behind her, weeds sprouting from banks that cut off her view of the fields, and she felt as if she'd wandered onto a disused section from which she might never find her way home. The sun glared down as the last of the haze dissipated, and ragged shadows of weeds groped over the edges of the motorway, growing blacker, blackness reaching out of the earth for her. She stared back at the lifeless concrete and fled.

By the time the motorway began to slope upwards, the sun had moved from her right to her left. The motorway climbed out from between the overgrown banks, and she saw Ellesmere Port ahead. Huge drums which she supposed were full of chemicals clustered like fungus, grey or white, beside the road. Pipes fatter than she was tall wound among the bunched drums, orange flames danced at the tips of tall thin blackened metal chimneys. Thick smoke squeezed out of stouter chimneys and seemed to stick like mould to the sky. The vista of metal and concrete and fumes went on for miles, but it had lifted Rowan's spirits. It was on the Mersey coast, and she could almost see home. She began to skip through the discoloured grass to the top of the overpass.

The distant cathedrals of Liverpool glinted across the grey river, under the gathering of smoke. She hurried down between the barriers. Drums and chimneys sprouted around her, flames leapt as if desperate to pierce the lowering smoke. Despite the time of day, orange lights shone harshly among the pipes and storage tanks. They made the landscape seem abandoned, pumping out its fumes and flames like a gigantic machine trying to be a volcano. The chimneys gave out as banks rose on both sides of the road. She was still between the banks when the sun vanished.

The shadow of the left-hand bank swallowed the shadow of the barrier that had been trailing over her path. The path was immediately colder, but the sensation seemed distant, separate from her. She was running to be somewhere other than the enclosed deserted stretch before night fell. She turned a long blank curve as the sky to the west grew glassy and sullen, and saw a sign ahead.

The intersection it mapped was below the motorway. Before she reached it, she was able to see over the banks. Ragged trees waited to finger the low sun, which had laid a path of dying light across the fields. The road that crossed the intersection would take her to Birkenhead, and it might be easier for her to steal onto the ferry there than onto the bus through the tunnel at the end of the motorway. Besides, there would be houses on the road, perhaps even people on their way to evening mass. She dodged across to the ramp and hurried down.

A long black car glided under the motorway, so silently that she wasn't sure she had seen it at all. Otherwise this stretch of the dual carriageway between Birkenhead and Chester was deserted. The trees beside the pavements were fossilised by the sky, the tall concrete streetlamps were clogged with shadow. In the distance ahead she saw houses and shops, the green neon glare of a fish and chip shop. She wasn't even surprised to realise she didn't feel hungry at all.

The shops must be further away than they looked. What felt like fifteen minutes' walking brought them no closer. Several were lit by now, and beyond them cars turned across the carriageway, flashing their headlights at each other. All of that felt like companionship, but she had only just started to run when she came to a signpost that brought her up short. It was a sign for Liverpool.

It appeared to be pointing down a side road. Vandals might have bent it, but the route made sense; it would be closer to the river. Beyond the trees that overhung the side road she saw a lamplit row of white cottages that looked inviting and safe. She ran across the road and under the trees.

They blotted out the sky at once. They were so swollen with ivy that she could hardly see between them. Sodden leaves flapped down, thickening the pavements and the narrow road. Rowan slid downhill on them, flailing her arms. Usually this would be a game, but not when you were sliding down a tunnel that felt dank and rotten, a dark tunnel with light at the end. As soon as she lurched to a halt at the beginning of the lamplit street, she looked back.

The rotten tunnel seemed much longer and steeper. She couldn't see the main road. The tunnel reminded her suddenly of the open grave, as if the world had turned upside down and the grave were hovering over her, waiting. She flinched away from that, towards the first lamp.

The white cottages multiplied as far as she could see, an unbroken shadowless terrace of them on each side of the road, beneath the lamps that looked exactly like household light bulbs standing on their heads. Since there were no front gardens and no gaps between the cottages, there was nowhere anyone could hide. She stepped forward almost confidently on the flagstones of the pavement, which were white.

So were the doors of the cottages, which opened straight onto the pavement, and the curtains at each small neat window. As the narrow glassy sky turned deep blue and then died out, the street grew whiter still, the outlines of the roofs and chimneys sharpening like ice. Rowan was glad that the street was deserted, but shouldn't there be sounds of people dining or watching television in some of the curtained rooms? Almost at once she reached the first cottage she could see into downstairs, into a room with rings of dancing fairies printed on the wallpaper. Perhaps the people who lived in that cottage had a child who couldn't climb stairs, though there was no furniture to show what the room was used for.

Rowan hurried past another dozen cottages or so, and then the silence made her glance back. The decaying tunnel was out of sight, but why wasn't the white street more encouraging? Perhaps it was the absence of any signs of life. Maybe she would see someone through the next uncurtained window, several cottages ahead on the opposite side of the street; just the sight of someone else might be enough. She went forward so quickly that she felt she was losing control, in danger of being unable to stop. Instinctively she reached out to the wall of the nearest cottage to slow herself down, and her hand sank in.

The wall felt chill and gritty, yet it made her think of softened flesh. She recoiled before she had time to gasp, but the sensations clung to her, swarmed through her. When she realised that she'd left a shallow handprint in the white surface, she was so embarrassed she wished there were somewhere to hide after all. She turned nervously to make sure that nobody had seen what she'd done to the wall, and then she saw that she had left faint footprints in the deserted pavement.

The street seemed to close around her, the long white street whose doors she had suddenly become more aware of. They appeared to be composed of the same substance as the cottages – the same as the pavement into which she hadn't noticed her feet were sinking. She backed away from the sight of the treacherous pavement that could only lead back to the rotten tunnel, and then she twisted round and fled. She had almost forgotten the uncurtained window, and when she came abreast of it she was caught by a shudder that seemed to pass through the street as well as through her. Beyond the window, the downstairs room was papered like a child's bedroom with rings of bright-eyed dancing fairies.

So was the next front room she fled past, and the next, and the next. It seemed that the cottages no longer needed to hide whatever they were now that she had come too far even to think of retreating. The lightless sky made the white roofs appear to crouch towards her. She wondered suddenly if this might be where Vicky had meant her to end up. Though the idea was dissociated as a thought in a nightmare, she looked back wildly in case Vicky was there. But what she saw was far worse. Every front door in the entire street behind her was wide open.

She thought she would never be able to look away. She stared at the vista of open doors as if staring were all that might keep the street deserted, and then she began to edge backwards. Suppose she was backing towards more open doors and whatever was beyond them? She whirled and saw that the doors ahead were still closed. She felt as though she had become pure panic, unable to think. All she wanted was to be out of the street that was like an endless dream about to turn into an endless nightmare. She thought she felt the pavement dragging at her feet, about to harden like concrete. Her panic seemed to blind her then as she flung herself forward, no longer caring how she escaped as long as she did. All at once, with no idea of how she'd got there, she was in the midst of darkness.

It was like falling into a pit and being buried at once. She twisted round so quickly that she lost whatever bearings she might have had. Across a field that glistened faintly, blackly, she made out streetlamps at the end of a line of white cottages. She turned and strained to see something, anything, else. She had lost her sense of staring and of herself when reddish light flared and showed her that the field was at the edge of water.

The light reminded her of a rocket bursting in the sky, but it couldn't be Guy Fawkes Night; it wasn't November yet, not even October. Green light flared across the water, silhouetting a few houses and confirming that it was the river across which she was seeing them, and then the dark rushed back. It seemed to engulf her like mud, and wasn't the earth underfoot growing softer, liable to suck her down? But she'd seen a wall at the edge of the field by the river, a wall whose top was level with the earth and which had railings to cling to. A leap so desperate she couldn't judge its distance took her onto the wall.

The stones were uneven, but more than wide enough to walk along. She didn't need to hold the railing. She peered at the field, which was utterly black now that she was closer to the glow of houses across the water. She began to walk as fast as she dared along the slippery wall above the slopping blackness of the river.

A mist was settling over the river, muffling the lights that branched across the sky and any sounds they made. Having consumed the far bank, the mist lay contentedly in the middle of the river. While she strained to see across, the black field was buried under concrete that proved to be the final resting-place of piles of torn cars. Whenever a wind set the rusty metal creaking she thought someone was creeping after her from car to car.

Eventually the scrapyards gave way to dockland. Lightless ships towered above her, weeds dangling from their portholes. Chains thick as her waist and gleaming sullenly like tar tethered the ships to the wharves. The stains and rust that glistened on the hulls, and the weeds that looked dredged, made her feel the ships had drowned and then been dragged up by their chains, especially when she heard water falling hollowly inside them. Catwalks railed with sagging links led across the mouths of docks, led her between ships which blotted out the night sky on both sides of her and which stirred ponderously, restlessly, in the dark. It was like trying to find her way through a maze whose walls threatened to collapse towards her. She felt as though the ships would never end by the time she saw a hint of open night beyond them. But when she came into the open on top of a thick rough wall, she saw the distant landing-stage at Birkenhead.

A glow the size of a hotel was gliding towards it – a ferry with passengers singing indistinctly and dancing on the decks. Rowan fled towards the landing-stage, a mile or more away. Long before she got there she heard the ferry thump the tyres at the edge of the stage. Revellers crowded up the ramp and into the night, and she hadn't reached the pay booths when the lights of the terminal were extinguished. The ferry was moored and dark.

All she could do was huddle in the chill glassed-in waiting room until morning. Up in the streets of Birkenhead people shouted and sang for hours, and then there was only the lapping of waves. But she was nearly home, where she and her parents would hug each other as if they might never let go, though when they did she thought she might sleep for days.

A dark bulk looming out of the fog brought her back to the moment. It was another ferry, carrying transport staff from Birkenhead to Liverpool. When they were out of sight on board she stole onto the deck and hid behind a funnel while the ferry turned towards a dull pink dawn over Liverpool. As soon as the men were under the awning of the Liverpool terminal, Rowan flew across the wooden ramp and up to the bus station at the Pier Head.

Three red-faced men were huddled on a bench, but seemed too intent on drinking from brown paper bags to notice her. Otherwise the Pier Head was deserted, even the dozens of numbered bays that ought to contain buses. The desertion made her feel as if the world might be about to play another trick on her, and so did what the three men seemed to be repeating as they passed a paper bag among them. All the same, she had to make for the dock road.

It was the most direct way home, but the loneliest. It led between warehouses for miles. When she heard children playing, out of sight on a cracked road beyond a pub where blurred garlands hung inside the frosted windows, she had to force herself not to go looking for company. She'd be in Waterloo by the time the sun was highest, she promised herself.

She almost was, though the sun stayed dismayingly low. Past the traffic lights at the end of the dock road she saw the radar station, its dish turning like a blind beggar's, and the yachts drooping on the marina. She ran past the silent overpass and the stone angel at the Five Lamps, and saw families coming home from church. Children were riding new bicycles in the side streets or showing off their other presents, and there was no doubt now what the day was or what she'd heard the red-faced men at the Pier Head wish one another. How could she have been lost for so long? Had Vicky done that to her somehow? She didn't care now that she was nearly home.

The street by the railway station shone with melted frost, a light that felt like a memory of warmth. She ran into the side road, past the house whose side said Thompsons Boot Repairers. Children whom she knew from the school turned away from her without noticing her, having been called home; it must be time for lunch. She'd be in time for hers, she thought, and wondered how she could have gone so long without food as well as sleep. She raced to her street and down it, past windows full of coloured lights, to the house.

It looked new. The walls had been pebbledashed, and gleamed against the dunes and the glittering bay. Her grandparents' car was parked outside; it must have been granddad who'd landscaped the garden with rockeries and curving paths. An extra strip had been tacked to the sale board: SALE AGREED, it said. She didn't care. Home was wherever she was with mummy and daddy, and she would tell them so. She passed beyond the open gate and went up the path.

The front door had changed. The walls were blue and printed with delicate blossomy silhouettes, and a large blue Chinese paper globe lit the room. The room was full of people: mummy and daddy and mummy's parents, Jo and Eddie and their children. Rowan had been looking forward to being with just the family, and surely the neighbours would leave them alone when she went in, the neighbours she could see and whoever else it was that the grown-ups and Patty were talking to while the children played near the Christmas tree. Rowan pressed close to the window and watched, letting the sight of the tree and the presents and above all her family make up for everything she'd gone through, waiting for someone to turn and notice her, enjoying the prospect of the moment when they would all be together at last, stifling a giggle as she imagined how surprised whoever saw her first would be. Waiting seemed like the best Christmas game of all, with the best prize ever at the end. But when she realised it had begun to rain, she raised her hand to tap on the glass.

Then grandma held out a wrapped present to the person whom the grown-ups had been talking to, and who stepped forward now. "Happy Christmas, Rowan," grandma said.

CHAPTER TWENTY-NINE

"Happy Christmas, Rowan," Edith said, and Alison echoed her under her breath like a prayer. It would be a happy Christmas, they would make certain it was. The family was all here, at least all those who had survived, and that was what Christmas should be. She and Derek and her parents had the present they had wanted most of all: they had Rowan, safe and sound. Today of all days Rowan must realise how much they wanted her, how they would have given anything to have her back the night she was lost in Wales. She must never feel unwanted again, and Alison would be happy to devote her life to making sure she never did.

Edith held out the large soft gift-wrapped parcel, and the child stood up with a rustle of paper from the corner where she'd unwrapped the Dickens novels she'd asked her parents for. Her movement, slow and graceful yet oddly tentative, and the sight of her – her eyes more withdrawn behind the long lashes than they used to be, the hint of a pout in the shape of her lips set firm now in an expression that looked constantly dissatisfied, her hair coiled tight on either side of her forehead – pierced Alison's heart, and she wanted to hug her as she had the night Derek had brought her back from Wales, hug her until the child knew how precious she was. But Rowan's gaze passed indifferently over her as the child glanced towards a noise at the window.

She was still nervous, Alison thought anxiously, and who wouldn't be after what she'd seen that night months ago? She turned to the window herself, but there was nothing except the abruptly grey day and an icy rain that was becoming sleet, large sad crystals shattering on the glass and trickling down it. She looked away as Rowan crossed the room. "Thank you, grandmama," Rowan said.

She sounded more old-fashioned than ever, and shouldn't that mean she was becoming more like herself again? They watched as she unwrapped the present, and Alison realised how tense all the family was, willing Rowan to enjoy herself. Derek asked Jo and Eddie if they'd like another drink, and then everyone was chatting, almost too eagerly. Eddie accepted a drink as Jo said they'd stayed long enough. "Oh, a pretty dress," Rowan declared. "Thank you."

"Try it on for us, sweetheart," Edith said.

Rowan bundled up the parcel and headed for the door. "Don't be silly, chick, you can undress in front of us," Jo cried.

That earned her a glance of such withering scorn that she covered her mouth and made a face, not quite comic enough to disguise her confusion. Rowan stalked upstairs, and Eddie murmured to Jo "Just let her alone, angel, let her be herself."

Derek gave Alison a wistful smile that meant he shared her hopes and fears and secret regrets that were still almost drowned in relief. Having Rowan back was all they deserved to expect, if not more than they had a right to. If she was no longer the child they had taken for granted then surely they were most to blame for that, but some nights Alison hardly slept for weeping quietly and telling herself to be grateful for what they had.

When they heard Rowan coming downstairs, everyone but Paul and Mary turned towards the door. As soon as she came in the women set about telling her how grown-up and elegant she looked in the long embroidered dress, and the men joined in less expertly. She did look grand, poignantly so, yet Alison was reminded of Hermione, not only because it was the kind of dress Hermione used to make but because she could imagine how dismayed Hermione would have been by Rowan's looking even more like Queenie. "She's only got books and a dress for Christmas," little Paul protested.

"That's because she's quite a bit older than you," Patty said. "You play with her a bit now, Mary. Just you remember how she gave you all her comics."

She seemed disconcertingly less mature than Rowan, especially since she was forcing the children on each other, Mary looking as reluctant to approach Rowan as Rowan was contemptuous of her. "I think we'll be going," Jo said and drained her glass. "We've kept you folk from your lunch long enough."

Alison watched her and Eddie and the children dash through the sleet and into their house. As they gained shelter she experienced an unexpected sense of longing, so intense that she stared about the street and the bedraggled garden. The cold, and the thought of being shut out in it, made her shiver. She closed the door hastily and went back down the hall.

Derek and her parents were carrying bowls of vegetables from the kitchen to the dining-room. Rowan was among her new books, and looked impatient, bored. Once she would have set the table, but she hadn't helped around the house since she had returned from Wales. They were going to have to discuss her unhelpfulness, Alison thought, but not today. "Come on, Rowan, join the family," she said.

By the time she took the turkey out of the oven, the heat of the biggest plate in the house penetrating her oven glove like a dull knife, they'd sorted out who sat where. Rowan had tried to sit at the head of the table until Edith shifted her with a joke. She obviously resented that and not being served first when Derek carved the turkey. "That's enough for me, thank you," she told him, so curtly that Edith gave her a look which would have been accompanied by an audible rebuke any day except Christmas. When Keith poured her a token glass of wine she disconcerted him by saying "Thank you, but I never drink."

"You used to have a sip as I recall," Keith said and frowned, perhaps wondering if his memory was growing senile or reminding himself of what she'd gone through since. "Clink your glass of milk with us, then. Here's to prosperity and happiness for us all in the years to come."

"Prosperity and happiness," the adults intoned over the chiming of glasses that touched an echo in the chandelier, and Rowan nodded as if acknowledging gratitude. "You've got those now, haven't you?" Edith said.

"Too right we have," Derek said, "thanks to Eddie for helping decorate the house and our estate agent for getting us a contractor who owed him a favour. And I got an accountant who's worth a lot more than that other prat, excuse me, and Ken who owed me all that money paid up just before he would have had to go to court. But nobody would have looked twice at the house if you hadn't done the garden, Keith."

"I only did the planning, old chap. You did nearly all the digging."

"I needed the break from doing my books. It'll be good to get back to Liverpool, and you don't mind changing schools again, babe, do you?"

Rowan glanced up when she realised he meant her. "I don't mind. I've no friends at this one."

"Well, just you make sure you find some in Liverpool," Edith cried.

Rowan stared at her with a blankness not unlike hostility, and Edith looked away. "Perhaps now you're doing well," she said to Alison, "I should be digging out my knitting patterns I bought when Rowan was on the way."

"Once we're settled, who knows?"

"I'd like to have a little sister, mummy," Rowan said. "I expect she'd be like me."

At least she was calling Alison mummy more readily now. Home from Wales, she'd been stiffly formal – not that Alison could blame her after all that she'd overheard – and then she'd begun to say "mummy" and "daddy" with what seemed to be concealed amusement, which Alison had found more hurtful still. Now she sounded so unexpectedly eager that Alison was confused, and lost control. "I liked having a sister," she said, and was close to tears until she realised what she was reminding Rowan of. She thought of Hermione, dead of being protective to the last, lying in the open grave while the night wind had its way with her, and Derek massaged her hands to keep her calm. After a while Keith cleared his throat. "I know what you're waiting for, Rowan. It's time we pulled the crackers."

She pulled one with him as if she was doing him a favour, and put on the party hat it contained. Her blank face beneath the paper crown distressed Alison, reminded her of Julius, the ageing child who'd occupied the side room at the hospital. Perhaps the sight upset Edith too. "Shall we have the curtains drawn?" she said abruptly. "I'm feeling cold."

The sleet on the window was losing its shape the instant it landed. Alison drew the curtains and went back to the table, where the conversation was becoming studiedly jolly. Rowan watched Keith dab gravy from his chin, watched Derek pick up a turkey leg to gnaw, and her contempt was almost palpable. She might have been a monarch tolerating her subjects, Alison thought in dismay: a queen with a paper crown.

After the pudding Rowan helped carry the plates to the kitchen, once Edith had suggested pointedly that she should. Later they played Monopoly on the dining-table. Alison had always liked playing board games with her family, but now Rowan scrutinised everyone else's moves as if she suspected them of cheating, and greeted any penalty she had to pay with a resentment that seemed almost dangerous. Alison was saddened to find she was glad when it was Rowan's bathtime, the day had left her so exhausted.

Ever since Derek had brought her home from Wales, Rowan had insisted on being left alone in the bathroom. Edith pursed her lips when she heard the child bolt the door, and was visibly uneasy until Rowan came downstairs, her brushed hair shining. "Let me do the honours tonight and read you your bedtime story," Keith said.

As soon as he was labouring upstairs after Rowan, Edith closed the door of the living-room. "Have you thought of seeing a doctor about her?"

"We did when I got her back," Derek said. "He was knocked out by how well she was doing."

"Then he couldn't have known her."

"She seems all right to me."

"How can you say that, Derek? What's become of her? I know she has to grow up, but I never expected her to turn out so much like—"

"She had to grow up, mummy, that's right," Alison interrupted. "We can't keep her a baby, can we? That's what Queenie tried to do to Hermione and me, and we don't want to be like Queenie."

"But Rowan used to be such a happy child. Call me overanxious if you like, but I wouldn't let her lock herself in the bathroom, particularly if there's anything sharp in there."

"Edith, love, that's the last thing we need to worry about," Derek said. "She's still getting over what happened, but I reckon I've never seen anyone who wanted to live more than she does."

Surely that will to live was worth all her sullenness and withdrawal, Alison tried to reassure herself. Besides, at times she seemed more like her old self, which might mean she was forgetting, though none of them knew precisely what she had to forget: Alison agreed with the doctor that they should let her choose her time to tell. When Derek had found her under the willow, the binoculars lying broken and rusty at her feet, she might have been hiding for hours. She must have smashed the binoculars in a rage at Vicky for taking or abandoning her there, and Alison was glad they hadn't even heard of the child since. She did her best to persuade Edith of all that. "Just don't leave her to herself so much she grows into someone you don't know," Edith said.

"I didn't, did I?" Alison reminded her, willing her to smile, and turned as Keith came in. "She fell asleep while I was droning to her," he said.

"I used to do that sometimes, remember?" Alison said. She poured everyone another festive drink, then went upstairs to check that Rowan wasn't troubled by dreams. Oddly enough, she had been sleeping more soundly since Derek had brought her back; she no longer talked in her sleep. She appeared to be deeply asleep now, her face upturned on the pillow in the midst of her spread hair, her long lashes shadowing her eyelids, her lips slightly parted, her fingers interlaced on the sheet over her chest. Alison covered her hands with the sheet and stooped to kiss her.

The night tapped at the window with melting fingernails, and Alison faltered, her hands sinking into the pillow on either side of Rowan's face. For a moment she thought Rowan wasn't asleep but watching her or at least aware of her. Worse, the prospect of kissing the child had made her shiver. She gazed at the smooth still face and bent to it as if she'd seized herself by the scruff of her neck, and planted a kiss on Rowan's forehead.

She whispered good night and went downstairs slowly, feeling ashamed to face her family. It seemed she had been so concerned about how Rowan's ordeal might have affected the child that she had failed to consider how the strain might have told on herself. She would have to keep watch on her feelings. If she was going to imagine things about Rowan, perhaps she would need treatment. It didn't matter what she went through so long as Rowan was safe.

CHAPTER THIRTY

"Happy Christmas, Rowan," her grandmother said, and Rowan told herself that her grandmother was pretending not to see her outside the window, prolonging the surprise they were planning to give her by turning and acknowledging her as if they hadn't realised she was there and running out to hug her tight before they carried her into the house. But her grandmother held out the parcel and gazed across the room, and in a few seconds that seemed to last as long as her entire trek home Rowan understood that her grandmother hadn't meant her. She felt herself beginning to fade like the sunlight that clouds were drowning as she saw herself step forward inside the room.

That isn't me, she tried to cry. You've all made a mistake, that's someone else who's tricked us. Mummy, look at me, why won't you look at me? Can't you see it's really me out here? Then her body that was stepping forward more elegantly than she ever used to looked straight at her. It was only a glance, yet it seemed to cling to her like dusty cobwebs and cover her with darkness colder than the shadow of the sky, for in that instant she saw Vicky looking at her out of Rowan's own face.

The look said that Rowan might as well not be there at all. Vicky had got what she wanted. Too late Rowan saw how everything Vicky had done with her up to the point where she had fallen in the graveyard had undermined her sense of herself. She'd trusted Vicky when Vicky had been the slyest liar of all: she'd made Rowan think her parents would be better off without her when all the time she had been plotting to take her place. Rowan wanted to fling herself through the window and confront the impostor, except that she was afraid she might pass through like a draught, with no substance and no control. Then her mother turned and looked at her.

If anything could give Rowan back to herself, surely that would. Rowan was afraid her mother would cry out with disbelief, but Rowan would tell her this was really herself, and the family would drive out the impostor – and then Rowan realised fully what she had become, for her mother stared straight through her and turned back to the child who was reaching for the parcel. The sunlight went out, and sleet that Rowan couldn't even feel slashed through her to shatter on the window.

So she was nothing. Even her feelings were suddenly more difficult to grasp, slippery and melting like the meaningless shapes of sleet on the glass. Her experiences since the graveyard were catching up with her: not only had the world around her turned into a dream that was often a nightmare, she had been little more than a dream of herself. As she realised that, her feelings grew exhausted, the exhaustion of her journey home, of being robbed of herself after all the time and effort she had spent. At least she could rest now she was home.

She wouldn't go to her room. Nobody wanted her there, and she wouldn't have gone near her bed even if it had been offered to her, now that her parents had given it to someone else. She would rather hide where it was darkest, sleep and sink into the dark on the top floor until perhaps she forgot who she had been. All that held her back was not knowing how to get into the house, unless she was scared of what she instinctively knew.

She watched the impostor unwrapping the parcel and lifting out a dress that once upon a time Rowan would have loved to wear. She was forgetting how jealousy felt, which seemed to promise that soon she would feel nothing at all. She watched her body take the dress out of the room, and lingered at the window. The thought that she would never see her mother and father again once she settled into the dark touched her with a distant sadness. She might have wept if she had been able to, but she could only feel thinner and more vulnerable. Her body came downstairs in its new dress and was admired by everyone, and then Jo and Eddie and their children made for the door.

As the five of them crowded out of the house and ran through the sleet, Rowan shrank back. The idea of their being somehow aware of her seemed agonisingly shameful, a feeling that cut through her as if the sleet were able to reach her after all. When her mother stared out of the porch under the splintering sky, Rowan huddled against the drenched wall of the house. She felt like a shadow full of sleet, but she didn't dare move until her mother closed the door.

The soaked dunes looked like mud now. The sky and the sea were a grey whirl of sleet with which she felt close to merging, being borne away in fragments on the wind. She drifted back to the window, but her family was blurred by the sleet that streamed through her onto the glass. She watched them and her body eat Christmas dinner, listened to everyone trying to make her body feel more welcome, until her mother came to the curtains and closed the light off from her.

Night was already massing like dark knives of ice, since this was almost the shortest day of the year. Rowan followed the light around the outside of the house from room to room, first to the kitchen and then the curtained living-room. Eventually the lights began to climb out of reach, to the bathroom and the room that had been hers. When the light in that room went out she knew her body was in her bed.

Would it dream? She wondered if the nightmare she'd had to struggle through in order to return had been Vicky's or her own, or a tangle of both. That confusion made her feel in danger of drifting back into the nightmare, until she concentrated on the house and made herself think of nothing else. Hours passed, and the sleet became thin icy rain. Lights climbed the house, bedrooms lit and were extinguished, and then the house was dark except for the lamps in the hallways.

Now that all the family must be falling asleep, the house no longer seemed to have sufficient presence for her to hold on to. She wanted to be inside, not cast out in the night that could turn into nightmare. She went to the porch door and gazed through the small latticed panes. Beyond them and the window of the inner door was the silvery hall, where suddenly she yearned to be. Her surge of yearning was stronger than her fear of making her way in. The next moment, easily as dreaming, she was in the hall.

The way the house felt came as a shock: old and stale, however new it looked. The silvery wallpaper on either side of her, and the new plaster on the staircase wall, were no more convincing than chalk sketches, already fading from the bricks. She didn't like the way the darkness of the house seemed to reach for her through the lamplit halls, but she was more afraid of the night outside. At least the dark here was familiar. She let herself go effortlessly to the stairs, and up.

She would have enjoyed the lack of effort if she had been dreaming, but it made reality feel slippery, made her feel closer to the darkness underlying the new paper and plaster. She settled on the first landing and gazed along the hall towards the room where her mother and father were. Another remnant of emotion flared in her. She wanted a last sight of them to take with her into the dark.

As soon as she thought of it, she was passing along the hall. She faltered by the door of the room that had been hers. Someone, presumably her mother, had left the door ajar. A dull helpless resentment and a compulsion to see what her enemy looked like in her sleep took her to the gap.

It was almost like seeing herself dead. Her still face was upturned on the pillow, the blankets were humped over her clasped hands. Only the slow rise and fall of the bedclothes showed that her body was alive. Rowan gazed at it until she felt she had forgotten how to move, until she began to feel trapped not by watching but by being watched. She felt as if her body had become the lair of the hidden ageing of the house. She was reminded of the shrunken thing she'd seen in the grave and afterwards; she felt as if it had become so shrunken that it could hide inside her body. The idea frightened her so much that it released her, and she fled to her parents' room.

Their door was ajar too. Rowan hesitated on the threshold; she didn't feel welcome enough to go in. Her parents were in bed, their backs to her. Her mother was closer to the door, one arm around Rowan's father, her face against his shoulder. Rowan watched them for a long time and hoped they felt safe in their dreams. She watched until she felt sure of remembering how they looked just then, together and untroubled. Perhaps dreaming of them in the dark would be like being with them. She ought to go up now, while the sight of them had made her feel peaceful. She was withdrawing from the doorway, lingering over her last sight of them, when her mother stirred restlessly. She let go of Rowan's father and turned towards the hall.

For a moment Rowan thought her mother was aware of her – that perhaps she was able to sense her because she was asleep. She shrank back until she realised that despite having moved, her mother was too deeply asleep to be aware of anything. Peace on Earth, Rowan thought with vague contentment, and then the sight of her mother seemed to lurch towards her as she saw how much older her mother looked.

She hadn't looked so old while she was awake, but she couldn't pretend in her sleep. She'd aged while Rowan was away, not by the months Rowan had taken to come back but by years. Her face looked pinched and lined and starved of colour, as if worry had dragged at it until the skin wore threadbare. Rowan wished she could give her just one kiss on the forehead to get rid of the lines that would always be there now, but what was the use of wishing? At least her parents had each other, and they would look after each other – but they couldn't keep each other safe when they didn't even know that their child was no longer their child.

Her father turned just then, groping blindly for her mother until his arm bent round her. The two sleeping faces lay on the pillows, aware of nothing outside themselves. Her father's wasn't as drawn as her mother's, but both seemed dreadfully vulnerable, at the mercy of the thing that was hiding inside Rowan's body. She couldn't bear to leave them like this. Somehow she had to waken them.

At once she was in the room, having slipped through the gap between door and frame without needing to sidle. This was the room she'd crept into during their first nights in the house, whose chilly emptiness had troubled her sleep. She'd snuggled between her parents and hidden from the huge dark. They had let her do that instead of telling her she was too old to be scared of the dark, and the memory made her feel closer to them, a closeness that ached. Might she even reach them while she felt like this? She went like a leaf on a wind towards the bed. She was almost there when she caught sight of the dressing-table mirror. The bed and her parents and the stretch of carpet leading to the door were in the mirror, but there was no sign of her.

That snatched away the last of her sense of herself. She was shrinking like a picture on a television that had just been switched off, she was being dragged towards a pinpoint by the nothingness on the far side, and the smaller she grew, the less strength she had to resist. There was nothing to hold her, nothing to contradict the absence of herself the mirror was displaying with a cold glassy glare like ice that was fixing her absence forever.

Then her parents stirred again. They moved apart and lay on their backs, their faces slack. They looked even more helpless, each of them alone in sleep. At least the dismay that seized her managed to hold her there in the room. She turned away from the mirror, blotted it out of her awareness, and tried to feel as if she were leaning rather than sinking bodilessly towards the bed. She was so close to her mother that she could see how dry her slightly parted lips were, how they trembled minutely with each breath. She could see veins sketched on her mother's forehead, under the skin that looked fragile and worn. Behind the long eyelashes her mother's eyelids looked bruised, and uneasy with a dream; a drop of moisture glistened at one corner. Rowan was suddenly desperate to hold her and be held. Without thinking, she stooped to kiss her mother's lips.

She jerked back just in time from the imminent sensation of falling and being unable to stop. Why was there so little of her, when Vicky had seemed so real? She mustn't give in to the sense of being outcast and bodiless. All she had to do was make her parents realise she was here, because then they must know that the creature they had taken for her was something else.

But when she tried to call out to them she couldn't even hear herself.

She tried to feel that she was standing by the bed instead of hovering beside it, in case that allowed her to reach out and touch them, but that didn't work; she wasn't even able to judge how close she was, since she couldn't see herself reaching. If she touched her mother, she might sink into her. The idea seemed warm and comforting, almost unbearably so, but it wouldn't keep her mother safe. She tried to scream at her parents and her helplessness instead, scream at her parents to waken while she was still there.

Trying to scream only made her more aware that she no longer had a mouth. She could feel the mirror reaching coldly for her, the nothingness beyond the mirror waiting to draw her in. She tried to hold on to the sight of the lit room that used to be her refuge. She remembered snuggling between her parents under the blankets and murmuring to her mother, who was always the one who wakened. "It's me, mummy. Can I stay with you tonight? It's too dark out there. I'm frightened." The memory was achingly intense, so intense that she could hear her own voice in her mind, the voice she hadn't heard for so long. "It's me, mummy. It's only me."

And then her mother's face turned towards her, eyes flickering within the eyelids as if they were fighting to see. Her mother's hands struggled out of the blankets and groped clumsily towards her. "Oh, Rowan, it *is* you, isn't it?" she said in a voice clogged by sleep. "I thought I was going mad."

CHAPTER THIRTY-ONE

On Boxing Day the family went for a stroll by the sea. The day was piercingly clear. The dunes were still pockmarked by yesterday's sleet, but the sea had drawn into itself all the pools the downpour had left on the beach. A few distant ships glinted beneath the cold bright blue sky from which seagulls fell like shards of ice. The men and Rowan led the way along the concrete promenade while Edith held on to Alison's arm and chatted about old times, the days she and Keith had spent across the river at New Brighton when there had been a pier and a fairground and a tower, when there had been a ferry to bring them back to Liverpool and the overhead railway along the dock road. "Happy days," she sighed, and Alison nodded and murmured agreement and stared ahead, barely hearing her mother. Perhaps she had been right in the first place about herself, perhaps she'd told herself the truth last night on the edge of wakefulness. Perhaps she really was going mad.

She gazed at Rowan's back and winced from her own feelings. The child was wearing the long dress Keith and Edith had bought her for Christmas, its hem swaying beneath her duffel coat. She was holding her father's hand and Keith's, and strolling gracefully. The combination of elegance and childishness made Alison's eyes moist, but did she deserve to feel that way? Suppose Derek had been right, and there was madness in the family, surfacing in her because she hadn't been able to cope with her fears while Rowan was lost in Wales? Perhaps she had been so riddled with the fear that Rowan might be dead that she was secretly unable to believe she had come back – but there could be no excuse for her suspecting her own child.

Yet she couldn't dismiss what she'd thought she had heard last night and what she had certainly seen. She'd heard Rowan calling her, sounding more like Rowan than she had for months, and the child had seemed so close that Alison had wondered why she was unable to touch her. She'd felt a surge of love for Rowan as intense as she'd experienced when Rowan had first been laid in her arms, and she'd murmured to her, welcoming her back as she blinked away sleep and opened her eyes. She had been so convinced she would see Rowan that the deserted room had looked like a dream from which she had yet to waken. The room had been real enough to make her eyes sting as she stared at it, and she'd been telling herself sadly that Rowan's voice had been the dream when she'd heard it again. "It's me, mummy. It's me."

Could it have been the last trace of a dream? She'd waited breathlessly to hear it again, until she'd realised that she felt as if Rowan were still calling her from beyond the door. Carefully, so as not to waken Derek, Alison had slipped out of bed and tiptoed to Rowan's room.

When she'd eased the door open she had been ready to sit with Rowan, to talk her back to sleep. Just then there had been nothing she would rather do, for she'd realised what she had missed most since the child had come back: feeling as if Rowan needed her, even a little. But there was Rowan, lying quite still and untroubled, and at first Alison hadn't understood why the sight had made her quail. Then she had realised what she was seeing, and she'd dug her knuckles into her mouth. Rowan had been lying in precisely the position she'd assumed when Alison had tucked her up in bed, hours earlier.

That wasn't like any child asleep, let alone like Rowan. She had been lying like a corpse – like Queenie's corpse. Alison had hung on to the doorframe for support, gripping it until she'd thought she felt it shift. The notion that the child in the bed wasn't Rowan, whatever she looked like, had seemed to illuminate the last few months with a clarity that made Alison's mind feel seared. She'd pushed herself away from the doorway at last and had crept into bed as if she could hide from her thoughts, telling herself that it was just the night that was telling her stories, that she couldn't think such things in daylight. But she had, and she'd been watching Rowan all day, waiting for proof.

She wanted to be proved wrong, she told herself. She wanted someone to catch her watching and ask why, and tell her how absurd she was being when she owned up. They'd tell her she was worse than Hermione for wondering why Rowan no longer let anyone see her naked: didn't she want the child to grow up? If Rowan seemed increasingly like Queenie, that must mean she'd needed her hereditary wilfulness to help her cope with that night in Wales. Good riddance to Vicky who Hermione had thought was Queenie, and what did it matter where she'd gone? What was Alison trying to suggest that she didn't dare put into words? Out here in the sunlight, where the shadows of the nursing homes pointed at her, Alison felt exposed to herself. That was Rowan ahead of her, and any other notion was grotesque; where else did she think the child could be – in the empty sky, on the stained dunes, in the shallow waves that plucked at the beach? Thinking that made her feel disloyal, cruel, more confused than ever.

When her mother grasped her arm more firmly Alison grew tense, waiting for her to demand what was wrong. But her mother said "Step out a bit and let's catch them up. We'll have them thinking we're past it."

Rowan and the men were nearly at the houses that marked the end of the promenade, where they would have either to turn back or continue along the beach. Suddenly Alison thought how she could prove herself wrong, and she was about to tell Edith when, for no apparent reason, Rowan and the men stopped short of the houses.

The day seemed to freeze around Alison as if it had become a photograph, pitilessly bright and unchallengeable. She was certain she'd seen Rowan halt the men. Rowan had stiffened as if she knew without looking back that Alison was about to speak – as if she knew what Alison would say. Alison swallowed dryly and stammered "Actually, I'm getting a headache. You catch them up and I'll go back."

She spoke so that only Edith could hear, and stared at Rowan's back. Her heart shuddered then, for Rowan turned at once, her face blank, and tugged at Keith's hand. "What's the problem?" he called.

"Alison's off home to nurse her head. I'll walk along with you if you give me the chance."

"We'll all go back," Derek said, and Alison was sure that Rowan was tugging his hand. "You shouldn't have let us tire you out, Edith. We aren't all as young as our Rowan."

Rowan's face stayed blank. Alison thought of a mask behind which a puppeteer was hiding while she worked the men. That seemed crazier than ever, but surely that meant she needed to be away from Rowan, to sort out her thoughts if she could. "My mother isn't tired, she wants to carry on, don't you?" Alison pleaded. "I won't be able to relax if I think I've spoiled your walk. At least you take Rowan a bit further, Derek. She needs the exercise after being inside for so long."

"We'll go on at least a little further," Edith said. "You deserve a rest before you go back to work."

Alison hugged her and let go immediately, in case Edith sensed that something was wrong. As she swung towards the house, her head began to ache. She took a dozen steps and glanced over her shoulder. The others were strolling down to the beach. Just as she glanced at them, Rowan looked back at her. Her face was too distant to be read, but Alison felt discovered, shamefaced, more paranoid than ever. She urged herself home, almost running.

The promenade was deserted. A breeze slashed across the dunes and seemed to sprinkle her legs with sand and ice. Ripples like cracks spread across the fringe of the sea. There was no other movement near her, and she felt alone and deluded, robbed of her child by her own doubts. The glare of sea and sand and concrete pierced her eyes, but she mustn't just lie down when she reached the house: she might be able to show herself the truth.

She slid her key into the lock and drew a breath that made her head swim. She turned the key, which numbed her fingers, and pushed the front door inwards. She stepped across the threshold and halted, gripping the edge of the door.

The house wasn't empty. Rowan was there, washing dishes in the kitchen or tidying her room, writing notes for her parents to find, reading so quietly that you mightn't know where she was until you heard her laugh. If all this was just a memory, it felt like a presence Alison had failed to be aware of. It felt as though Rowan had been with her all the way along the promenade, hoping to be noticed when they were alone. Closing the door behind her, Alison paced along the hall.

The sight of the deserted rooms didn't make her feel closer to Rowan, nor did the smell of stale books that lingered in the house – but she had something that would. She ran upstairs to her bedroom and rummaged in her handbag for the note. *Dear mummy and daddy, I love you and I realy dont mind if you dont buy me things becose you cant aford them...* It was her last link with Rowan as she used to be. She blinked fiercely as her vision blurred. The note should help her see the truth.

She was at Rowan's door when she had the panicky notion that Rowan was already home and waiting for her, the new contemptuous watchful Rowan. She flung the door open and stalked in, appalled to feel she was venturing into a lair. She hurried to the window and pushed up the staggery sash, in the hope that she would hear when the family was close, and then she began to search.

She found the diary almost at the bottom of a pile of books. All the spines were turned to the wall. It seemed a cunning way to hide the diary without appearing to do so, she thought, and heard her paranoia like a shrill whisper in her head. Much as she'd wanted to read what Rowan might have written about her last night in Wales, she had never asked; she would never have considered reading the diary without asking – but if it could prove her wrong, surely she mustn't hesitate.

She sat on the bed and laid Rowan's note on her lap, and found that she was afraid to open the diary. Her throat felt parched by a smell of stale paper, her hands were cramped by dread. She made herself a vow: the diary would show her the truth, and she would act on whatever she found; if it proved her wrong she would seek treatment while her parents were here. She turned the diary over and let the blank pages scrape past her thumb until writing appeared. She forced herself not to close her eyes, to see what was there, the truth.

It was the entry for Christmas Day. *Today I got three books by Dickens and a new dress. Then we had Christmas lunch and pulled crackers. Later on we played a bored game and I won, and then it was time for me to go to bed.*

Alison blinked rapidly, and hardly knew what she was feeling. The tone of the diary was so cold that it didn't even mention who had bought the presents, and yet there before her eyes was all the evidence she could ask for. The paragraph in the diary and Rowan's note were in exactly the same handwriting.

So that was that: the truth. The child who'd written the last entry was the only Rowan now, and that was what Alison hadn't been able to cope with, perhaps because she blamed herself for losing the child she had brought up and loved. Rowan was growing up, away from her, and Alison could hardly blame her. As for herself, perhaps the treatment wouldn't be too drastic, since she was facing the truth. She closed the window, shivering at a breeze that felt as if it had frozen hope. Thank heaven she had noted where the diary came from – the child must already feel spied on. Alison gave the diary and the note beside it a last look, as if that might help her relinquish the past and accept Rowan as she was now.

Then she jerked as if someone unseen had caught hold of her. The sensation vanished before she could be sure she had felt it, faded like a snowflake, except that its touch had been warm. It might have been the shock of realisation she experienced as she stared at the pages on the bed. She let out a moan of hope or despair. It wasn't over. She had almost missed seeing what the pages showed.

She sat down so heavily that the bed creaked, and leafed through the diary, her fingers shaking. She found the last entry Rowan had written in Wales, about a photograph of Vicky that Hermione had shown her. Most of the subsequent dates had entries: how she was glad to be home, how most of the books in the school library weren't worth her attention, how Miss Frith pretended to know more than she really did... The only emotion they expressed was impatience, and impatience had betrayed the writer. In the earliest entries the spelling was as erratic as always, but by yesterday Rowan was able to spell Christmas and crackers and sometimes. It wasn't possible. Rowan might enjoy reading Dickens, but Alison should have realised that she couldn't spell his name.

Alison clenched her fists to make her fingers work, and leafed through the diary again. The spelling improved as the entries came up to date. The progress might have been convincing if it hadn't been so rapid, but now even the token misspelling of board game looked insultingly obvious, if indeed it was a misspelling at all. The writer had grown tired of the pretence, or perhaps she couldn't bear to seem to spell as inaccurately as Rowan had.

Alison folded the note and closed it inside the diary. She put the diary in her handbag, which she hung over her arm. For the moment she felt nothing but a mounting sureness that made Rowan seem closer, the Rowan whom she'd borne and loved, however imperfectly, and whom she wanted to come back to her. She'd vowed to see the truth and act on it, and deep in her heart she knew there was only one explanation for the changes in the diary and in Rowan. But if she believed that, she had reason to be as nervous as she was growing. She was wondering why, when the child out there had seemed to know what Alison was planning, she hadn't tried harder to prevent her from coming back to the house.

CHAPTER THIRTY-TWO

Derek thought Alison was about to speak when Edith came into the living-room and said "Rowan wants you, Derek."

Alison bent her head to Edith's magazine and retreated into silence. "What were you going to say, Ali?" he said.

"It'll wait. You go up and find out what she wants."

She sounded too bright, like a radio with the treble turned right up, and he didn't like it at all. First he should see about Rowan. She was lying in bed, hands folded on the blankets, head raised slightly by the pillow. As he stepped into the bedroom her eyes turned to him, and he had a disconcerting notion that he should have knocked before entering. "What's up, babe?" he said.

She seemed to find that overly familiar. Even when he'd found her in the graveyard she had been aloof, reluctant to let him hug her, and since then he hadn't often tried. She raised her clasped hands as if she were praying and leaned towards him with an intimacy he no longer expected. "Will grandmama be staying in?"

"She will, and your mother. You know we'd never leave you alone in the house."

"I know mother will be. But grandmama will too."

"That's what I said. Why are you asking?"

She gazed at him as if he ought to know. Worse, he thought he did. "You go to sleep now, all right? Everyone loves you," he said awkwardly, and stooped to kiss her forehead. It was cold, and wrinkled as his lips touched it. When he looked back from the doorway, her eyes were closed. He hurried downstairs, full of a protective rage and praying that he needn't feel that way.

"What did she want?" Alison said, too casually.

"Just making sure we weren't all going out, as if we would. What did you want before?"

"Only to remind you not to get my father too drunk. Remember they have to drive home the day after tomorrow."

Derek sensed that she was concealing at least as much as he was. It seemed a denial of everything they'd shared and built together since before they were married. He could feel his dismay swelling into words, forcing his lips open, and then Keith said "Come on, let the poor man show me his local. I haven't had a proper talk with him all Christmas."

She wanted Derek to be closer to her family, after all. He wanted it himself, though not under these circumstances. He followed Keith into the night, where a wind swooped down like a sluicing of ice from the roofs. Pinched edges of foam rose jerkily on the dark bay, ships flared like heaps of coal as they pitched through the waves. In the pub Keith's glasses clouded over. Derek bought the beer while Keith wiped the lenses and muttered "I hope you aren't going to be difficult, you two" and a tape sang "God Rest Ye Merry Gentlemen" through speakers draped with streamers in all the alcoves of the bar. Keith sat behind the fruit machine and clinked tankards with Derek. "Well, that's another year nearly over and the world's still in one piece."

"And most of us still are," Derek responded, and was wondering how to sidle towards the subject they had to discuss when someone gripped his shoulder. "Stag night, is it?" Eddie said.

He put down his tankard and roved not quite steadily around the neighbouring tables in search of a chair. "To tell you the truth, Eddie," Derek called, "this is sort of a family conference."

"Where's the rest of them, already under the table? I thought you never talked about them, too perfect or something. Don't worry, I'm going, I won't show you up in front of your arty gardener, though you were glad enough to know me when your mansion needed decorating." He picked up his tankard and raised it towards them with exaggerated dignity. "Don't mind us," he said to Keith as if each word were a toffee he had to unstick from his teeth. "We're always going on like this."

When he'd swayed away Keith said "Are you?"

"It's news to me."

"He could join us by all means. Unless you really want a private word, in which case I'll stop droning." He frowned encouragingly at Derek and supped a mouthful of beer. "If Edith and I can help in any way, you've only to ask."

"That's kind of you, Keith. You're a good friend." He was also Alison's father, and how might he react to what Derek had to say? "It's how we've been since things went wrong, how that left us." He took a gulp of beer to wash away the taste of inadequacy. "Maybe you've noticed."

"There's always the future, old chap. I think you have the kind of marriage that rebuilds itself, even if your troubles make you think you can't stand each other sometimes. Is that what you mean? Just last night Edith and I were saying how well we thought you were coping."

"Yesterday I'd have agreed with you."

"I see it's hard for you to talk, old son, but I can't help unless you tell me."

Derek almost drained his tankard. He let the blurry warmth of alcohol sail into his brain, then waved Keith down as he made to buy another round. "Wait and I'll tell you. It's Alison. I think what happened upset her more than she's letting on."

"It might have, don't you think? After all, she lost her sister and may have thought she'd lost her only child." His eyes clouded until he blinked away the memory of his bereavement. "But it can't be good for her not to share her feelings with you. If Edith and I hadn't helped each other over losing our Hermione I don't know where we'd be. I'll have a quiet word with Alison if you think that would serve."

"We mightn't want her to know we've been talking. She's got sort of mistrustful. I don't think she believes Rowan has really come back."

Disconcertingly, Keith looked relieved. "What makes you say so?"

"Didn't you see how she was watching her today?"

"I may have now you mention it. Let me replenish your mug. I should tell you now it wouldn't be the first time with Alison, so cheer up."

Derek stared after him while he waited at the bar to be served. A large bald man tore mouthfuls out of a turkey sandwich and fed the fruit machine, which chirped like a ravenous bird. Keith returned at last, balancing tankards. "Not the first time," Derek prompted urgently.

"No. No, I don't think it is." Keith set his tankard and then himself down gently. "When Alison was three Hermione had to spend some time in hospital, and her mother stayed with her, of course. You had to make a fuss to do that in those days, and the hospital wouldn't let Alison go visiting, out of spite, we thought. Anyway, when they came home Alison was very wary of Hermione and not a great deal better with their mother. We found out she thought that when you'd been anaesthetised you could be someone else when you came round. Hermione had to remind her of things the two of them had done together. I'd say it was being separated from her mother and Hermione that made Alison feel that way, and I'm sure the same applies now and she'll get over it, don't you think?"

"But she isn't a child any more."

"No more than the rest of us, at any rate. Still, can't you see why she might feel uneasy with Rowan? Rowan's not the child she was, and I think we can understand why. Perhaps you should let Alison know you sometimes feel the way she does."

Derek felt as if he had to tear down a wall between himself and Keith without knowing what the wall might be supporting. "But I don't," he cried. "She doesn't just think Rowan's not herself, she thinks Rowan's somewhere else. She talks to her when she's not there, for God's sake."

"Yes, but that needn't mean—"

"I haven't told you what happened last night. I woke up and she was sitting up in bed, and then she started talking. She said 'Rowan, it's you' to the empty room, do you understand? Then she got up and I sneaked a look at her, and believe me, she was wide awake. She went along to Rowan's room and I heard her stop outside, and I'm telling you, Keith, if she'd gone in I'd have been there like a shot, the way she looked. Maybe you think I'm exaggerating." He faltered, feeling cruel to the old man. "Except do you know why Rowan called me upstairs before? She wanted to be sure her grandmother was staying in. She's afraid to be left alone with her mother."

He still hadn't told Keith the worst – that he'd heard Alison say she thought she was going mad. Keith raised his eyebrows and blinked at his knuckles, and then he said "Would you like us to stay longer?"

"I don't think Rowan's actually in danger. I can't believe that."

"Alison might know we've been discussing her if we change our plans, you mean."

So this was how it felt to be one of the family, sharing thoughts and each other's distress. He'd gained a relative, but what might he be losing? "Or if Rowan went home with you while I try and sort things out," he said.

"We'll have her any time you like, you know that. I only wonder what you have in mind for Alison."

That was exactly what Derek dreaded putting into words. "Maybe she'd talk to the doctor. I would as well if it helps. He might give her stuff to take, do you reckon?"

"That sounds about right to me, old son," Keith said, but his obvious relief made him less reassuring. "This must have been building up since that business with poor Hermione. I expect Christmas brought it to a head because Alison will be missing her."

"You don't think she's blaming Rowan for what happened to Hermione?"

"God knows how her mind may be working with all this death and stress. I do wonder if we shouldn't have Edith talk to her."

"It ought to be me. I only wanted to check with you."

"I'm glad you did. I feel I know you better and like what I know. I won't tell Edith until we're home or you might never see the last of us. Maybe things will improve once we're out of the way and Alison can devote more time to Rowan. But any time of day or night you need to get in touch, one of us is bound to be awake."

Derek drained his tankard and stood up to buy another round. Having someone to confide in seemed to have helped more than he'd dared to hope. "Just look after them both, as if I needed to tell you," Keith said as if there could be no question of protecting one at the expense of the other. The crowd at the bar pressed around Derek, their smoky breaths massed overhead and dimmed the lights, and he prayed he wouldn't have to make that choice.

CHAPTER THIRTY-THREE

Left alone, the women talked about the family. Edith wished Richard had joined them for Christmas – nobody should be alone at this time of year – but when Alison had called him he'd declined with a calm she'd taken to be sorrow that he wanted to preserve undisturbed. He hadn't been at Hermione's funeral. Hermione's cottage was for sale, the proceeds to be divided equally between her sister and her parents according to her will, and Edith thought they should all spend some of the bequest on a Spanish holiday. "Then at least some good will come of all this grief." Alison murmured as agreeably as she could without committing herself so far into the future when she didn't know where the present would lead. She poured large drinks despite her mother's token protests, and was glad when her mother turned to reminiscing about Alison's childhood: at least the past was over, no longer threatening. It was a while before she wondered if her mother was avoiding the subject of Rowan.

Was she nursing the doubts she'd had on Christmas Day? She had been afraid for Rowan, though only that the child might harm herself. She'd thought they should take Rowan to the doctor because of the way she had changed, because she seemed too old for her years, too much like Queenie. Alison had done her best to dissuade her mother, but now she hoped she'd failed. She was sure that the longing for reassurance she felt wasn't hers alone. She was thinking of a way to resurrect the subject when Edith did; at least, she cocked her head towards the door. "Has Rowan come downstairs?"

For a moment Alison thought that the intruder had come to prevent her from speaking to Edith, and then she realised that she didn't feel at all nervous. "Did you hear something?" she said.

"Not exactly. You can just feel when someone's there, can't you?"

"Of course you can," Alison said, willing her to be receptive. "I expect you were right. Go and see."

She held her breath as her mother went to the door. Edith touched the handle and bent her head towards the upper panels, and then she snatched the door open. Alison glimpsed movement beyond it, and her heart seemed to twist like a knife – but it was the reflection of the door on the silvery wallpaper. Edith glanced both ways along the hall and looked dissatisfied. "I was sure she was here. Let me see if she's nipped back upstairs."

"I'll come with you."

Edith glanced sharply at her and made for the stairs. Couldn't she sense the yearning that seemed to fill the whitewashed stairway, the yearning to be noticed? She hesitated in sight of the next floor, then shook her head as if to convince herself the corridor was empty. She tiptoed to Rowan's room and peered in, and stiffened.

Alison went quickly to her side and saw what she was seeing: Rowan's body lying face up in the bed, hands folded on its chest, the way it always slept now. "My dear lord," Edith whispered, "she looks just like—"

She was ready for the truth. It was time to show her the diary. Alison steered her away from the door, pretending that the occupant of the bed was unaware of them. She put her finger to her lips and ushered Edith to the stairs, bracing herself to speak once they were in the living-room. But she hadn't reached the downstairs hall when she realised that she couldn't tell her mother.

Lance had known something, and he was dead. Hermione had known a great deal, and so was she. How could Alison put anyone, let alone her mother, in such danger? Just now she didn't want to think what risks she might be taking herself. In the living-room she smiled carefully at Edith as they reached for their drinks, but Edith demanded "Did you see her? Did you see how she was sleeping?"

"She always has, mummy." Alison felt disloyal, both to Rowan and her mother. "At least, ever since she was a toddler."

"Well, I've never seen it before." Her mother pursed her lips and put down her glass. "What aren't you telling me? We've never been able to pretend with each other."

"I'm just trying to stop you worrying when you needn't, mummy, that's all. What does it matter how she sleeps so long as she's able to? She's back with us, isn't she? What else could we possibly want?"

Her mother gave her a long look. Eventually she picked up her glass and held it out for a refill, and turned the conversation back to Wales, where Gwen and Elspeth had taken over Hermione's shop. Now and then she glanced towards the door, and Alison found herself praying that she would think she was only imagining a presence. She was glad when Keith and Derek came back, until she saw how deliberately they were chatting and realised they had been discussing her.

She had to persuade them that nothing was wrong, or they mightn't leave her alone with the child. She wished they could all confront the intruder, but even as a family they might be too much at risk, though it seemed ludicrous and demeaning to be so wary of a child. "Coffee for two?" she said lightly, and headed for the kitchen. A sense that they were listening to be sure she didn't sneak up to Rowan's bedroom made her want to laugh and weep.

She was in bed with Derek, both of them pretending to be asleep, when she realised that he must have heard her last night after all. Perhaps he thought she was going mad. She wanted to hug him tight and talk to him until he believed her, she wanted to recoil from him for thinking that about her, but all she could do for his sake was lie still, cursing the intruder in the next room for separating her from him. Wasn't she herself as much to blame, for failing to heed her sister? But someone was telling her that it didn't matter now, someone close to her in the room, closer if she shut her eyes. Someone loved her for what she was, and that soothed her to sleep.

In the morning she was dismayed to think of leaving Rowan in the unwelcoming house with the intruder. "Come with me," she whispered when there was nobody else to hear. As she drove to the hospital she kept glancing at the passenger seat, hoping to see what she could already feel. Once, as misty sunlight flashed from a side street and through the car, she thought she glimpsed Rowan's face smiling wistfully at her. It vanished instantly, like a star so distant you couldn't be sure you had ever seen it.

All the children in the ward wanted to show Alison their presents, and Rowan seemed to merge with the way they were demanding Alison. Throughout the day she found herself distracted from her patients by trying to feel that Rowan was still there, not lost in the corridors that smelled too much like Queenie's sickroom. It wasn't fair to the patients or to Rowan. She couldn't go on like this.

At home Derek and her parents were eager to tell her how well Rowan had behaved all day. She was glad they didn't suspect and saddened by their determination to convince her. "I know you're there," she reassured Rowan silently as the eyes of the child of the house stared at her, blank with triumph.

That night she dreamed she lost Rowan. She was in Liverpool for the sales, struggling through the crowd that filled the street of shops from wall to wall and eddied sluggishly around the traders' stalls and open suitcases. She was thinking that at least Rowan needn't struggle to keep up with her when she realised that Rowan was no longer there. She glanced about wildly as if she could see Rowan, she craned her body to see over the masses of faces indifferent as masks, she cried Rowan's name as she thought she heard her voice beyond the wordless murmur of the crowd, she tried to force her way through the crowd that was packed too tightly now to let her pass. Soon someone would offer to help her search for her lost child, and when she admitted that they couldn't see her they would burst out laughing, the whole streetful of people, laughing so loud and so cruelly that they would drive Rowan away for ever. Alison woke trembling, icy with sweat, knowing that the dream was hardly even an exaggeration of the truth.

Her parents left before dawn to avoid some of the traffic. "I hope we'll see you all soon, Derek. And just you look after our Alison, she's all we've got now," Edith said with a misty dragon breath.

"Keep in touch," Keith told him and stopped in the act of shaking his hand, for Rowan had appeared in the silvery hall.

"Go back to bed," Alison cried, in a rage at the sight of Rowan's body not even being allowed to sleep. "Say goodbye to your grandmother and grandfather and then go back until it's time to get up."

Alison hugged her parents and made herself let go, and watched the car's red lights shrink, turn the corner, vanish. The child was just behind her on the pavement, gazing at the stars that the approaching dawn had begun to extinguish. Her breaths stained the air grey, and filled Alison with sudden loathing: they weren't Rowan's breaths. "Get inside when you're told," she almost screamed.

"Try and get a bit more beauty sleep, babe, not that you need it," Derek said and pushed the child gently into the house, though Alison was sure she stiffened as he touched her. "Don't be too hard on her, Ali," he murmured as they heard her footsteps overhead. "She's been through a lot, remember. I know you have too, but let's just try and be glad we got her back, all right?"

"I will be," Alison said, aching with the impossibility of telling him more of the truth. She took his hand as they went back to bed for an hour. She wanted to make love to him, to bring them closer, but she couldn't when she sensed that Rowan had taken refuge in their room. They lay in each other's arms as the dawn draped the sky with gold. Rowan was part of her calm, which felt like a wall that shut out the intruder in the next room. It couldn't last, but perhaps it was a promise, and she kept it secret and safe when the alarm warned her it was time to go to work.

She was brushing her teeth when the phone rang downstairs. She hurried down, but it had been the school, for Derek. "Vandals have been at the electrics. Rowan won't want to come with me, so she'll have to stay at Jo's."

"All right," Alison said, hushing her thoughts furiously, making her face into an agreeable mask. "Will you take her over? I'd better be heading for work."

She scraped the silvery ferns off the windows of her car and prayed that it would start. While she pumped the pedal and listened to the spluttering of the engine she had time to watch Derek hurry the child across to Jo's. At last the car lurched juddering towards the main road. She drove for half an hour at random through the thawing streets, past parked cars with blinded windows and children skating on the pavements, and then she turned back towards the house.

As she came to the crest of the overpass beside the bay, sunlight pierced the car from back to front. In the dazzle beside her she glimpsed Rowan's face. Rowan looked anxious, close to fear. "We'll be all right," Alison murmured fiercely as the glimpse was extinguished. She parked the car outside the house and called the hospital to say she was too ill to come to work, which she had never done before in her life, and then she strode across to Jo's to fetch the child.

CHAPTER THIRTY-FOUR

The vandalism wasn't as bad as Derek had feared, at least as far as his work was concerned. Rewiring the school had been his most demanding job so far, especially in disentangling the labyrinth of wires the original builders had buried in the plaster. The school governors wouldn't let him wait until the holidays, presumably because they wanted to reassure parents that the school was being made safe after the accident that had gained him the job. It had taken him almost a month of nights and weekends. The job had made his reputation locally and brought him all the work he could handle, but now he realised he'd seen far less of Alison and Rowan than he should have when they'd needed him.

The deputy headmistress came across the schoolyard as Derek climbed out of the car. A glazier was repairing a window by the infants' entrance. "Thank you for coming so promptly," the deputy, a thin woman in a purple track suit, said to Derek. "I hope this hasn't sabotaged any plans you had for today."

"No, you're okay." He followed her into the school. Children's paintings had been torn off classroom walls: someone had set fire to a pile of them in an open desk. "Stupid bastards," he muttered.

"Thank heaven for children like yours. Not that most are bad. There's always been a minority like this."

"Rowan's doing all right then, is she?"

The deputy smirked as if she took him to be joking. "Considerably better than that, Mr Faraday. Hasn't Miss Frith let you know how impressively she's done these past few months? Our only fear is that she may grow bored."

"You heard what she went through? I suppose her teacher's making allowances for that."

"Miss Frith didn't need to. In all my years in the profession I've never seen a child so mature. You've nothing to worry about there, if I may say so." She stepped aside as they reached the assembly hall. "I believe this is what you'll need to look at."

All the lights were smashed, and someone had pulled down a wire and a chunk of plaster. The pointless stupidity dismayed him. Rowan would never do anything like this, he thought as he discovered that the vandals had stuffed the wall sockets with plasticine and tipped a bucket of water over the fuse box. Perhaps when Alison heard about all this it might help her accept the way Rowan was developing. He brought the old hairdryer from the car and used it to dry the box before he replaced the fuses, then he unscrewed the fronts of the wall sockets so as to poke out the plasticine. He'd replaced the wire and was packing his tools before he went to mix some plaster when he heard a woman's footsteps hurrying down the corridor behind him. "Nearly finished," he called. "Could have been worse."

The footsteps halted, and the silence made him glance back, the snapped wire dangling from his hand. The woman in the corridor was Jo. Apprehension brought him to his feet so clumsily he kicked the box of tools away. "Where's Rowan?"

"Alison took her."

That jerked his nerves tighter, and he found it hard to speak. "I thought she was at work. Where've they gone?"

"Back to your house."

Derek grabbed the toolbox and made for the corridor so quickly that Jo flinched. "She's Rowan's mother. I couldn't stop her," she said defensively, and as if she wanted to deny her reason for coming to him "I thought you should know, that's all."

CHAPTER THIRTY-FIVE

As Alison reached Jo's gate the children in the house fell silent. Wind hissed through the sharp grass on the dunes under the grey sky and made her shiver, but most of what she felt was a determination so fierce that she grew a little afraid of herself. She could no longer sense Rowan beside her. Perhaps fear of the child in Jo's house had driven her into hiding. The thought made Alison feel cold and hard as metal. She strode up the short path and rang the doorbell.

Jo was wearing a housecoat and slippers. She opened the door halfway and stopped it with her foot. "Now you see how us ladies of leisure dress when we aren't receiving guests," she said like one of the historical romances she enjoyed reading. "Aren't you at work?"

"I was mistaken. I'll take her home now."

Jo didn't step back. "Nothing's the matter, is there?" Alison said sweetly. "Can't I come in? I won't be shocked by anything I see, I promise, even if you haven't tidied up after the monsters."

"Come in for a chat and a cup of something if you like," Jo said, her face reddening. "But really, you can leave her, I don't mind. They're playing."

"It sounded to me as if they were arguing." As Alison marched along the hall into the main room she had time for one deep breath that stiffened her chest and her throat. "Say goodbye, miss. You and I are overdue for a talk."

The child was sitting at the table, Paul and Mary at her feet. She raised her head unhurriedly and stared at Alison. "I'm playing hangman with them."

"You would be, wouldn't you?" Alison saw that she wasn't even taking the trouble to ensure that her look of innocence was convincing.

"I'm sure they can manage without you now," she said, forcing her teeth not to clench.

"She keeps saying we can't spell," Mary complained.

"You can't," the child said, "and so you were hanged."

Alison went to the table that was scattered with sketches of gallows, stick figures dangling from them above uncompleted words, and made herself grasp the child's shoulder, which stiffened at her touch. It felt exactly like Rowan's, and yet she shuddered at the feel of it as though it were full of worms. "No more arguments," she said.

"What's she done?" Jo queried.

Almost as soon as she began nursing, Alison had vowed that she would never be drawn into that collusion between adults that makes children into property and victims – but she wasn't using it against a child, she thought, appalled. "Don't ask," she said in a tone that told Jo they both knew what children were like.

Jo was staring at her hand on the child's shoulder. "Wouldn't you at least like a cup of tea to give things a chance to calm down?"

"I couldn't be calmer, Jo, and we've embarrassed you quite enough. Now we're going home this instant, miss."

Might the child pretend to be frightened of her and tempt Jo to intervene? But the child shrugged off her grasp and stood up. Without another glance at Alison, she stalked down the hall and out of the house. "Thanks for keeping an eye on her," Alison said, and ran after her.

She was staring back from Queenie's gate. Her faintly mocking look enraged Alison, all the more so when she realised Jo was watching her run across the road. She unlocked the house and would have shoved the child inside, except that the child strutted in, head held high. Alison followed her into the hall and leaned against the door to shut it. "I'm surprised at you," she said at once, "trying to use people you've so little time for."

The child turned, leaves shifting on both sides of her. "Why, mummy, I thought that was how you felt after what she said about me."

"How clever you think you are." Alison could see from the child's eyes that she hadn't needed to say those words out loud. "Who do you think I was talking about?" she said through lips that felt cramped. "It must be hard for you to have to depend on us even as much as you do."

"Because I heard you say you didn't want me, do you mean? I hoped you might want me now. I thought at least you'd be glad I came back."

She was taunting Alison because she knew Alison couldn't risk injuring her — injuring Rowan's body. Or perhaps she wanted to provoke Alison, because if Alison marked her that would be evidence that she wasn't fit to look after the child, a reason to send Alison away and leave the child with those who believed in her. Alison could only just control herself, and she would be no use while she felt like this. "Don't you dare speak like that to me. Go to your room and don't you say another word."

The child glared sullenly at her. In the dimness her eyes looked like a sky before a storm. She was about to stop pretending, Alison thought, apprehension flashing through her like an electric charge and springing her mind alert for the least chance. But the child smiled faintly, derisively, and did as she was told.

Alison listened to her footsteps going up. They sounded measured and confident, the footsteps of the owner of the house. Alison imagined her curling up on Rowan's bed, safe in her lair that was the entire house, satisfied to be alive. The thought jerked her upstairs like a knife driven deep into her.

The child had reached the next floor. Her shoulders hunched as Alison ran up behind her, as if she expected Alison to hit her or shove her, but Alison told herself that the child knew perfectly well what was coming. She dodged past her and blocked the doorway of Rowan's room. "Don't try to come in here. This isn't your room."

"Why, mummy, who else could it belong to?"

"To my child, and you aren't my child."

But it was Rowan's face that was gazing at her, so sadly that Alison wondered if she was wrong after all, if she was going mad. How could she have said what she'd just said when Rowan had already run away once because she felt unwanted? How could she believe in a Rowan she wasn't even able to touch instead of the evidence of her own eyes that

Rowan was standing in front of her, her small face stiff as a mask, perhaps because if it moved it would burst into tears? Her whole body ached to step forward and hug the child, to feel that she was still Rowan after all and needing her, even after what Alison had just said. She could feel the step she was about to take, the step that would rush her forward to the child.

Then she felt the sadness in Rowan's bedroom, a sadness that was ready to be cast out for ever, and she didn't have to see the child's eyes narrowing to know where Rowan really was. "You aren't my child," she repeated in a voice that felt like ice against her teeth. "I read the diary and you know I did. You couldn't be bothered to spell like Rowan for long, but I love the way she can't spell, because it's her."

"Don't you want me to grow up?"

"You haven't grown up, you've done the opposite," Alison cried with a laugh that tasted poisonous. "This is your second childhood."

"I won't listen to you if you mean to be horrid to me. I want to go in my room."

"I'm not preventing you. You know where it is."

The child stared dully at her through the dimness that seemed to seep out of the dingy walls. "If you won't let me pass I'll go upstairs. I like looking across the water."

As soon as she began to climb, Alison followed her, trying to ignore the smell of rotten books and stale brick that met her, as if the house were no longer bothering to seem renovated. "You won't be able to use the binoculars, will you? They disappeared like Vicky as soon as you didn't need her."

The child didn't look back. She climbed towards the dark, refusing to be hurried, in possession of herself and the house. She was ceasing to pretend, since Alison seemed incapable of harming her. She oughtn't to have made her contempt so evident. It sent Alison leaping upstairs after her, hands outstretched. She had to see what the child was hiding, though she was sure she already knew.

She'd hoped to make the child show her, but now she realised that the only advantage she had over the child was greater physical strength. That was why she was rushing at her, even though she saw herself as

Derek or her parents or any observer would see her, charging wildly upstairs to attack her own child. If this was madness, at least it felt like being closer to Rowan than she had felt for months. She swung herself around the bend in the stairs without touching the walls and onto the darkest stretch. The stench of rotten bricks and books swelled out of the dark, and the child turned to face her.

The eyes that glared down at her were far older than a child's. Had she waited to turn on Alison where a push would do her the most harm? Alison flung herself at the small figure. "Let's see what you're hiding," she gasped.

The child's hands flew up as if they meant to peck at Alison's face. The darkness of the top floor seemed to step down towards Alison. She knocked the hands aside and grabbed the neck of the long dress. "You'll have to kill me to stop me," she cried.

Whatever she expected, it wasn't what the child did then. She sat down on the stairs, lowering her hands to steady herself. Alison followed her down, still fumbling at the dress. Mad, you're mad, a voice wailed in her mind, there's nothing there, nothing to see. But then why wouldn't the child let anyone see her undressed since she'd come back from Wales? Alison tugged at the neck of the dress so impatiently that the button flew off and struck the whitewashed wall.

The child's neck was bare. Alison peered at it, at the tendons that stood out through the pale soft vulnerable skin above her collarbone, and then she undid another button of the dress. Still there was nothing. She was growing desperate to say she was sorry, to tell the child to run to Jo or to anyone who might protect her from her crazy mother. She glanced up, afraid to see what the child thought of her behavior. Deep in the determined innocence of the child's eyes there was a glint of triumph.

"Don't be so sure," Alison breathed, and reached through the child's hair to the back of her neck. She found the chain at once. She lifted it, and the locket appeared like an insect crawling out of the child's dress. Alison's hand clenched on the chain, which tightened around the child's neck and then snapped.

Alison sprang to her feet, holding the locket fast, and saw that the gleam of triumph in the child's eyes was unconcealed now. So was the sound of it in her voice as she said "You hurt me."

"You made me," Alison cried, appalled that the intruder had made her do that to Rowan's neck. "You think you can show someone now, do you? I wonder how you'll explain this."

The child raised her eyebrows. "Hermione wanted me to have it," she said.

"You'll tell them she gave it to you in the graveyard, will you?" Alison's voice scraped her throat raw. She took a step down so as to be unable to lash out at the child, but even now she could flail at her with the chain. The lock of Rowan's hair glinted dully in her hand like neglected gold. The intruder didn't care that she had found it, Alison realised defeatedly: perhaps she had been wearing it only because it had been hers for so many years; now that she was safe in Rowan's body, it didn't matter. Nothing could touch her, Alison thought – and then she knew that wasn't so. If the intruder were certain of her safety, why was she trying to provoke Alison?

A movement made her look up. The child was climbing into the dark. The thought that she was fleeing sent Alison after her, up the stairs where she could barely see the new plaster, which felt cold as ice and as capable of shattering under her hands. On the top floor all three corridors looked extended by the gathering darkness. The small pale figure was already at the door of Queenie's room. "What are you scared of?" Alison said.

The child turned, one hand on the doorknob. Her face, Rowan's face, looked sad. "Of you, mummy, while you're behaving like this."

She sounded like Rowan, and so did the sadness. That and the sight of the small figure in the midst of so much darkness made Alison feel achingly protective of what she could see and touch, instead of what she had only sensed. "No," she whispered, "I know my Rowan," and then her voice came out strong and chill. "What about your father? What must he think of you now?"

The child pulled at the doorknob as if she meant to sidestep the question, and then her look of innocence hardened. "You'll have to ask him when he comes home."

"When the workman comes home? That's what you mean, isn't it? You can hardly bear to pretend you're his child. I wonder how long you'll be able to keep it up." She was saying too much, losing her advantage; that was clear from the way the child had let go of the door. "We both know who I meant. You may not know where your father is, but that doesn't mean he can't see you. Perhaps he won't let you find him because he's ashamed of what you've been doing."

The child clenched her fists. All at once her eyes looked swollen by rage, and darker than the windowless corridor. Alison had got to her at last, and now Alison was about to learn how dangerous she could be. The empty floors below seemed suddenly cavernous, cutting her off from the world. She thought she felt boards shift underfoot, but that might have been her inadvertent shiver. Then the child looked away as if Alison weren't worth the effort. She opened the door and stepped into Queenie's room.

Alison threw herself forward and reached the door just as it met the frame. She shoved at it with both hands and felt it fling the child backwards, and then she followed it into the room. The bare floor and the newly plastered walls were saturated with the darkness that was massing above Wales and flooding across the bay. The smell of stale books hung in the air, and Alison thought the whole room looked rotten with darkness. But the child stood in the middle of it, arms folded, drawing herself together from the shock of being thrown backwards. Perhaps the shock made her careless of what she said, or perhaps her contempt for Alison did. "You stay out of here unless I say you can come in. This is my room."

"It's your father's room," Alison said deliberately. "If there's anywhere he can see you, it must be here."

"I don't know what you mean. I think you're going mad, to talk to me this way."

Alison laughed. However small it sounded in the bare darkness, her laughter felt like an outpouring of relief. "Rowan would never say that. I don't think any child of her age would. You may as well stop pretending, Queenie. You know you can't fool me."

The child's face wrinkled with rage. It looked as if she had aged in an instant, as if a shrunken old woman were standing there, a woman so senile she'd put on a child's dress. Then her eyes glinted like coal, and she sneered, stretching Rowan's lips into a grimace, spoiling her face. The door slammed behind Alison, sealing the dark.

"That didn't scare me last time, Queenie, and it doesn't scare me now." Alison hesitated and then took the risk: she had to. "Is that the best you can do?"

The child's lips writhed. "Don't try me," she hissed.

Alison thought she glimpsed something besides a threat: restraint in case the father might indeed be watching, or even a limit to the harm she was prepared to wreak? "I don't want to, Queenie, can't you understand? All I want is my child back."

"You've got her. You should thank God you have."

Alison's fury felt like a charge her body could barely contain. "Where's God in all this? If you'd seen God you wouldn't have come back, would you?" Suddenly there was a question she couldn't help asking, however grotesque it seemed to ask this of Rowan's face that shimmered in the dark. "What did you see, Queenie?"

The child's eyes widened, with glee or with terror. For a moment the answer seemed to be in them or beyond them, a vast darkness that led somewhere Alison would rather not see. "I know you couldn't find your father," she said hastily, trying to reassure herself that all she'd glimpsed was loneliness. "Perhaps you were going about it in the wrong way. You've got to try again. You must realise you can't go on like this."

The child's eyes were blank again, the face was a dark mask. "You'll have to go through everything you loathe all over again," Alison persisted. "Having your periods every month and being surrounded half the time at school by other girls who are. And then your menopause, and growing older, and all the diseases you may pick up in the meantime – who knows what I'll bring home from the hospital?" Rage flashed through her as she remembered what she'd almost forgotten. "You'd better understand one thing, Queenie, in case you're still hoping. I'll never have another child for you to influence. I'd have an abortion first."

The small face looked shocked. "You wouldn't kill a child," it protested shrilly.

"What do you think you did to Rowan? Believe me, I'd do anything I had to not to have a baby you could get the better of." Yet her rage was turning to sadness, some of which she thought was Rowan's, wherever Rowan was in the growing darkness. Might Queenie's loneliness have been so terrible that she could only take refuge in being a child again, with all the selfishness she had been indulged in as a child? Might she have needed in her loneliness to befriend the only child she had ever cared about, however selfishly? "Queenie," Alison said as gently as she could, "I did love you, however hard you made it for us to. But I can't love you while you do this to my child."

The eyes were contemptuous again, brimming with disbelief. "Nobody will love you unless you give this up," Alison said, quieter still. "Not even your father."

"You just stop talking about my father," the child screamed. "You aren't fit to have his name in your mouth."

"Then I'll talk about Rowan. You'll permit me to talk about my own child, will you?" There was already more sadness than anger in her voice. "Maybe you don't want to believe any of us loved you, but you know she did. She loved you and felt closer to you than anyone else did, and that was how you were able to come back, not because of this locket at all. She loved you, and in return for that you stole her life."

For the first time since they'd entered the bare room, the child's eyes seemed to falter. She looked momentarily ashamed, and more like a child than she had since that night in Wales. "Is that the best you can do with so much will?" Alison demanded. "Can't you use it to find your father? If he sees you've let Rowan back, don't you think he'll make certain you find him?"

She'd claimed too much too quickly. At once the child's eyes were impenetrable as the clouds that had blotted out the sky. Alison reached behind her and pressed the light switch, to prevent the child from hiding her thoughts in the dark that was swelling into the room, but the bulb failed with a sound like a single note of a distant bell. The child grinned, teeth glinting in the dark, and Alison cried "Did you do that too? Can you honestly be proud of it? You may still be able to play that kind of trick, but you'll have to do better than that to scare me off."

She took a deep breath, though it tasted stale, and regained control. "Or are you trying to impress yourself? Are you trying to forget what you can't do? You can't stay alive forever like this. If you stay where you are you'll have to die all over again. And this time you'll know what's coming."

Was that a glimmer of fear in the child's eyes? But she shrugged with a defiance that seemed both childish and senile, and Alison realised too late that such a fear would make her more determined to stay where she felt safe. "Maybe you needn't start worrying yet, maybe you've a lifetime before you need to, but it's Rowan's life, not yours," she cried. "You just think of her for a moment, that little girl you tricked into giving up her life, and ask yourself if you can bear to live with knowing you've left her out there alone in the dark."

The child shook her head almost reprovingly. "She needn't be alone, you can keep her with you. Anyway, you should have taken better care of her while you had the chance."

Perhaps she saw for the first time in all her years that she'd said too much, for she stepped back towards the window, the oncoming dark. She wasn't trying to provoke Alison now, she was afraid of what an adult could do to a child. That fear drew Alison forward, feeling charged and dangerous. She reached for the child, ready at last to do whatever she had to that would drive Queenie out – and then the old eyes glared at her, seizing her, and the floor vanished.

The whole room did, and the house. They seemed to rot away instantly, letting the dark rush in. It felt like utter blindness, but worse too: it felt like a threat of rottenness you might smell if you even stirred and disturbed the total stillness, rottenness that would come creeping from all sides if you betrayed that you were there. That was yourself, or all of yourself that you'd left behind, outside this oasis of peace that was the nearest you could come to the state of not existing. Was this how

Queenie had felt when she hadn't been able to find her father, or was it why she hadn't dared to search, to reach into the dark? The question was enough to brighten Alison's mind and give her back her blinded senses: she wasn't dead yet, she couldn't be supported by nothing but darkness. The endless dark withdrew into the old eyes, and the room took shape vaguely in the blackness that was only winter gloom after all.

She thought she knew what to say. "Queenie, that didn't frighten me either, and you mustn't let it frighten you. There must be something more than that. Surely you've still got the strength to find out what it is."

"No, I won't." The child's voice shook with wilfulness, or perhaps with secret fear. "Nobody can make me. Just be grateful that things are no worse."

She meant that Rowan had been able to come back, but she was ignoring how vulnerable Rowan was, far more so than herself, to that waiting dark. In a moment Alison felt ablaze with horror and rage and grief. "Come and take her. You brought her up to be like this," she cried at the dark in case she might be heard, and flung the locket away from her so violently it shattered the window. Yet when she seized the child she thought at first that she was being almost gentle as her hands closed around the slim soft neck.

CHAPTER THIRTY-SIX

Once Jo had given Derek her message she seemed not to know what to do. She trailed after him while he went to tell the deputy headmistress that he had almost finished and was going home for a few minutes, and then she followed him to the car. He slung his toolbox in the trunk and knew instinctively that the engine wouldn't start at once, not when the day was suddenly so cold under the blackened sky. It might be quicker to hurry along the promenade, and he did.

The low sky squeezed a glow out of the tall pale nursing homes that overlooked the dunes. Many of the rooms were lit, but their light didn't reach far. Above the huddled dunes the sharp grass looked like scrapes on the dark air. Derek felt as if the dark were mud, especially since Jo was panting to keep up and making him feel bound to slow down for her. "If there's anything I can do..." she panted.

He had to feel grateful, though the interruption had hardly been worth slowing for. "I don't know yet, do I," he said, trying to keep his voice neutral, as if that might make his fears unnecessary. He could see the pebbledashed house ahead, and it looked somehow wrong, a huge rock covered with pebbles and the shells of parasites, upheaved under the black sky. "What do you think you can do?"

"I'll take Rowan again if you like. Alison was shouting at her after she took her away."

"You shout at your own sometimes, don't you?" A sense that she might be leaving as much unsaid as he was made him even more nervous. "You didn't come and get me just because of that."

"It sounded as if they were at the top of the house."

"For Christ's sake, Jo, if you've got something to tell me——" He faltered, the chill of the concrete promenade striking up through his shoes at once. He could see what was wrong with the house – what Jo had left unsaid. "I thought I heard that," she told him.

One pane of Queenie's window was broken. Alison and Rowan must be in that room, beyond the window that gaped among the chimneys and stony protrusions like monuments in a graveyard. Under the doused sky the rectangle of window looked black as an upended grave. His rewiring had been no use, he thought in the midst of a larger dismay he was afraid to comprehend. He lurched off the promenade and onto the dunes, towards the house.

Sand fitted itself to his shoes. Where he had to struggle upwards, his efforts sank his feet deeper. He dragged himself free with handfuls of grass, tearing blades out by their roots. At last, prickly with sweat and desperation, he reached the solid pavement that seemed to spring him towards the house. He was digging the key into the lock when Jo arrived, red-faced and pressing her chest with one hand, at the gate. The idea of her seeing what was wrong as soon as he did appalled him. "I know where you are if we need you," he called, almost snarling, and let himself into the house.

He closed the door so carefully behind him that though his ears were ringing with the strain of trying to hear whatever was to be heard, it seemed to make no noise. The house was so stuffed with darkness that all sound was choked. He ventured forward between the walls that unfurled dimly as he passed, and was opening his mouth to shout to Alison, already hearing how enraged his fears would make him sound, when he heard her voice at the top of the house. "Rowan," she was pleading.

He drew a shaky breath and closed his mouth. She sounded desperate, and he was afraid to learn why, more afraid than he had ever been in his life. He paced to the end of the hall and gazed up, and heard Alison say Rowan's name again like a prayer. He began to climb, and might have prayed himself if he had dared think what he would be praying not to have happened at the top of the house.

Before he reached that floor he was having to grope over the new plaster, which was so cold and smooth it felt aloof, as if he had no place here. The darkness made his senses more acute, and he heard how Alison's voice broke as she repeated Rowan's name. Even if he'd dared to call out now, his throat was too tight to let him speak.

He had to force himself to step into the top corridor. He was terrified to find out why Rowan hadn't made a sound since he had entered the house. When a board creaked beneath him, he flinched and froze there, one foot raised – and then Alison pleaded "Rowan, come on" beyond the door. However much noise he might have made on his way up, it seemed she would have been too preoccupied to hear. All he could do was pace to the door of Queenie's room and push it open.

Alison was kneeling on the bare floor near the window. One arm cradled Rowan's shoulders while she stroked the child's forehead and peered at her closed eyes in the faint light that seeped out of the sky. Nothing else moved except her hair and Rowan's as a thin chill breeze whined at the broken window. "Rowan?" she said with a kind of hopeless gentleness, her voice rising and breaking. "Rowan?"

Derek stumbled into the room. "Ali, what— what's happened?"

He couldn't quite bring himself to ask what she'd done, but her expression when she looked at him told him that he might as well have asked. Her mouth was trembling wordlessly, her eyes sparkled darkly with tears. He should have taken more care of her and Rowan, he thought numbly: he should have known sooner that things were going wrong between them. When he trudged forward, Alison clutched Rowan to her as if he meant to take the child.

He tried to tell her with his eyes that she could rely on him, not to dodge away from him as he was afraid she meant to, though he felt as if he might begin at any moment to shiver uncontrollably. Everything dismayed him, even the dark at the window; the window seemed more like the mouth of a tunnel. He fell to his knees beside Alison and held out his hands to her. She mustn't close him out now, that would be worst of all. Surely she would either take his hands or give him the child, and couldn't she be mistaken in her hopelessness even if she was a nurse?

She didn't take his hands, but she leaned towards him as if she were giving way under her burden. He'd support her whatever she'd done, he vowed, because he loved her and because it must be his fault too. He wished they had never come to this uncaring house; it had helped cut them off from each other. Then Alison jerked away from him.

"Don't, Ali," he pleaded, but she didn't hear him. She was gazing into Rowan's face, lifting the child's head and stroking her hair that shivered in the chill wind. The tunnel whose mouth was the window seemed longer and darker than ever. The pale blur hovering out there must be a bird, like a vulture, he thought agonisingly. He hadn't time to look, he must get through to Alison, even if it meant acknowledging that the movement she imagined she'd sensed had only been the wind in Rowan's hair. "Ali," he murmured, "look at me, love, I'm here," his body growing tense when her gaze didn't leave Rowan's face, which looked more still than sleep. He would have to let out the cry that was gathering inside him, because otherwise he would seize Rowan, anything to break the spell of not admitting the worst. He reached out again, his legs trembling with cramp. "She's my child too," he was going to cry out, and he had no idea what would happen when he did.

Then he heard a whisper. "It's all right," it said, and he froze despite the pain in his legs. It was Rowan's voice.

He thought it was only in his head, even when Alison stooped closer to Rowan, cradling her head and kissing her closed eyes, murmuring her name urgently. "Don't, Ali," he muttered, desperate to stop her before his heart broke at the sight of her forlorn hope, "can't you see—" And then Rowan's eyelids fluttered, and she blinked up at her mother as though she was unable to focus. "I'm all right, mummy," she said.

Alison reared up, almost dropping the child. She was drawing back, but only to be sure what she was seeing. She gazed at Rowan's uncertain smile and cloudy eyes, then she hugged her so tight Derek was afraid she would bruise her. "Oh, Rowan," she said shakily, "don't ever make me feel like that again."

"Don't worry, mummy, I never will," Rowan promised, and the two of them burst out laughing and weeping as they clung to each other. They seemed hardly to notice when Derek struggled to his feet, rubbing his thighs. He couldn't help resenting having been made to suffer such anxiety for apparently no reason – or were they trying to convince him there hadn't been one? A movement at the window drew his gaze there, just as the pale watching shape dwindled out of sight down the tunnel that he could see now was the sunless sky. He'd never known a bird to be so swift, but the broken window was more important than a bird, and needed explaining. "Is someone going to tell me what's been happening?" he demanded.

The two of them looked up at him. Rowan got to her feet as if she had to remember how, stretching out her hand until he helped her up. She closed her eyes and nestled against him. She hadn't for months, he realised, and felt she was thinking that too. "It was Vicky," she said slowly. "She's gone now. She won't come back."

He stared at Alison as she wavered to her feet. "What was?"

"The window," Rowan told him. "She broke it when mummy said I mustn't see her again, and then she pushed me over so hard I bumped my head, and then she ran away."

He was still waiting for Alison to speak. "I don't get any of this," he said. "Jo came to tell me you'd got Rowan. We couldn't understand why you'd come home from work."

She glanced at Rowan, and an understanding that he couldn't grasp seemed to flash between them before she looked at him. "I saw Vicky hanging round near here when I was on my way to the hospital. I knew she'd be trying to approach Rowan again, which I don't think you'd have wanted either, and so I came back." Her voice was almost steady now, and so was the plea in her eyes. "Besides, it was time to have it out with Rowan about her."

"And while we were talking Vicky came and wouldn't go until mummy made her," Rowan said. "She was why I've been so nasty all these weeks. She kept being with me and you never knew. There's just me now, though. You still love me, don't you?"

"Of course we do, babe." Yet he felt that questions he should ask were slipping away from him in the dimness. "Where does the little bitch live?"

"I can't tell you, daddy. I never knew. I'll tell you if ever I see her again, but I'm sure I won't." She lifted her face and gave him a wide-eyed look he couldn't glance away from. "Aren't you going to cuddle mummy as well?"

Questions squirmed in his head, but they seemed shameful now she was gazing at him. He took a long breath and gave up. If Rowan trusted her mother as she obviously did, how could he do otherwise? He reached for Alison almost blindly. "Come here, Ali, if you can still put up with me. I don't know what went wrong with us."

"Vicky did," Alison said fiercely and, leaning against him as if she were near to fainting, put her arms around him and Rowan. They stayed like that long enough for a knife-edge of blue sky to lever up the lid of cloud across the bay. As the room began to lighten he looked down at Rowan, and was still searching for an injury when she glanced up at him. "Daddy, will you let me come and watch you work again sometimes? I won't be in any danger really, will I?"

More than anything else, that made him feel she was herself again. "I wouldn't ever let you or mummy be."

"You'll have another job to do when you've finished at the school," Alison said unevenly, hugging them tighter than ever. "I'm afraid the lights on this floor have gone up the spout again." She shuddered, and at first he didn't realise she was laughing, so helplessly she had to struggle to make a sound. The sky opened above the sea, and Rowan started giggling too. The afternoon light seemed to reach for them, and Derek relinquished the last of his unanswered questions. Without the least idea why or any need to know, he began to laugh until he cried.

EPILOGUE

They moved on a Saturday in May. Rowan went to the edge of the dunes for a last look while the men were loading the furniture into the van. Shoals of sunlight basked on the rippling water beneath the cloudless sky. Wales stretched along half the horizon, a green serpent scaly with cottages. Ships seemed to sail past only inches from the dunes, and their names felt like voyages to her: *Tamathal, Knud Tholstrup, Essi Silje, Atlantic Compass*... A Russian ship with several of the letters in its name turned backwards glided by, and she remembered the endless night in Wales, when she had been unable to read anything. She hurried back to her mother and father, away from the whisper of sea and windblown sand.

She wouldn't be sorry to leave here after all. None of the children played much with her, because of the way she must have seemed to them before Christmas. Miss Frith was disappointed in her and felt she wasn't trying, since she had been spelling perfectly last term. Mummy knew why, and daddy felt it was part of what she'd been through: he said he'd rather have her like herself even if she had to learn all over again to spell. They knew she was trying. Only her mother knew that she'd thrown away last year's diary, with the entries that looked as if an impatient teacher had been showing her how to spell but in Rowan's own handwriting. Rowan had no longer been sure whose diary it was.

Mummy knew what had happened. Perhaps that was why they never talked about it, or perhaps she was waiting for Rowan to be old enough to want to; perhaps she was even embarrassed that Rowan had had to lie on her behalf, though Rowan thought that doing so on behalf of someone else might be part of growing up. It made her feel protective of her parents. Just now she was glad she was still a child and able to rely on their protection, though the years during which she would be a child seemed like almost no time at all.

The van was loaded. Her father had been helping the men, and now he was sharing coffee from their vacuum flask. "Mummy's checking the house if you want a last look," he told her, "and then wagons roll."

Her mother was coming downstairs as Rowan trotted along the leafy hall. "Ready for the adventure?" she said with a smile that wavered as she reached out gingerly, almost automatically, to touch Rowan's throat. She hadn't forgiven herself for that, though it had never hurt much: Rowan had only been bothered in case her father might have noticed that at first she'd found it hard to speak. She took her mother's hand and moved it up from her throat to her cheek. "Please may I say goodbye to my room?"

"Of course you may." As they passed on the stairs she added "Just don't be long, or I'll come to find you."

Rowan ran to the middle floor and glanced into her bedroom. It was bare and unfamiliar, and looked much dustier now that there was no furniture for dust to hide behind. Only the view of the bay remained, and she shed a tear for that before she tiptoed quickly up to the top floor.

She wasn't sure why she needed to go there. As she stepped into the central passage she felt almost as frightened as she had in the weeks after Christmas, when falling asleep had felt like falling out of her body into the waiting dark. She'd taken refuge in her parents' bed for weeks before she'd felt safe enough to sleep by herself. Surely she was safe now: her mother was downstairs and within hearing. She ventured along the stale corridor where sunlight never reached, and pushed open Queenie's door.

There seemed to be nothing to make her afraid, nothing to explain why her whole body seemed to shrink around the sudden pounding of her heart. The room was bare, and nothing moved except a tanker and the seagulls in its wake beyond the window. Yet she could feel how short-lived all this was, how if she gazed for long into the room it would turn into the mouth of a tunnel that led to the dark. She closed her eyes and, groping for the handle, shut the door tight.

She'd come up here as if that would tell her what had happened last time she had, but she was as uncertain as ever. Had her mother been able to drive Queenie out because the old woman had turned herself back into a child, or had Queenie relented at the end and let Rowan return? If she had gone to look for her father again, mightn't she find him this time or at least believe she had, since she deserved to? All Rowan knew was that when her mother had let go of her throat she hadn't known where she was: she had been falling out of the sight of her own body in her mother's arms into darkness, falling as if she would never stop, except that the fall had ended inside her body, a life-size weight she'd had to learn to move, to see out of and to make speak. In the instant of returning she'd sensed Queenie soaring away into the dark, Queenie's dark – and it had taken her months to realise that if that bare scoured dark was Queenie's, the place Rowan had passed through in her efforts to come home must have been her own.

Things could change, she told herself. The house would soon be a nursing home, where people like Queenie would be cared for, made to feel less lonely, she hoped. She was beginning to think she might like to do that kind of work herself. Whatever was waiting at the end of her life, surely it needn't be what she had already gone through, unless she gave in to the fear that it would. She opened her eyes and ran downstairs, and breathed easier once her surroundings felt less flat, more real.

As her mother's car turned in the shadow of Queenie's house, the shadow seemed to gape like a long pit in the road. Then they were in the sunlight and following the van, and the sight of Jo and her children waving goodbye dwindled. As soon as Rowan finished waving she clasped her hands together to make herself feel she was still holding on to her mother and father. The last thing she heard in the road was the sound of the waves beyond the house, so distant that she might have been hearing them in a shell, the thin blue shell of the sky. The car turned out of Queenie's road towards the future, and she whispered "I'll never come back."

ACKNOWLEDGEMENTS

A good few people helped me with this novel. While I prepared it for writing, Dennis Etchison took me to the Dark Country, where Tony Mendoza bought me a pen in Ensenada so that I could work on my notes. During the writing I benefited greatly from the hospitality of Tom and Barbara Doherty in Connecticut and Doug and Lynne Winter in Washington, not to mention the World Fantasy Convention in Providence. I've a special word of thanks to Howard Kaylan, Mark Volman and Joe Stefko of the Turtles. As always, my wife Jenny was the midwife, and our children Tamsin and Matty helped ease the passage of the novel too.

FLAME TREE PRESS
FICTION WITHOUT FRONTIERS
Award-Winning Authors & Original Voices

Flame Tree Press is the trade fiction imprint of Flame Tree Publishing, focusing on excellent writing in horror and the supernatural, crime and mystery, science fiction and fantasy. Our aim is to explore beyond the boundaries of the everyday, with tales from both award-winning authors and original voices.

•

Other titles by Ramsey Campbell include:
Thirteen Days by Sunset Beach
Think Yourself Lucky
The Hungry Moon

Other horror titles available include:
The Haunting of Henderson Close by Catherine Cavendish
The House by the Cemetery by John Everson
The Devil's Equinox by John Everson
The Toy Thief by D.W. Gillespie
One By One by D.W. Gillespie
Black Wings by Megan Hart
The Playing Card Killer by Russell James
The Siren and the Specter by Jonathan Janz
The Sorrows by Jonathan Janz
Castle of Sorrows by Jonathan Janz
The Dark Game by Jonathan Janz
House of Skin by Jonathan Janz
Dust Devils by Jonathan Janz
The Darkest Lullaby by Jonathan Janz
Will Haunt You by Brian Kirk
Hearthstone Cottage by Frazer Lee
Those Who Came Before by J.H. Moncrieff
Stoker's Wilde by Steven Hopstaken & Melissa Prusi
Creature by Hunter Shea
Ghost Mine by Hunter Shea
Slash by Hunter Shea
The Mouth of the Dark by Tim Waggoner
They Kill by Tim Waggoner

•

Join our mailing list for free short stories, new release details, news about our authors and special promotions:

flametreepress.com